THE HAUl

C. A. DAWSON SCOTT

TABB HOUSE
Padstow, Cornwall

Published in the ENCORE Series 1985 by Tabb House
11 Church Street, Padstow, Cornwall, PL28 8BG.
in cased and limp editions.

First published by William Heinemann in 1921

Introduction copyright © Francis King 1985

This book is sold subject to the condition that
it shall not be lent, re-sold, hired out or otherwise
circulated without the publisher's consent.

ISBN 0 90718 37 8 Cased
ISBN 0 907018 38 6 Limp

The Tabb House 'ENCORE' Series of Reprints

The Haunting
C. A. Dawson Scott
with a Foreword by Francis King

Malachi's Cove, and other Stories and Essays
Anthony Trollope
Edited and with an Introduction by Richard Mullen

One Poor Scruple
Mrs Wilfrid Ward
with an Introduction by Bernard Bergonzi
and other titles to follow

Typeset by Inforum Ltd., Portsmouth
Printed and bound in England by
Robert Hartnoll Ltd., Bodmin

INTRODUCTION
by Francis King

TODAY Mrs C. A. Dawson Scott is chiefly remembered as the founder of the international writers' organisation, P.E.N. The feat was a remarkable one. There were writers better known, there were writers richer and more influential. Yet hers was the original bold concept, and hers was the determination that, with John Galsworthy as the first President, brought it to realisation.

It had always been her role in life to be (as Rebecca West once put it to me) "a kind of literary telephone-exchange", so that, long before the establishment of P.E.N., she had already been the means by which writers of widely varying backgrounds, aims and achievements had kept in touch with each other and so had felt themselves to be part of a fellowship of comrades, instead of being rivals. It is a cliché to say that writing is the loneliest of all professions; but, like most clichés, it happens to be true. Some writers are glad of that loneliness and would not want any intrusion on it; but many more see it as the chief disadvantage of a chosen way of life. For those in the second of these categories, Mrs Dawson Scott, constantly eager to bring people together, was a friend to cherish.

But her role as invaluable literary catalyst should not obscure her achievements as a novelist on her own account. Though she is now less regarded than they, her place is along with such other regional novelists as Sheila Kaye-Smith, Winifred Holtby, Constance Holme, and Mary Webb. She combines the same robust story-telling skills with the same sharp eye for a setting and the same sharp ear for dialect.

The Haunting, first published in 1921, is one of a series of Cornish Tales: *Wastralls*, *The Headland*, *The Haunting*, *They Green Stones* and *Blown by the Wind*.

Mrs Dawson Scott was intensely interested in what we today would call the paranormal, and this interest is clearly evident in a story about a previously staid, hard-headed and self-controlled man driven first to the verge of madness and then to suicide by the ghost of the brother whom, in a moment of rage at being betrayed and forsaken by him, he is driven to poison. For those with a taste for the occult, this story—how well Mrs Dawson Scott's talents would have been suited to television!—is a gripping one. With its secret passage, its hoarded gold and its account of two decent women, mother and daughter, each suffering for her love of one of the two brothers, it is also a gripping one for those with a taste for adventure or romance.

But for me what remains most interesting in it is its vivid picture of a small Cornish seaside town at a time when people still travelled on horseback or by coach or carriage, when Jamaica was still a place where a young Englishman might expect to make his fortune, and when Rhoda Broughton was a novelist as highly regarded and as popular as Margaret Drabble or Iris Murdoch today. (Her influence is everywhere evident in Mrs Dawson Scott's own work). In such descriptions as those of the Saturday market, with its stalls displaying pasties, butter, eggs, cream and fresh bread and cakes "for hussies too lazy to bake their own", of the witch who is thought to have caused one of her neighbours to be infested with lice, or of the little shop kept by Mrs Liddicoat and her daughter, Mrs Dawson Scott evokes a whole world long since destroyed by the arrival first of the railway and then of the motor-car.

The 'haunting' of the title thus becomes not merely the haunting of Corlyon by the brother whom he has killed, but also the haunting of a modern Cornwall of holiday bungalows, caravan parks and luxury hotels by the ghost of its far more secluded, individual and 'foreign' past.

Francis King

CHAPTER I

I

MR. CORLYON stood before the mirror in his white shirt-sleeves, the razor in his hand, and lather covering his cheeks. He must hurry. He had to shave and dress, and at any moment Antiks Hellyar might call up the stair, "Young Maister be comin' down street."

He must be at the front door to welcome his brother. Not once during the years of Pascoe's roving had he failed to be there. He had opened the door as the lad walked up the path, had drawn him into the warm, bright house, had closed the door on the accomplished fact of his return.

Of the long family only they two—the eldest and the youngest—were left and it was for Mr. Corlyon, abiding in the little waterside town, to remind his brother that the walls and roof to which he returned from his voyages were not only a shelter. The boy, while adventuring on blue and green and grey seas, should bear the brown house in his mind as something glowing, a something to which his heart of a wanderer must eventually turn.

He might come at any moment and Gale Corlyon was not ready. That business of Buddle's horse had kept him longer than he had supposed it would. Difficult to convince Shugg that as he had let the animal down he must pay, that to do otherwise would be unprincipled.

He wiped the lather from pale smooth cheeks and taking the scissors clipped his moustache a little closer. A moustache gave the final touch of masculinity to a face. He liked the rough feel of his. Other men had moustaches that stuck out, or hung down; but his curved in, lying above his thin well-cut lips like a defiance. He cut the edges of the hard black-grey hairs. He would not have his lips hidden.

It was fortunate that he had brushed his suit before going to meet Shugg and Buddle, for now he had only to change out of his work-a-day clothes. He had worn the same suit last time

Pascoe came home. As he fastened the smoked-pearl buttons of his waist-coat, he glanced at his reflection. It paid to have your clothes cut by a good tailor. They were growing shabby, but they still set off his young figure of a middle-aged man. He pulled his waistcoat into place, settled the new tie. Blue was becoming to his clear skin and clear eyes, while the small white spot added a note of gaiety. The old well-brushed suit, the steep hard collar, the fresh tie. Pascoe should feel that the stay-at-home was as well-looking a chap as any he had seen on his travels; that he was not necessarily dead to the ferment of life because he had chosen to remain in Stowe.

He smiled, confidential fashion, at the reflection—extraordinarily black and white—in the mirror. Pascoe's life of a wanderer made him the pebble rolling on the floor of the seas. He might learn something of human nature, but what did he *know*?

People did this and that, but what made them do it? He, Gale Corlyon, had spent his life in Stowe and he knew not only what was done in the houses huddled at the head of the harbour, but why it was done. Oh, how much he knew . . . the men and the women . . . they made their faces into shop-windows, but behind, on shelves and in drawers, were the goods, the secrets of their interesting lives.

When the shutters were up, the shop closed, he could lift the latch of the side-door. He could go in because he had a finger in the little pies simmering on the various hobs. Fifty years in Stowe and he the cleverest man in it. To whom else could people turn when they were bothered? The parson would have admonished, doctor and lawyer would have sent in a bill, but he . . .

He liked being of use and, because he never talked, he was safe. The people knew that.

They could trust his wisdom and, also, his discretion.

And the secrets . . .

It was godlike to know, to have behind his white silence, like sheep under snow, this knowledge. After all, his was a more interesting life than that of Pascoe who, though for ever seeing new things, saw only the surface of these things, who never penetrated, who knew, dear lad, nothing.

A scatterbrain . . . would have scattered money too, if it had not been for Gale . . . did scatter what he earned. A pity that, but as long as he remembered to buy where his ship touched and to bring home what he had bought, Gale would be able to fill those brown skin bags of his with the proceeds, able to "fatten his pigs," to fatten them against his and Pascoe's old age.

This time Pascoe, in his letter home, had said "emeralds." An intriguing word—emeralds.

II

If the ship had got into Plymouth yesterday, he should have been home by now. He had, of course, to dispose of the emeralds; but he knew the byeways of Plymouth better even than the highways, and was no bad hand at a bargain.

He would not have let the buyers detain him—not long. Perhaps, though, he had reached Stowe and had been button-holed by some gossip as he came through the streets. He knew everybody—had known them since his babyhood.

Mr. Corlyon looked from his window. Men were unloading a collier on the other side of the harbour, a smack was heading for the wharf of the fish market; but, on the road that ran along the side of the quay, there was no sign of the familiar figure.

He could only see as far as the opening of the street through which his brother must come. No one! But the house had a side-aspect. From Pascoe's room he could see up French Street as far as the Cornish Arms.

He crossed the landing, the shadowy landing with the white curtains and the plants and, further down, the doors of disused rooms. That, opposite to his, belonged to Pascoe. During the three months of his absence it had been a chrysalis, now it displayed hangings and coverlet and the shining surfaces of walnut wood. Mr Corlyon looked between the dimity curtains, looked over the bushes of purple veronica, and up the road.

At the head of the quay, on the old men's bench Spargo and

Abel Prior were sitting. A cat, careless of dogs and men, was sauntering across the road, a great grey cloud, pregnant with rain, hung over the town. The shops, low bands of colour on either side of the way, ran from the opening of the street, up hill and over. Mr Corlyon looked sharply for what he sought. Instinctively, he had glanced first at the baby-linen shop. There, if anywhere, but no, no horse was tethered to the wall-staple.

It was evidence Pascoe was not in the low-raftered shop, talking to Jenifer Liddicoat. Something in the man checked and resumed at a lesser speed. Pascoe must be still on his way.

But he had better hasten or he would be caught by the rain. Anyway, as the roan mare had not yet topped the hill that sloped to the flat grey edge of the harbour, his brother would have time to go round the house, see everything was in order.

Pascoe's room . . . clean, neat . . . Antiks knew her work. Mr. Corlyon stopped at the mantelshelf, looked at the row of cartes-de-visite behind the opaque blue vases. Jenifer Liddicoat's photo . . .

He had not taken it with him, then?

III

In the kitchen, Antiks Hellyar was wetting flour for cake. She stood in front of the table, her sleeves rolled above dimpled arms, a big plain apron covering her blue cotton frock, rounding up over her breast, out from her jimp waist, out over her hips. Mr. Corlyon on his tour of inspection had reached the work-a-day centre of the house. He smiled at Antiks. She was not young now, the hussy, but she was still pretty. That dark hair of hers, curling round her forehead and her softness—he did not wonder the men could not leave her alone—and she worked in his kitchen.

"Push in a few sticks, Maister, your fire don't go ahead like our'n do."

On the pane the quick rain drummed, streaming down the glass, blurring the view of grey outhouses, of the lane at the side, changing the hill at the back into a dark wall. Mr. Corlyon, crossing to the big basket of fuel that stood under the window, thought of Pascoe, riding across high open land, pushing through the rush of water. Poor weather, indeed, a poor welcome. They must see he had his favourite food . . . open a bottle of wine.

"Did you buy a hog's pudding?"

Antiks' mouth, lifting at the corners, revealed strong regular teeth. So many women, old and young, were snaggle-toothed, but not she. "'Ow do 'ee think I can get 'og's-puddin' when ole Billy 'aven't killed the pig?"

"Thought he was going to do it, Saturday?"

"Ole sow wadn't fit to kill—you knaw moon's batin'."

"So it is."

She shook her head at him. "You a country-man and not know. Us'll 'av to wait till next week for puddins."

The warmth of the kitchen, as well as a certain inner stir, made him linger. His feet were always cold. He would sit for a moment in the corner of the settle, stretch them to the fire.

There was no hurry. Pascoe, if he were on the road, would house-up somewhere . . . some farm . . . cottage. "What have you for supper?"

"There be the bit of bacon boilin' and this rabbit-pie is ready to bake." Antiks fetched the round black baking iron, put pie and cake and pasties on it, and fitted the baker over all. A fire of stick embers, roofed in with turf . . . nothing better. She opened out a space, pushed in the baking iron, covered all with the dark sods.

"By time 'e come, it'll be done lovely," she said and stood at ease. After the long hours of work, good to have an idle moment, a craik with "Maister." Her blue eye turned appreciatively on the lounging figure, found that he was studying her, found that in some fascinating way his face had changed. He had come in cold and with his snowy look, now he was young, eager. Her heart seemed to sink under a happy burthen, to fall away.

"Come over here, Old Easy-Daisy," and he pulled her onto his knee.

"Now, give over, do."

He turned her face deliberately, put his lips to her mouth, found it ripe, willing.

"Who is after you now?"

"Don't 'ee talk about it, there 'edn't no one."

"What about Jacky Trudgian?"

She stirred in his arms. Jacky . . . if she had cared for Jacky and she was not going to admit it . . . anyway that was away back last winter! Nobody now . . . unless . . . yes, she did like the "Maister," but he did not care for her. He only took her because she was there. If she had had any sense, she would have married Jacky, settled down with him; but no she could not, not while the "Maister" . . .

"Jacky be goin' to Mexico and I be glad. Don't want any of they bothering round."

He smiled down at her. "No, you don't want any of them, do you, Antiks?"

He was teasing her, but it was the truth. She had not run after the men, and yet, somehow, she seemed to get mixed up with them. Difficult to say "No," difficult to go on saying it . . . yes, especially when you liked them. If it had not been for the children; but poor little dears, they came . . .

"There be one thing I can say; I never made nobody pay for what 'e 'ad and I've been always able to work for the children as God sent me."

"Is that the way you take it? The children are nothing to do with the men?"

"Oh, don't 'ee be silly, Maister, talking such stuff."

She had four children and he knew the men who had fathered them; but he knew, too, that easy as she was, her easiness had dropped away since she had been working in his kitchen. His hand, stroking, slightly pinching, passed up her arm. Pretty, every bit of her, and warm, made for love.

IV

In the brown sitting-room, the fire had been lighted, the table

laid for supper; laid with silver, with cut glass. The best cloth
had been got out, the old Sunderland ware. Antiks had understood that for Pascoe he wanted the best. The lad was to see he
was thought of, prepared for.

Mr. Corlyon looked about the room. The peat in the fire-
basket was burning dully. That last load from St. Wenn had not
been worth the cost, the sods were both thin and damp. He
must speak to Henwood about it. If he paid good money, he
wanted money's worth. A few sticks, a dry motte, and the fire
would blaze.

At the end of the room was a heaped yet tidy desk. Business
meant papers, and Corlyon not only had his business of an
auctioneer, but that quiet finger-in-every-pie business, the
business that brought him interesting information, which
brought him—was it power? If it was, he made no use of it. Of
course not. He was a man of principle.

A few rubber bands and the mass was so much reduced that
the lid could be shut and the key turned. Not that Pascoe was
curious, but when you were the repository of other people's
secrets, you could not be too careful.

He glanced from the well-brushed floor-cloth to the rubbed
mahogany sideboard, from the sideboard to the curios on the
wall, the curios Pascoe had brought from foreign parts. Antiks
had wanted to rub the blood from the head-hunter's spear, and
had been told that on no account must she touch the weapons.
Her master looked at the spear closely—the one dirty thing in
the room—dull dark metal and darker smears. A man's blood.
A queer world where the soldier got honour and love o'
women for taking life, while if the civilian saw red he swung at
Newgate.

That was because the odds were uneven. When the soldier
slew it was nation against nation; but the ordinary citizen,
avenging his private quarrel, was fighting, not his enemy, but
the community. A man might no longer take his spear in his
hand, challenge his enemy, and fight with him to the death. In
such a contest the winner would be the loser, for the community would hang him. The dirty old spear stood for a clean way
of fighting, for something at once fierce and jovial.

Above the spear, higher on the brown wall, was a quiver containing half a dozen tiny arrows. A more deadly weapon that—one scratch and you were as good as dead. Mr. Corlyon, looking from the spear to the arrows, dwelt thoughtfully on the latter. The weapons of the pigmy, of the out-classed. Not a clean way of fighting . . . why not though? A man fought to kill.

Idly, his glance on the dusty quiver, he thought of Africa; of books he had read. He could imagine what happened . . . a narrow path between walls of growth, a black speck in the sky and a man walking . . . quickly . . . along the path. He did not know why, that man, but he was afraid. He would try not to quicken his pace, would tell himself that either side of him was only jungle, that the jungle was . . . untenanted.

Yet away back in the wood was the other man, the pigmy; and at the appointed moment a tiny brown shaft would wing out of the green. Its poison point would graze hand . . . cheek . . .

The sweat would break out on the man, his quick walk turn—in spite of him—into a run. He would be running, poor devil, from what he carried in him . . . and above, in the blue, the one black spot would be joined by others; and below, near the place where, at last, he dropped, the ant, the bone-pickers, would hurry out of their ant-hills.

He would die there and would not know to whom he owed his death.

Gale Corlyon looked from the slim brown arrows to the heavy spear. The pigmy has grasped one to the tenets of civilization. A man wanted to match himself with his opponent; but when the odds were unequal he strengthened his arm . . . as best he could . . .

V

On the sideboard Antiks had set out a decanter, a decanter of cut glass.

When he had fetched the wine from the cave at the end of the cellar, Gale would have made all the preparations he could.

Taking the lanthorn from its nail in the passage, he lighted the candle and went down the stone stairs. A grating revealed some boxes and barrels; revealed also a flagged passage leading to a low door. The cellar was under the garden, a narrow garden which ended abruptly at the foot of the hill; and the low door, being at the end furthest from the house, seemed as if it must open upon some elfin palace. It led, however, into the bluff which stood between Stowe on its estuary and the open sea.

The wood of this door was black with age and consisted of heavy timbers that had been salved from a wreck. The ends of these rose above and sank below the oblong aperture. It had no keyhole. Mr. Corlyon, when he set it in place, had preferred to padlock it with chain and staples to the wall. Opening the door, he let himself in and fastened it again on the inside.

He was in a rock cavity of some size, a cavity which pre-historic man, discovering, had adapted to his need. On one side, near another low door, was a raised place, a sort of giant bed. Made of stones, the spaces between had been filled with clay and the whole levelled. People sitting or lying on it would not suffer from the damp of the floor. On this primitive and ancient couch stood a chest, also primitive, for it had been hollowed from a tree trunk and bound with iron. As Mr. Corlyon passed in quest of the wine, he took the sight of this chest to his heart. The wine lay in casks and bottles at the dim end of the cave-dwelling; and his business was not with the chest, but—if Pascoe were further delayed, if indeed time served—he would like to waste it there.

A bottle of Bordeaux from a hollow in the rockface . . . a flagon of rum, stuff which Pascoe had brought in the smack, that he and his brother had carried through the fogou and stored in this old hiding-place.

He put the bottles in readiness by the door of entrance, then, crossing to the other, opened it on a low twisty passage. The lanthorn showed this to be of the height of a man, and about three feet wide, showed it running forward—tunnel-wise—into the bowels of the hill.

The fogou—this passage—lay like a black snake between Stowe and a sheltered cove where sea met estuary. As Mr. Corlyon stood to listen he heard the faint distant rumble of the tide, and it seemed to him that the familiar sound was dull, duller than usual.

Could anything have happened to the passage? His mind considered the length of uncoiled serpent thrusting mysteriously through the hill: and he remembered that in one place the rock roof had cracked a little, had let through stones and earth. Not much had fallen, surely not enough to diminish the sea thunder. The hush must be due to the state of the tide, or to the wind being off-shore. It was, however, a reminder. He must get Pascoe to help him shore up the bulging strata. One or two baulks from the wood weathering in the garden, and the fogou would be good for another thousand years.

With his mind's eye Mr. Corlyon regarded that velvet-black crevice. The fogou this work of an ancient and forgotten folk, intrigued him. It had been a means of egress or escape—a secret way. When Stowe was a stockaded fortress, its inhabitants had been able, in extremity, to escape by means of it, to get away from the oncoming, irresistible foe. The chieftains had handed the secret from father to son, and now it was his. The secrets of his fellow citizens were known to him and them, but this secret of the fogou was his unshared.

There was, of course, Pascoe; but Pascoe was his brother . . . no one else in the town of Stowe, in the duchy, in England, in the world, knew of the fogou; and, after all, a brother was your own flesh and blood.

He was the cleverest man in Stowe, and he held the old secret of the rulers. He wondered whether, perhaps, he were descended from them, whether his fine-sounding name . . . Corlyon . . . had some tribal meaning. He wished he knew.

Turning back into the cave, he went over to the giant bed of welded stones and clay. The chest that stood on it was, by comparison, a thing of yesterday, and yet the tree from which it had been cut had done its leafing centuries ago. Mr. Corlyon, unfastening the two locks, raised the lid, but the interior thus revealed showed, at first, entirely commonplace. A piece of holland had been folded to fit the oblong. It was thick, a piece some yards long. Lifting it out, he laid it before him on the dry ground.

Beneath it, in two rows, were a number of pigskin bags, the mouths of which were fastened with leathern thongs. Gale, on his hunkers by the chest, touched each with a slim finger, counting. The number was correct. So many fat-sided bags, so many waiting to be filled. He picked up an empty bag, laid it by. The money Pascoe received for the emeralds should be dropped, coin by coin, into that happy bag; it should no longer suffer among its fellows the reproach of emptiness. Pascoe was coming home, and Pascoe would bring money, money that should be added to this store his brother kept hidden in the depths of his dwelling. He lifted a full bag, unfastened the thong, poured the sovereigns on to the holland.

His business brought enough for his comfort, and he had not tried to develop it. What occupied his mind was the finger-in-every-pie work which brought no return, no monetary return; but being a good citizen he had to take thought of his old age, also for that of Pascoe.

He had told Pascoe what to buy and where to sell, had received from him the proceeds of these deals, had stored them in the pig-skin bags, and the bags in the shaped iron-bound trunk.

His savings.

A voice called to him from the top of the cellar stairs, "Maister! Maister!"

He shovelled the gold into its bag, fitted the bag into its place, the holland over all, and locked the chest.

"Maister, your brother be just comed. He'm ridin' down the street."

Pascoe, the young brother who went out empty and came back full, whose every voyage added a fat sum to the provision Mr. Corlyon was making, Pascoe was come.

Snatching up lanthorn and wine, Mr. Corlyon fastened behind him the door of the cave, and ran up the stair.

CHAPTER II

I

ANTIKS HELLYAR had lifted the cloth from the table, had washed the dishes, and gone home to her children. The men, desire of meat put from them, were smoking and talking. They lay back in deep chairs east and west of the hearth, and between them on the table the many facets of a cut-glass bottle sparkled in the radiance of lamp and firelight.

On the lamp was a green shade. Save for a little moon of light above the chimney, the upper part of the room was in darkness, but from the edges of the shade brightness flowed over table and floor, over Pascoe's short stuggy body and bronzed face, over the shining blackness of Mr. Corlyon's boots.

"I was looking for you quite an hour before you came."

"The rain!" and Pascoe reached for the square bottle.

"You—you stopped somewhere?" Not till Pascoe affirmed it could he believe what he already knew.

"At Treveglos."

A farm some way out of the town, a farm at least two miles from the baby-linen shop. "You did not see anything of the Liddicoats as you came along?"

Pascoe measured himself a tot of rum, and his brother noticed that the tot was ample. Of course, the lad had had a long ride, and he fresh from board-ship life. Tired, no doubt.

"Came down Main Street."

Main Street was the midmost of the three that opened on the harbour. Pascoe, riding into Stowe, must, if he came by way of it, have made a detour.

"Joe Gregor had asked me to order him a case of winter fruit. I thought I had better tell him it was on the way."

His excuse would hold water. "As you were late, I thought you must have stayed at the Liddicoats for supper?"

Pascoe understood that old Gale was curious; he wanted to be indulged with the truth of the matter. He was like that, a digger, and always at it.

"Thought you would be waiting for me . . . "

That ought to satisfy him, but no. "You were fond enough of dropping in there last time you were home."

Pascoe nodded. Why try to keep things to himself? Gale must know, and as well first as last. "Lot of water has flowed over the wheel since then." He smiled to himself, his mind shifting from adventures in Jamaica to his amusements when last in Stowe. Out of that three-months-old holiday a possibility stared at him. "How are they? How is Jenifer?"

The older man passed his hand over the pocket of his coat. He could feel the hard oblong of the carte-de-visite he had taken from his brother's mantelshelf. He would not acknowledge he had it, and nothing should induce him to give it back; but he noticed uncomfortably that Pascoe's voice was quick with interest.

"Jenifer?" She had seemed to him a little paler of late, less blooming. It made her only the more attractive. He would not tell Pascoe that; the fellow might find it out for himself. Mr. Corlyon, his impassive face a screen, said Jenifer was much as usual.

"Ah, then, that is all right." Oblivious of his brother he fell back into a dream. "Seemed," he said, "as if that shipwreck brought me luck."

"Brought you a broken leg and the loss of all you had."

Pascoe glanced at his loose blue trousers. "It brought more than it took. Leg is as good as ever, and while I was lying in hospital I—well, I thought things over a bit."

Mr. Corlyon felt his heart sink, Fool that he had been to think even Pascoe could forget her, forget such a maid as Jenifer? Sea-eyed, wheat-haired, and . . . her lips! The vision of her seemed to pass—a brightness—through the dull room.

He pulled himself up in his chair, and the light, cut off sharply by the green shade, showed only the steep hard collar, the dull black of his clothes. To Pascoe, on the brink of confession, it was as if he were speaking to someone who had suddenly become headless.

"It—it is about time I settled down."

"You think so?"

The voice, the still voice that came out of the shadow was disconcerting. Pascoe wished his brother had not withdrawn himself, become invisible.

"I mean it is time I got married."

In order to show himself companionable, Mr. Corlyon had been smoking. The pipe was in his hand, but his arm remained stretched along the edge of the chair, and gradually the tobacco began to dull.

"Time? But—my dear lad, you are only——"

"Twenty-eight, last March!"

"I am forty odd," the voice had changed, had become charged with some emotion to which Pascoe could not put a name, "and I . . . have not married."

"A born old bachelor! I can never think of you with a wife and children."

"No? And yet men of my age——"

"Oh, I know." Gale was not old, not really old, still . . . he could not hope for the freshness of feeling that he, Pascoe, had. The man had gone past that. "Fact is, old chap, I wish you would marry. Don't like to think of you all alone here. Why not look out for somebody of your own age, somebody who has got a little money? A widow, say . . . "

"Like—Mrs. Liddicoat?"

Why should Gale's voice have an edge to it? Mrs. Liddicoat was all right. "You might do worse."

"Or better. I might, for instance, marry a woman that I was fond of."

Linking his hands behind his head, Pascoe smiled into a peopled darkness. His brother was incomprehensible, but what did it matter? Plump, kind Morwenna Liddicoat or another . . . the pale emotions of middle age! It was, anyway, a matter of slight importance. "Ah, if only you knew what it is to want a maid as I want Grizel."

Mr Corlyon sat forward, his face showing in the full light, showing the astonishment which possessed him. "Who?"

"Grizel—Grizel McVitie. Didn't I tell you that was her name?"

"You told me nothing." The voice rang out sharply. "I

thought you had come home to—to marry—to marry someone in Stowe."

"And of course you would rather I did?" Gale was naturally annoyed, would be more so when all was told. "Sorry, old man, but a chap can't marry to oblige his brother; and Grizel . . . there is not a maid in Stowe fit to hold a candle to her."

"Go on," said Corlyon, "let us have it all." He had taken a spill from the mantelshelf, and was busy refilling his pipe. Presently, he sat back, puffing.

"Out with it," he said, cheerfully.

"The McVities," Pascoe told him, "were kind to me when I broke my leg. They had a place at Constant Springs. As soon as I was able to get out of bed they asked me there."

"Jamaica people?"

"Old McVitie went out as a young man, went out from Scotland. He is a ship's broker."

"Married out there?"

"Lord, no, married an Englishwoman. Get this into your noddle, Gale, the McVities aren't dark, they are as white as you and me."

II

Gale had taken it just as Pascoe, conning his confession on the voyage home, had known he would. The one thing in the world he wanted was to see Pascoe happily married. With his eyes full of handsome interest he had shaken his brother's hand. A sweetheart in every port had beem Pascoe's way, but this was better.

And the other, an obscure doubt laid to rest, opened his heart. Gale, being so much older, had always been like a father. A fellow could speak out to him. Being only, after all, a brother, he could not go back on you.

Sitting at ease, smoking placidly, even sipping the hot rum and water at his elbow, Corlyon listened. He had never felt more comfortable, more like a warm, full-fed, purring cat. Pascoe with a wife! A little house, and in it Pascoe's young

wife, and presently Pascoe's children! Good . . . it could not
have been better.

As the sailor talked, his words shuttling about the figure of
that distant girl, Corlyon gradually became aware of the
McVities. They drifted in and out of the tale. A kindly shrewd
father, a mother who kept her eye on her two daughters, sons
who were away, one a doctor, one ranching in Florida.
Alexander McVitie had made it plain that he would tolerate no
"hole-and-corner" love-making. All open and above-board.
Come forward with your offer, or clear out. And Pascoe had
lost his heart. "Nothing new, that. You've been in love a pretty
many times."

"I mean it now." The other women hadn't counted, this was
the one . . . he only wanted to get back to her . . . couldn't eat
or sleep for thinking of her. There was a ship sailing on
Monday . . .

"On Monday? Come, come!"

But Pascoe had made up his mind. The emotion compelling
him was too strong. When a chap felt like that, he did not waste
time. Gale could not be expected to understand, but he,
Pascoe, must go.

"And when you are tied up good and tight, you'll bring her
home?" He must find them a house; must have it papered and
painted in readiness. No trouble that, he would enjoy it.

Under his kindly planning was a secret warmth, the hope of
similar adventure. Pascoe and his over-seas maiden; but he,
Gale, would be content with one who had spent all her walking
and sleeping hours in little old Stowe. If only she would have
him, and she might . . . now that Pascoe was out of the way.

As in a dream he saw the young man's face change, grow
apologetic. "Bring her home—here? No, her father would not
hear of it. He made a point of our living out there."

"In Jamaica? But you are not going to, are you?" What
about the secret trade, the articles Pascoe invested money in as
Gale's agent? What about bags that had still to be filled?

"Can't help myself. Both McVitie's sons being away he
really needs another man in the business."

"But you—you wouldn't know enough—a sailor like you."

"He says my knowledge of shipping will be useful to him."

"And you really think of settling in Jamaica?" His thoughts were with his hoard. The fat bags represented a goodish bit of money, but he had looked forward to many more of Pascoe's laden home-comings. It seemed to him that his brother was acting shabbily. Without warning, without even seeming to realize what he was about, he proposed to put an end to the trading that brought him yearly such a comfortable sum. How selfish were even the best! A girl shyly lifted her blue eyes, and you might whistle for your money. That was Pascoe all over . . . unstable.

But then, if he had not been happy-go-lucky he would have traded for himself, and he had a wonderful eye for bargains. Gale did him justice. The lad bought in a cheap market, and always turned in to him, Gale, the difference. Yes . . . all these years. And it was a goodly sum. If he had chosen to lay it out . . . invest it . . . buy land . . .

But there had been no need. He earned enough for his bachelor requirements. Now, perhaps . . .

"You see, Gale, he has offered me a share in the business."

The pebble rolling hither and thither for so long had found a rich hollow.

"He is doing well," Pascoe said. It's a good business. I should be a fool if I did not take on the job."

Gale had almost uttered the words behind his lips, "And what about me?"

Had Pascoe no thought for anyone but himself? Gale dwelt on the long affection he had borne his young brother . . . apparently it was no more to Pascoe than ballast. For the sake of this girl he would jettison it without hesitation.

"I congratulate you, but," he must try him a little further, make sure, "you'll be back here, now and again?"

"Daresay I shall, though old McVitie says, 'where a man makes his home, there he should bide.' He has never been back. But I am different. Fact is," he laughed at his fatuousness, "I want you to see Grizel; and I want to take her around, show her places, the fogou, and so on . . . the places I've told her about."

"The places in some way connected with you?"

"That's it, She'll be interested. She'll want to see them." He went on talking, and Gale, half listening, let his eyes rest on the straight handsome features, the moving lips. Pascoe was entirely occupied with the girl and his relation to her. That Gale would miss his home-coming had hardly occured to him. It was of no importance. He had put it on one side and forgotten it.

III

"How did you get hold of the emeralds?"

"Ship was at Cartagena for cargo, and I met a miner from up-country, a Cornishman, and stood him drinks. He had the stones. I don't know how he came by them, but he needed to pass them on, and pretty quick, too."

If Pascoe was showing a cold disregard for Gale's future, at least he had done him good service up to date. Queer chap, Pascoe, he put your suggestions into practice, made money for you, and thought nothing of it. All in the day's work. The adventure of a bargain as good as any other adventure, but no better.

"You sold the stones in Plymouth?"

Pascoe saw he was expected to render account, and he was willing. The tale of his secret earnings had always been poured into Gale's ears, Gale, the trustworthy old buffer who took care of the money. "Malet gave me fifty for the two biggest. They were worth more, but he wouldn't part."

"And the others?"

"Twenty for the others, seventy in all."

"That's not so bad."

"I gave ten for them!" He chuckled over the easy money, thought of the one stone he had kept back, the stone which was to be set in a gold band for Grizel. Seventy pounds and a fine ring . . . all that for a tenner . . . not so dusty!

Gale looked over his shoulder at the window. The curtains hung brown and straight across the aperture. The brothers

were as safe from prying eyes as if they had been in the Cave.
"Let's see the colour of it."

That, too, Pascoe would give. With an effort—because of its
packed rotundity—he pulled a bag out of his trouser pocket.
"Seventy pounds," he gloated, and, untying the neck of the
canvas bag, poured them on to the black tray.

They slid over each other with a sweet metallic sound, they
twinkled in the yellow light of the lamp. Gale, stretching a lean
finger, would have stirred them, but . . . he did not realize how
. . . Pascoe was before him.

"Seventy pounds that I have earned," he said.

IV

Gale was thankful for the long training in discretion which
listening to other people's private affairs had given him. At that
amazing utterance of Pascoe's he had felt something fall away
inside, but he had not spoken. He had sat, tensely silent,
apprehension growing apace; but, growing behind the still
mask of his face, growing invisibly.

"Seventy pounds that I have earned!"

The necessity was on Gale for some sort of movement, some
outlet for the rush of emotion. He got up, a tall thin man who
looked his age. "The fire wants mending. I'll fetch a motte."

In the basket under the kitchen window were a couple of big
tree roots—mottes. Gale took the hatchet, and carrying the
bigger piece into the yard, shaped and trimmed it. The passion
of him went into the blows. He came back to the brown
sitting-room his usual pale but debonair self. He was ready
now for this new Pascoe.

His glance, as he entered, went to the tray; but the shining
heap had vanished.

Pascoe must have put the gold back into his pocket.

V

"Come," Gale began roughly, then pulled up short. With this new Pascoe he must walk warily. "I mean . . . move aside, the motte is heavy."

He thrust the root deep into the hot smouldering turf, thrust so fiercely that it was as if he would have pushed it through the fire-basket. That money . . . a strange thing for Pascoe to have done . . . what did he mean by it?

If he were short of cash, wanted some to buy his girl a present, wanted some for furnishing, he had only to ask for it. Gale had always, well . . . not given him money to waste . . . but been generous. If he were treated properly, no one was more open-handed.

From behind him, still busy with the fire, came Pascoe's fresh-air voice. "We must settle up, I think."

"Settle up?" What was there to "settle up"? The old brown house on quay-side had been their mutual home, the expenses of its upkeep Gale's affair. He had never grumbled at the cost, had been glad to think Pascoe should have a home to which he could return.

Pascoe might have offered, if not to share expenses, at least to pay a little, but he had not. Where money was concerned, he had always been a bit careless. Gale had had to think for them both.

If he had not, they might have drifted into Poverty Street. He turned his back on the fire. From his lean height he looked down, questioningly, on his brother. "Settle up?"

"You know, father left this house between us," Pascoe said. "We'll get it valued, and you can buy me out, or we'll sell it."

The house—so solid, so long Gale's house—thinned suddenly to paper. Though built on "Hard country," it heaved under his feet. The house in which he had been born, in which he had spent the forty odd years of his life, the house which, since the death of his father, he had looked on as indisputably his . . .

Pascoe had put in a claim: Pascoe, who, for ten years, had paid nothing—

"You've lived in it rent free," Pascoe was saying. "Of course, that is no matter, you were welcome."

Rent free? Was that how he had looked at it? The revelation of his mind was bewildering. Had Gale been mistaken? Was Pascoe not the happy-go-lucky sailor, indifferent to money, keen only on adventure? Was he not the affectionate lad . . .

But he had had proof already that Pascoe cared for him, Gale, not so much as a snap of the fingers. Grizel filled his heart. He could bid farewell to the brother who had fathered him, who had been devoted to him, without so much as a backward look. He was, indeed, only impatient to be gone.

A bitter awakening . . . but Gale must not think of that now. A situation had arisen with which he must deal. That first. Pascoe, no longer the easy, semi-dependent young brother, was demanding his . . . rights. Yes, the unconscionable dog, that no doubt was how he looked on it. The letter of the law . . . but law was not justice . . . and law between brothers . . .

Why, law was not even common sense! It would have been wiser to have left things as they were, to have kept the old house on quay-side as a refuge to which Pascoe could always come. You couldn't tell . . . life was uncertain . . . he might be back, wife and all, within a twelvemonth. This talk of selling . . .

That Pascoe could contemplate it for a moment. The house was—home.

Mr. Corlyon could not imagine himself dislodged, a snail from whom its shell had been taken. Why, he would do extra work, do without comfort, live on bread and tea rather than turn out. Alarming, this talk. Not that it meant anything, for he would, of course, have the house valued, find the money to buy Pascoe out; but the suggestion had opened a vista of possibilities.

"And," pursued the cheery voice, "and there's the money."

Gale found his lips dry. The money? What money?

"I should think by now it will be a brave sum."

"But father did not leave any money." A mistake somewhere. Pascoe could not mean, impossible that he should mean . . .

"I know . . . poor old father; if he had not been so fond of his glass, he would have left us more than the house."

Us!

"No—I mean the money I have made; the money I gave you to take care of for me." He smiled at his brother. "I knew it would be safe in your hands. Get milk out of a cheese, easier than money out of you. How much is it? I'll be bound you know."

In the turmoil of his wrath and excitement, Gale clung to one thought. He must be wary. He must not show what he was feeling. He must not give anything away, not information, not hinself. This unheard of, egregious, abominable demand . . .

"I don't, though."

Was the effort that he was making palpable? He glanced at Pascoe, at the smiling happiness of him, and felt he could no longer endure the sight. Turning, he pushed his chair a little back, and sat down. He wanted time . . . a few moments' grace . . . self-control was sometimes so very difficult to compass. But he mustn't speak. It was imperative that he should keep the words back.

"Let's have a squint at it, then. Some fun counting it up."

Gale leaned back in his chair, his face once more a paleness in the green dusk of the lampshade. "I would not bother about it to-night. To-morrow will be soon enough."

"If you don't want to stir out of this, give me the key and I'll go get it."

Go get it . . . down the cellar stairs, into the cave . . . Gale's sanctuary! Pascoe put out a hand, but Gale, sitting back in the shadow, did not move. How much longer would he be able to sit there . . . silent . . . hiding his bitterness. And it was more than bitterness. Something had broken . . .

"What's the hurry to-night? Business in business hours. You have trusted me all these years, surely one night more isn't going to break the square?"

Pascoe sat there, contemplative. Of course, just as Gale liked, but he had been thinking of it during the voyage home, wondering how much he had. "You see—I have to buy my partnership in McVitie's business."

Gale's groping mind had found the solution to the problem. Pascoe would not get his wife unless he stood in with the girl's father. An obedient . . . obedient? Perhaps even, she was the scheming daughter of this canny Scot. McVitie wanted money, and Pascoe was to supply it. Not having any of his own, he had bethought him of Gale's money. An unscrupulous lot, and Pascoe as bad as the others. He would never have thought it of his brother . . . still, when a woman stood at the turn of the road, beckoning . . .

How did Pascoe know that McVitie's business was flourishing? The fact was, he did not know. He had accepted McVitie's statements, and McVitie, of course, had put his best foot foremost. Without inquiry, Pascoe was going to hand over Gale's money . . .

From start to finish the trading had been Gale's idea, carried on under his direction, and the proceeds handed over. He thought of the double row of pigskin bags in the chest. His savings, ten years of carefulness, of slowly mounting addition, and now a hand stretched towards it, a greedy acquisitive hand.

If only he could have struck it down.

He could not trust himself much longer—this outrageous claim!

He would not give up the money . . . his money . . . that, at least, was certain. But how would he fend off those eager fingers? He must think, must have time.

The night lay black about him, and he felt thankful for the long hours. Before the grey of morning he would know what . . . not what he would do . . . no indeed, but how he should set about it.

An unconscionable, a wicked demand . . . yes, and a mercenary pair. Pascoe was playing into their hands. The fool . . .

"I think," Gale said, and he rose with a certain fierce briskness, "I think we'll go to bed."

The other laughed apologetically, as he followed.

"I haven't half told you about Grizel, still—there is always to-morrow."

CHAPTER III

I

"Good night!"

On the threshold of his room Gale Corlyon yawned as if he were tired. Hitherto, bolting the front door and putting up the chain, he had felt he was shutting himself and Pascoe in, that they two were united against a world of marauders. Now, suddenly, horribly, the situation had changed. Pascoe, with whom he had thought of himself as standing shoulder to shoulder, had become hostile.

Gale was conscious of a desire to be alone, the only wakeful creature in the dark house. He wanted to be surrounded by thickness on thickness of dead opaque night . . . he wanted to bar out Pascoe.

It had come, all of a moment, to that. He wanted, not to shut Pascoe in, but out.

This was not the brother whom a few hours earlier he had welcomed with such a show of kindly preparation; and the only way to be rid of him— of this intruder—was to feign a drowsiness he did not feel.

If the fellow thought he, Gale, had taken his demand as a matter of course, had not been bothered by it, had, in fact, gone off casually to bed, he also would sleep; and, once asleep, the irritation, of his presence would be, in part, removed. He would become, if not a nothingness, at least only a tooth which, though it held possibilities, did not ache.

Gale could wait. It seemed indeed as if he must, as if his brain were numb, had been stupefied; as if with that flame of alien consciousness burning so close to him, he could not think, He must—that was it—he must have the house to himself.

His house, his poor house, his house on which a sacrilegious finger had been laid.

The house which, if Pascoe had not been saved from the wreck, would have been legally his.

He had so nearly, so very nearly, not come back.

Gale visualized that long swim, those hours in the water. At the moment of failing endurance, a big wave had rolled Pascoe up the beach, left him there. It might so easily have rolled him under.

And if he had been drowned . . .

If—if! Ay—but "if" is a crooked letter.

Pascoe had come back to show Gale the sort of man he was, to claim half of the house on Quayside, and all the money.

He would strip his brother, and then bid him good-bye. "A man should bide where he made his home."

Gale, holding his head in his hands, in his long nervous hands, which were so capable, groaned to himself, groaned softly lest Pascoe should hear.

He had thought to know his brother as he knew the little limewashed rooms of the house. Light, easy, ay—but loyal.

Across the pale, candle-lit room his eyes sought an old and fading photo that hung on the wall, the photo of Pascoe that he had had taken on his first voyage. He had had that photo—for how many years? It must be over a dozen.

He drew a long breath. More than a dozen years, and during that time he had set the clock of life by his brother's comings and goings.

And Pascoe had seemed . . .

That was it—seemed; good Lord, yes, he had only seemed. His loyalty, his affection had been no more a part of him than his clothes.

The real Pascoe . . . Gale could not see him clearly, could not see all of him, but what he saw . . .

The world seemed to Gale bottomless as Dozmarè Pool, a black hollow through which one sank and sank. He had lost something, but it was not Pascoe.

The Pascoe to whom he had been so much attached had never existed. In his place stood a stranger, a stranger who, under a breezy manner, had hidden fierce and predatory thoughts, who had regarded Gale, not as flesh of his flesh, but as an "old buffer" away back in Stowe, who might be plundered.

It hurt . . . it was as if splintered glass were running into his flesh, were letting out warmth and red blood and some sort of stored emotion.

On the cane chair by his narrow iron bed, his bed of a bachelor, he sat very still, his heart crying out in him.

He wanted the old illusion, the old happy belief.

He wanted, not this new Pascoe with the hard smiling eyes, but the young brother who had come to him when in trouble, who had borrowed his money, and been at home under his roof.

The years of comradeship, so many and now that he was looking back, so short!

From the room across the landing came sounds of movement, the sudden dipping creak of a bed. Pascoe, his demand made, and his affairs in order, was settling to happy dreams of his sweetheart, would dream, perhaps, of the money he was filching from Gale, the money that was her price.

Very soon now he would be asleep.

And then Gale might go, through the silent house, down and down.

He needed to see the treasure at which Pascoe had snatched, to touch it, to comfort himself with it.

It was all he had.

Why, when Pascoe made that outrageous demand, had Gale not said that he had speculated with the money, lost it?

He had, of course, been taken by surprise; but he was not a liar. The money was his, and he would fight for it. Fight, but not deny the existence of it.

Going quietly to the door, he pulled it open.

II

From Pascoe's room came the sound, rhythmic and slow, of deeply drawn breath. He was asleep, asleep with his door left casually ajar. Gale, candle in hand, saw the oblong and in that pocket of blackness, the dim outlines of furniture. For the time being his enemy was, as it were, buried. Sleep had covered Pascoe, rendered him deaf and blind and the house was once more Gale's. He went down the bedroom stairs, the cellar stairs. At the other end of the flagged path, the low black door scowled from the hill-side. Letting himself in, he did not close it behind him. He had the feeling that he must not be shut away from the house, that he must be able to hear what went on in it.

Once, inside the cave he went directly to the great bed of clay-fixed stones. The old chest, banded with rusty iron, wore for him a friendly aspect. Here, at least, was something that would not change, not in a lifetime, not in many. Its seeming was the real thing. Grey wood from the outside to the in, grey wood that had been hollowed to hold what man wished to store.

He threw back the lid, spread out the holland, emptied on to it the pigskin bags. His fingers were trembling as he untied them. Ten bags . . . the savings of ten years. With the contents of those bags he might have hired himself servants, taken a larger house, married a wife; but he had been content to slip coin after coin into the little greedy mouths; to save until bag after bag was full, over-full, until he might thong it about and start on the next.

What were figures on paper to addition in the concrete, to that adding of sovereign to sovereign? No emotion so satisfying.

The flame of the candle burnt steadily in the still air of the cave: its light fell on the pyramid of shining coins.

Gale felt his heart swell, felt that his chest was not big enough to contain it, that it must choke him.

Here was substance which would not change into fairy gold . . . into withered leaves.

Affection? No, only this was real.

He stretched his arms, curving them round the glittering heap. He wanted to lay his cheek on the cold smoothness of the metal. The money was his . . . his . . .

Within him something hard began to push, to grow.

III

"Hullo, Gale!" cried a voice from the doorway. "So this is where you are?"

Pascoe, dark hair in a tousle, but no hint of sleep in his eyes, stepped up to the giant bed. He was looking, not at Gale, but at the money and he was smiling.

What did it mean? Pascoe's door had been ajar . . . on purpose? He, too, had been waiting?

"After all," Pascoe said, "you wanted to know. Come on, then, we'll count it."

He seated himself on the edge of the raised place, sat with his back to Gale; and Gale, watching him, thought how singularly unprotected people were who had their backs to you. No scaly armour, not even a thick hide.

To take what a man had, to sit as a matter of course with your back to him, showed the esteem in which you held him . . . the lack of esteem. A fangless lion whose claws had been cut; an old cat by the hearth.

The candle-flame had swooned in the breeze of Pascoe's sudden entry. It climbed again, a yellow flame about a thick inordinately long wick and the smoke rippled blackly to the rook roof. Gale, staring at Pascoe's back, at his head bent over the coins, at the busy movement of his hands, wondered how he could ever have thought the fellow good-looking. Too wide and thick for his height, why, he was almost squat; and his hands . . . the dishonest thumb . . .

IV

Having separated the sovereigns from the half-sovereigns, Pascoe was heaping the former in tens, the latter in twenties; and behind him the older man waited.

"My word, old fellow," Pascoe said at last and, leaning back, looked up with the old affectionate glance. "If it had not been for you I should not have saved half as much."

Gale let out a careful driblet of words. "You would not."

"You have looked after my interests mighty well. Could not have done better if they had been your own."

The breezy manner, genial, hearty, was that with which he was familiar—but Gale was wondering how he had been taken in by it. The veneer of walnut on plain wood . . .

"I put the money by. Yes, dragged in the chest and had the bags made and filled them. I filled them till they brimmed. Every pound they hold, I saved."

"You did." Pascoe smiled an acknowledgment. The little rouleaux, the tens and twenties, would give him his wife and a home worthy of her. "Mean a lot to me, these do. Never thought I should be as glad of them as I am."

"Pascoe—" Gale caught at the blurted word, tried to dam the black tide, failed. "If you didn't think to marry and the maid's father hadn't bought you, never a word should I have heard about this money." Sweeping his arm out towards the gold he spoke with more deliberation. "You spent what you earned, you would have spent this. It isn't yours and until it suited your book you never thought of it as yours."

"Not mine?" Pascoe said, a little breathlessly. He was ready for old Gale. The chap was fond of money, but he had always been straight-dealing. When he came to think it over, he would see he had not any right to this. "Oh yes 'tis mine right enough. I earned it."

"You? You bought where I told you to, sold as I bade you and brought me the proceeds. You were my agent."

"Not a bit of it, I kept account of every halfpenny I gave you, the dates and all. Believe I got it on me," he searched his pockets. "No, must have left it with McVitie."

Gale was taken aback. "You kept an account, you gave that account to McVitie?"

A fresh revelation of under-currents. Pascoe, handing over sum after sum, had not commented on them, yet had kept an account; and the paper of figures had been left behind—with McVitie—carefully. Pascoe had not needed to count the coins in the box, he had known as well as Gale what the sum total should be.

"Why, yes. No harm in that, was there? It was as well for the man to know how much I could put into the business. It would have been more if you had invested it, or put it on deposit at the bank."

There it was, just as it had been handed over, a lump of dead metal; and what was the use to anyone of bottled money? He had a sense of injury.

"My God!" Gale said.

"Don't look at me like that." Sitting between his brother and the money, he seemed small and gnome-like. The candle which was behind him was reflected in Gale's eyes, twin flames in eyes as darkly bright as agates. Pascoe felt a momentary doubt. Old Gale looked . . .

He could not put a name to it but ancestors of his had been ill-wished by men who had looked at them, who had looked like that.

"Come!" said he, with propitiatory glance and smile. "Money's mine and I've got to have it, but no need for us to part bad friends."

"I'm the wrong man to rob," Gale answered him.

Pascoe, sweeping the gold together, made a bag of the holland. Absurd, of course, but he felt queer . . . daunted. He must get back to his room, to the security of those four walls.

A good thing—as he had the money—to turn the key in his door. With the door locked a man might sleep sound.

Money or no money, a good thing to have a stout and locked door between you and . . .

And what?

CHAPTER IV

Jenifer

I

"WHAT, Jenifer? All by yourself?"

Gale Corlyon coming through the shop had noted Mrs. Liddicoat's absence. Nor was she in the half-parlour, half-kitchen, at the back. Only Jenifer, blossoming golden and rose-red in the obscurity.

"Mammy's overstairs." The girl was sitting on the window-bench, and the light, falling on a slope of garden that was always green, fell also on Jenifer, on her bent head, her warm smooth cheek. She had looked up on Mr. Corlyon's entrance and her glance had been welcoming. He noticed, however, that it slid past him, down the shop to the door, that when she returned to her needlework it was with a faint sigh.

"What are you doing?"

"'Tis an order we've had for embroidery, order from young Mrs. Pendragon." Between her fingers she held a tiny cap. She was embroidering on it a design, the crest and arms of the Pendragons.

"Ah," said Gale and seated himself beside her on the bench, "I call that a waste of time. You should be minding your own work and leave doing other peoples'."

His nearness affected her unpleasantly. It was not Mr. Corlyon who should have sat there. But that was always the way. The wrong man came, while the one for whom you looked till you were so restless you did not know how to sit still, he was late.

Where was Pascoe? He had said he was coming to supper, that he would come in with his brother.

Why then had Mr. Corlyon come in by himself? Did it mean Pascoe had gone elsewhere? She glanced at the other. She would have liked to question him, but could not quite get the words past her lips.

Over her tilted face the sun poured a revealing clarity of light. Gale looked at her lips. Soft full red lips. He put out a hand . . .

He would take the round white chin in his hand, pull her nearer.

"Don't," she said, her voice harsh, but instantly she repented. She was being rude to Mammy's friend. "I—I don't like being touched."

He leaned forward, came within that radiance of sun. "What! not even by me?"

Grey hairs at his temples . . . old as her mother, older . . . and his hand! The skin on it was loose, the knuckles were large, the flesh had gone from the bones. It was an old hand

"No."

A quality in his voice that she deprecated. "Why not, Jenifer?"

She might not tell him, not yet. Perhaps after to-night . . .

"You are Mammy's friend." She had got up, moved away.

"I'd rather be yours."

"You can't be."

"Don't you say that to me." He spoke with a vehemence that was startling and on his face was a plain nakedness of desire. Jenifer shrank from it. Not Mr. Corlyon, no.

"You are too old," she said, fending him off with the weapon readiest to hand.

"I am not. It isn't that." The new difficult voice beat harshly on her reserve. She had not known, had not even dimly suspected, had always thought of him as a quiet old boy, Mammy's friend. Yes, and he was old; but, as he said, it wasn't that. Her heart was full . . . full of secret trouble . . . why did he come bothering?

"'Tis, then."

"Jenifer, 'tis you I want and nobody else."

The tears . . . annoyance, shame, even a vague pity for the man because of that urge in his voice, because she understood too well, stood in her eyes.

"No."

"You can't care for anyone else?" He searched the soft face, trying to look through it into the girl's heart. "Surely not—you are too young?"

Too young—she!

And the last three months, the longing, the fear.

"Don't!" she said and lifted her hand as if the words were tangible, were sharp, stabbing things, as if she would shield her heart from them.

But his need of her was blinding him. "I've come here week after week———"

He had come to supper with her mother and after the meal they had played cribbage or sat one on each side of the hearth talking or had gone for a stroll—he and her mother.

"I've come thinking to have a word with you? Even a look would have been enough. I used to wonder sometimes whether perhaps my brother———"

Ah, now . . . she and Pascoe, they had tried to be secret; but love is a red flag in the breeze and how can it fail of being seen?

"But, last night———"

"Yes?"

He missed the wherefore of her sudden keenness.

"I made up my mind, last night, not to let it go on any longer . . ."

Let what go on? Had Pascoe said anything?

"At any rate you should know . . ."

Know? Know what?

"That 'twas you I want."

That he wanted her, he who mattered to her no more than last year's roses. She could have cried with vexation; and, suddenly, she felt that his grey hairs, his old hand, did really matter. She wanted Pascoe, his divinely rough hard kisses; and, for the moment, with a swing of emotion, she hated Gale. "Don't be so foolish as to think anything about me," she cried, in the exasperation of her longing. "I don't want you to. I can't bear that you should."

The stair creaked under a quick tread. The latch of the green door lifted and, conscience-stricken, Jenifer realized that the table was not yet laid for supper. What would Mammy think? She flew to the drawer for a clean cloth as Mrs. Liddicoat in a gown of dark purple with a ruffle of lace at the end of discreet sleeves, with a gold glint on the French lace of her collar, stepped down into the room. Her bright glance gathered in, at once, the girl, collecting in haste glass and cutlery, the man on the window-bench. They would have been chatting and that would have made them forget the time . . . a good thing Jenifer liked him well enough to chat with him.

"And where's Pascoe?"

But the long longed-for was at length come . . . the sailor, genial and hearty, had stepped in out of the chilly street.

"Ah," said Mrs. Liddicoat in her comfortable way, "Needn't ask because here he is now, coming in."

But she could have wished her daughter had not glowed with that quick increase of life. When she came down it had been a folded Jenifer, a Jenifer shadowy under the eyes, now it was a maid flowering. And Pascoe? The mother could not tell . . .

No use worrying, the young people must do as they would.

She glanced away from Pascoe and Jenifer, glanced at Mr. Corlyon. Was it her fancy or did he look tired? Been working too hard, perhaps. Ah well, she knew what should be waiting for a man at the end of his day's labour, and she smiled reassuringly, for the chicken had been in the oven just long enough, it would be done to a turn.

II

"There is someone in the shop, Jenifer."

The girl, still busy with the embroidery, was sitting by the white lamp.

"I think," Mrs. Liddicoat added, "it must be a man from Caer."

"I have got six done," Jenifer said. She was to have the money for them; and, until Pascoe came home, had worked briskly on the fine cambric. Since then the time had gone, she did not know how.

"Tell him you'll have the others ready by the next time he comes into Stowe."

It would be Denny Manhire, the groom; and he would have come to see Jenifer. Mrs. Liddicoat did not offer to go in the girl's place. Jenifer managed her own affairs.

And Jenifer, laying down the cap, wished her mother were not always so thoughtful. She had been sitting by Pascoe, listening to his sea-talk and she knew that the lamp-light, falling on her work, on her bright loose hair, on her full figure, was doing her a kindness. But, in the dimly-lighted shop, Denzil Manhire, the hard sprig of a stem of heather between his teeth, was waiting for her and he didn't care how long he waited.

"I will be back in a minute," she said, looking up with eyes that not so long ago Pascoe had found disturbing, that he still thought were fine.

Jenifer, handing Denny the little parcel of completed caps, explained that the others had yet to be embroidered. Perhaps . . . next time he was in Stowe . . .

That would be all right. Mrs. Pendragon did not need her "traäde," not yet; and he was coming over next week, would see to it that it was he, not Trispin Job, who came.

Meanwhile he had something to tell her.

"Have you, then?" She wanted to get back to Pascoe . . . this was the first time she had seen him, really seen him to talk to, since his return home. Still . . . there was no real hurry . . . not a bad thing to let him know that others liked her.

"Maister say I can have the rooms over the stable . . . four good rooms and a stove." Before that he had been only one of the grooms, now he had a home to offer.

Though Jenifer wanted to say the kind thing, she did not wish him to think those four rooms could mean anything to her.

"I suppose your mother's coming to do for you?"

"No, she don't want to leave Bloomfield." She had said that nothing would induce her to live over a lot of horses . . . "the noise of they things stanking up and down and the smell." But he withheld her comment. He wanted Jenifer to see the little rooms as comfortable, handsome.

"Well, if you can't get your mother you must get somebody else. I daresay there would be plenty who would like to come."

He was big and fair. Plenty of maidens in St. Ryn who would be walking on the headland, Sundays, if Denzil Manhire lived over Caer stables.

"If I can't have the one I want, I'll do for myself."

"Well," she said non-committally, "you know your own mind better'n anyone else. You must please yourself."

"Jenifer——" He leaned towards her across the painted deal of the counter, "can't 'ee come out for a walk?"

Against shop etiquette to turn a customer away, but she seized the opening. "No, I can't to-night, because we have got somebody in."

"Well, will you the next time I come over?"

"I dare say I shall be busy."

"You might as well, just for old time's sake. Won't 'ee now?"

She wavered. No harm in that, and she and Denny had been friends this many a year. "We'll see," she said, "but don't you build your hopes too much."

Better than nothing, he thought, as he mounted and, with the little packet safe in his pocket, rode from Stowe. The Master was in good humour these days, willing to give other men a chance, and the four rooms . . . Denny was some hand at the carpentering, he could put together a bacon rack, a bench for the wall, a cupboard. He rode warm, thinking of winter evenings. . .

Jenifer following him to the door, had watched him ride away. The street was empty, but the shops still glowed, a little riband of brightness, along the edge of the dark houses. "Pascoe," she called softly over her shoulder, "come and get a mouthful of fresh air."

III

As it was past closing time, Jenifer turned the lamp lower. It flickered for a minute or two and went out, but the place was not altogether in darkness. From the room in which Mammy was playing cribbage with Mr. Corlyon . . . "fifteen two, fifteen four and a pair's six . . . " flecks and beams of light. The biggest, falling through the square opening that raked the shop, lay like moonlight along the floor. Pascoe crossed it as he joined Jenifer at the door.

"Terribly hot in there," she said, turning her face to the breeze that came up the street from the harbour.

"You like the fresh air, Jennie?"

"I like the breeze," she said, "it blows you home to me."

Pascoe's tongue seemed to be stiffly hung . . . if only he could have trusted Gale to send out the money, if he had not had to return! He wondered, with a sinking heart, what was immediately ahead of him . . . discomfort, of course, and he deserved it; but, if everybody got their deserts, it would be an ugly world.

"The three months," Jenifer said, "have gone slowly. I only got one letter from you——"

"Which?" said he.

"The letter you posted at Trinidad and after that never a word."

"I told you about my time in hospital." Although the long immersion had not been death, he had come from it into a new phase of life. Until this evening he had not wasted a thought on the old existence, at least hardly a thought, not any on Jenifer.

Even now he saw her as across a dark space.

"You've been in Stowe two days," she said, "yet you never been to see me."

A rainbow bridge was being laid across the darkness. "Don't bother about that," he said, putting his arm over her shoulders —shoulders firm as warmed marble.

"You've got me, now."

She put her hand against his breast, not harshly but so that he should see she had found him negligent. "Do you mean that?"

"Kiss me . . . " that wonderful mouth of hers! His arm tightened and, though she doubted, she saw no reason to resist. He was come back, he wanted to kiss her, surely she had him

still? Her arms went up round his neck. "I've wanted you so
terribly."

IV

"When I came to myself, I was . . . laid out to dry and pretty
warm!"

"I might have lost you." The details of that life and death
adventure were poignantly interesting, but he was safe . . .
given back to her . . . She looked at the dark face, clear in the
many broken lights that had lifted night from the street. "I
wish you wasn't a sailor."

"Well," he said easily, "perhaps I have been knocking
around this old earth long enough."

"You are going to stay home?"

"I've had a job offered me and I hardly know what to do
about it."

"In Stowe?"

"Out there."

"Should you have to live there?"

"For a bit."

"I shouldn't like that then."

"D'you want to stop here all your life?"

"Please, Pascoe."

And she could, for all he cared.

"I'll have to go out again——" He knew instantly that he had
made a mistake. Why couldn't he have held his tongue? "To
settle up," he concluded, lamely.

"But not just at once?" Her tone was anxious.

"Oh, no."

"Can't we be married before you go?"

He remembered, as if it had been an occurrence in a former
life, that he had promised to marry her. To think she should
have taken him so seriously!

"Married before I go? Well, we will." Best to agree. He did
not want a fuss. It was quite enough to have his brother
unreasonable and ill-tempered . . .

She snuggled closer. "You'll see about it, then?"

"It?"

"The——" he might have helped her out, "the banns, Pascoe."

"The banns?"

"You'll have to see Mr. Stokoe, to put them in."

"I'll see him on Monday." His hand tightened on her, and he laughed. She thought she had him, but he had arranged to leave Stowe on Sunday night. By Monday he would be aboard ship.

What a rare old joke!

CHAPTER V

I

By the draped toilet table Jenifer was brushing her hair. Parted in the middle, it fell in smooth bright waves on either side, and Mrs. Liddicoat, already in bed, watched broodingly.

Behind her was the comfort of three pillows; and, lying down, she yet commanded the room, the big low room that spread over shop and kitchen, filling the space between Tippett, the watchmaker, on her right, and Rabey, the newsagent, on her left. Strange, she thought, to have other people within a yard or two on both sides, and yet be cut off from all but a dim knowledge of them. She and her daughter, though closely encompassed by the many people of Stowe, were absolutely alone in the small space of this room.

Yes, and each of them was shut away from the other. Mrs. Liddicoat's middle-aged flesh was folded about secret hopes. Time made only one difference. You still wanted things, but now you feared it was too late, that you would not get what you wanted.

Not you . . . but also not Jenifer, who was young. Ah, the poor maid, yet before her were the years that had gone by for you, the years in which things might happen, good things, the supreme good.

She was very quiet, had not spoken since they had come upstairs together, but she did not seem unhappy. Mrs. Liddicoat meditated on her daughter's dreamy withdrawn expression. She and Pascoe had stood for a long time in the dusk at the shop door . . . voices and silences, and then voices, the mother had taken note. If it had not been for Mr. Corlyon's news she might have thought Pascoe was still fond of Jenifer; but the older man's annoyance had revealed a sincere belief. And Jenifer was in ignorance . . . Pascoe would have told her a parcel of lies.

Mrs. Liddicoat did not want to make the girl unhappy; but no good came of keeping people in the dark.

"Well, dear life," she began, "had a pleasant evening?"

Jenifer, with quick fingers, began to plait the shining hair into a long tail. "Very," and she drew a contented breath, "I—I was a bit worried not hearing from Pascoe for so long, but he've made it all right."

"Have he?" Then it was as she had guessed . . .

Jenifer, blowing out the candle, jumped into bed; and, between her and her parent the big feather mattress rose in a soft curve.

"We are going to be married," she said.

The room was not altogether dark, for a greyness had slipped through the slats of the venetian blind; a greyness that tempered the velvet of the night. Mrs. Liddicoat, however, could not discern the features on the other pillow. "Married?"

"Pascoe promised before he went that, as soon as he came back, we'd be married. Why, Mammy, you knew that, I didn't make no secret of it."

"Ah, my dear, but three months makes a lot of difference to a man. They don't come back same as they go."

"Pascoe have."

"Jenifer, dear, was it he who spoke of the marriage, or was it you?"

"Why, Mammy, what's the matter?" Her fears, dispelled for a little, crowded back. The talk of marriage . . . it had been she, not Pascoe; still, he had not hesitated.

"Mr. Corlyon been talking to me."

Jenifer felt, of a sudden, angry with him. "Old gossip, then!"

"No, my dear, he don't gossip, and what's more, he don't lie."

"What have he said?" She did not want to know, for what her mother had said in his defence was true.

"He say Pascoe's going straight off back to Jamaica."

"Yes, he'm going back, but not for a bit."

"Mr. Corlyon told me ship was sailing Monday."

"It may, but Pascoe won't be in it."

"Why is he going back at all?"

"He've things to settle up."

"He have, indeed, there's a maid . . . "

"Mammy!"

"They'm tokened." She had dropped back into the vernacular. "Iss, my dear, they be, and he've come back to fetch what be 'is'n."

"No!" Her denial was violent. "I don't believe it. Why——" With his kisses still warm upon her lips how could she believe?

Mrs. Liddicoat, leaning against the three pillows, said no more. Best to let it sink in.

"Mammy—it isn't true! Oh—you don't think it true? Mammy . . . " A hand came out, caught at her shoulder. "Oh, Mammy, say it isn't true!"

"My dearie . . . what would be the good?"

II

"But why did he . . . " Jenifer, looking back, was noting straws. To begin with, her mother, having learned from Mr. Corlyon when Pascoe was expected, had told her, and she had watched for him to pass down the street.

Watched and watched, but he had come by way of the quay.

That morning she had met him by accident in the fish market, and he had declared he was on his way to the baby-linen shop . . .

Anyway, he was coming to supper, he and his brother.

She had been ready early, and Mr. Corlyon had come, but Pascoe had been late.

He had explained why, and the explanation had seemed . . . at the moment . . . to hold water.

Home after three months' absence, and he a lover? He should not have been late.

He need not have been. Not if he had really and truly wanted to come.

Well, avoidance . . . she must grant that; but surely it only showed she was not powerless, that the woman in Jamaica had no very strong hold.

Why should she have him? He had been Jenifer's and there were reasons . . .

"I don't want for him to go back." Mammy would help. When you got through your own strength, your own resources, there was always . . . Mammy!

"He promised——"

"Ay, men'll promise. It don't mean nothing."

"What can I do?"

Mrs. Liddicoat stroked the hot head. Was Pascoe worth keeping, Pascoe who so evidently had meant to leave his old sweetheart in the lurch? The boy was some handsome with his hair, curly as the middle of a sheep's back, but he had a many fancies, never stuck to no one. If Jenifer married him it would be a case of losing him, first to this woman, then to that. Better lose him now, for good and all.

"To-day's Friday," she spoke tentatively, "and Sunday evening he catches the coach at Triggyveal. There edn't much time."

Jenifer realized that Pascoe had meant to creep into Stowe, gather up his belongings, and be gone. Her heart swelled. He was her man, but someone else had put a spell on him.

"He wanted to get away quick," she said, with a fresh rush of tears. How could he behave so? She had been sweet to him, always sweet, and this was the return he made. How had he had the heart . . .

"Would you like me to speak to Mr. Corlyon?"

"'Twouldn't be no use." If Mr. Corlyon knew, he would see reason to hasten Pascoe's departure. No, they must manage without his help. Her indignation with Gale flashed into flame. Why, at this moment, when she had so many worries, did he want to add to them?

"Shall I see Pascoe, then?"

Jenifer, her head in the hollow of her mother's shoulder, was silent for a little, thinking. See Pascoe? If anyone saw him it had better be she. Having the knowledge that he had meant to desert her, she could be explicit. He should know what he was doing.

"Mammy, I'll see him myself. I can say things to him that you can't. But I dunno . . . he's a slippery one . . . "

"He's a proper dragon."

"I want to make it so that he just can't go." She was silent again, and this time for so long that Mrs. Liddicoat thought she must be getting sleepy.

She stirred at last. "There's the charmer to Springs . . ."

"Isaiah Quinion? Yes."

"I believe he can do anything he've a mind to."

III

Mrs. Liddicoat thought little Maddicott, of the Cornish Arms, might know the way to Springs. It was on the downs, fifteen to twenty miles from Stowe. She knew vaguely the direction in which it lay . . . somewhere among the hills east of the town, the round hills, visible on a fair day from the back window upstairs, but she had never had reason, hitherto, to visit Isaiah Quinion, or, as the town called him, "the ole feller what charm."

She told Mr. Maddicott that the mole on her cheek was giving trouble, and moles were unsightly, and she'd like it gone. Would he drive her over to Springs in his wagonnette? And he agreed.

From a country of deep lanes the party gradually came to wide stretches of country. The hedges thinned away, the trees shrank into furze. In an unhurried trot the shaggy pony carried the Liddicoats past Bogee and Mount Misery, past Crack-ruddle and Music Water and Wynnards Perch and Rosevannion. The moorland air brought them the scent of the heather, and Mrs. Liddicoat, sniffing, wondered what it might be that smelt of honey.

"'Tis some time since I been out here," little Maddicott said, stopping to ask a man where he should turn off the highway. "I've forgot whether we go through this farm or the next."

"But you've been here before, Mr. Maddicoat?"

"Oh, iss—drove Emma Pollard out last feasten. She had a running sore in her head, tarrible bad it were; but Isaiah Quinion charmed it, he did, and you should see it now. Lovely head of hair. They say she was the last person he cured."

"The last? Why, what do you mean?"

"You know he is dead, don't you?"

"Dead? No, I never heard."

"Died last Christmas. 'Tis his daughter, Elizabeth Brenton, do the charmin' now; old man taught her before he died."

"Ah, they say the 'gift' go from man to woman," but she was a little troubled. She had come to consult an old and experienced man, a man who though he lived remote from towns, was famous as far as Bodmin, perhaps even Truro, for his cures of ringworm, wildfire, adder's bite, and for his wisdom. Did the gift really go from father to daughter? Could young Mrs. Brenton have inherited the wisdom?

Mr. Maddicott turned through a farmyard on to the open moor. A trackway crossed the unfenced land which was dark with strange vegetation, dark, and yet richly coloured. The slopes were red with heather, and yellow with gorse. The many waters ran chuckling and gurgling over brown beds. It was indeed a land of great space and many waters, a land strange to Mrs. Liddicoat. She looked with interest at the gushing springs, at the gleams between the black stems of the plants. Where a stream ran over the trackway, a clapper bridge, a bridge made of a single moor stone, had been laid above it for the foot traveller, but the pony splashed indifferently through the water.

"'Tis no wonder this place is called the Springs," she said, and Maddicott told her he, for one, would not try to walk to the Quinion's farmstead across country. It was marshy, sodden, with unexpected pits and quags.

The house lay some miles beyond the last moorland village, a lone building of grey stone, widely visible upon the restless moor. About it the springs burbled, breaking from the healthy ground, spreading over the stones, busy with their singing and pouring. Mrs. Liddicoat and Jenifer left the wagonette at the farm gate, and went on alone to the knoll on which the house was built, and so to the glazed porch at the front.

A homely, middle-aged woman led them through a stone hall, the blue grey walls of which were unbroken by a peg or nail. Throwing open the door of a parlour and ushering them in, she said she would fetch her daughter.

"There are children here," Mrs. Liddicoat said, pointing to a boy's whip which lay across the books on the table. She spoke softly for she was nervous.

Jenifer, who had been thinking over what she had to say and ask, seemed to awaken. "Why, yes, I've heard Elizabeth has a boy. Her husband teals Springs for Mr. Quinion—I mean for her."

"Saving man, Mr. Quinion, if he bought Springs with what he made by charming. But there, people'll pay anything if they get what they do want."

The door opened, and the young woman, on whom the mantle of Isaiah Quinion had fallen, came quietly into the room.

IV

"I don't do this sort of thing," Elizabeth Brenton said. Jenifer had gone with her to an upper room and, sitting on the one chair while the other leaned against the chill white bed, had explained her wishes. "I cure disease. I can make that mole drop off your mother's face; but I don't meddle with what might not be right."

"You could do this for me," Jenifer said, "I know you could." The dark eyes under winged brows gave her confidence. This woman, young, remote, and yet a mother, had the power to help her.

"There's bad charms as well as good, but I only learnt the good ones. My charms are prayers."

Jenifer was convinced that they were more than prayers. Without doing anything Elizabeth Brenton made you conscious of her power. It was a power for good. You saw her, and knew at once that she could heal, that she could help you. "Then pray for me," Jenifer said.

The dark eyes scrutinized her, the witch pondered over what she saw, and Jenifer waited anxiously.

"You say he promised to marry you?"

"He promised solemnly that he would come back and marry me."

"And there is a good reason why he should keep his promise?"

Tears came easily to Jenifer. "Yes," she said, and the big drops splashed down on to her clasped hands.

"Have you anything of his with you?"

Having come prepared, she produced the long-hoarded treasure of a clean white handkerchief.

"I promise nothing, but——" the steady eyes were making Jenifer increasingly conscious of the something in this woman which would make her help efficacious, "I'll do what I can for you—I will charm this handkerchief, and you must give it to him. See it does not touch wood before you put it into his hands." She sat down, unfolded the handkerchief, and laid it diamond-ways across her knee. "Your name?"

"Jenifer Liddicoat."

"And his name?"

"Pascoe Corlyon."

Murmuring the names, Mrs. Brenton, bent her small dark head over the white square. "I have to say the charm three times," and turning in the opposite corners, she folded the handkerchief lengthwise, so that it resembled a long bandage.

"I can't hear what you say," Jenifer said, anxiously.

"That is right, you must not hear the words, for they are the charm." She smoothed the linen with workworn hands on which the nails were short and small; then began to mutter a sing-song of phrases. It seemed to the watching, deeply-impressed Jenifer as if Mrs. Brenton were saying them into the handkerchief, and that her voice held a note of command. It was calm, unhurried, it performed a ritual, but behind it lay force, a peculiar sort of withdrawn concentrated strength. At the end, she uttered an audible invocation—"in the Name of the Father, and of the Son, and of the Holy Ghost."

The smoothing, by the two hands from the centre to right and left, continued for some time. Jenifer felt as if the will of the young dark witch were being made manifest in that chill and silent room. She was convinced that what Elizabeth Brenton willed must come to pass; that once the handkerchief had been given to Pascoe he would forget the overseas woman.

The hands ceased their earnest, irregular, and yet rhythmical movement. Mrs Brenton lifted the long folded strip and breathed upon it, breathed into it her spirit. The ends were then folded over charm and breath.

She turned to Jenifer, her grave face full of kindliness. "You must have faith," she said, "the love he had for you is still there, underneath."

"And if I give him this it will come back?"

"I will do all I can to bring it back; . . . and," she repeated it, "you must have faith."

V

"'Twill be all right I b'lieve if I press this with an iron before I take it over to the Brown House?"

The Liddicoats, starting late for the moor, had been all Saturday about their business. When they reached home the evening was advanced, and neither thought of disturbing the brothers. Sunday lay before them, the whole of a white day, a day on which shops were shut and man seen in the streets.

"Iron isn't wood, my dear; but, whatever you do, don't let it touch the table or the ironing board."

Jenifer flattened the handkerchief into its unusual folds. It made a square, looked indeed much as usual, would look, she thought, all right to a man's eye. She was a little uncertain as to how she was to obtain the necessary interview with Pascoe. Keep watch at the bulging front window of the bedroom until he came out, then meet him, as it were, by accident? She put on a hat, and seated herself behind the long Nottingham lace curtains. She could see the Brown House and the warehouses beyond it on Quayside. It was the last of the houses, behind it a path climbed the green hill and ran beside the estuary along the cliffs. Jenifer had memories of that quiet lane from which the path sprang. She had waited in it for Pascoe, had gone there to meet him. So close to the heart of Stowe, yet unfrequented; a little green place, not overlooked by any window.

Mrs. Liddicoat went up the road to church, and when she returned Jenifer was still at the window.

"Come and eat your dinner," she said. "They won't be going out now. If I was you, dearie, I'd just go straight in this afternoon and ask for him."

But Jenifer wished to see Pascoe alone. She could not utter what had to be said with Mr. Corlyon listening. She was shy of Mr. Corlyon. She wanted him out of the way.

"Oh, go on," her mother said, "he won't eat you. I lay he know Pascoe has been courting ye."

But he didn't know, and he mustn't. Jenifer could not bear that he should. After dinner, she resumed her vigil, but that afternoon no one either came out of or went into the Brown House.

Jenifer waited in what was almost a stupor of anxiety; but at last, her patience exhausted, she decided that whatever might be thought by an observant public of her going to the house, go she must. As smoke was rising from the kitchen chimney, she knew someone must be at home, and she could only hope it wasn't Mr. Corlyon. She had waited so long now that the roads were filling with shadows. Perhaps, her flitting figure might pass unnoticed, anyway, the need was on her. Pascoe would be going soon, and she must see him, give him the handkerchief, tell him the truth. He would not go when he knew . . .

The gate at the end of the short garden creaked as she pushed it open. No one at the parlour window. She wished that she dare look over the brown wire blind and, if Pascoe were alone, signal to him. But Mr. Corlyon would probably be there too, and he would think. . .yes, seeing her, what would he think?

She rapped on the door with her knuckles, but though she heard some sort of stir within, it died away and nothing happened. She waited two or three minutes, then rang the bell, and now was certain that she could hear voices.

Why did not one of them come to the door? Probably Pascoe was busy packing, probably, too, on this, their last evening, they did not want people to drop in.

She couldn't help that. The white witch had told her to give the handkerchief to Pascoe, and she would do it. She rang again, and in the silent house the bell gave out a hollow reverberation. They did not mean to let her in.

For a moment she was blindly angry. She must see Pascoe. It was immensely important. Her future, her happiness, hung on the interview. She must reach him, tell him . . .

Had Mr. Corlyon seen her at the gate, guessed the reason of her visit, and decided that she should not see his brother? She had always been a little afraid of Mr. Corlyon. He was so taciturn, and behind his quietness, his smoothness, was a strange vitality. He would not want her to see Pascoe. Oh, but she must.

She stood thinking. No one about. No one to see what she did. She could run down the little secret lane till she reached the jutting stones, the stones in the wall. Pascoe had come over by those stones to find her waiting for him in the green dusk, and she knew exactly where they were. She could go in that way.

She must give him the handkerchief.

CHAPTER VI

I

THE tide was in, and as the Corlyons, on their way home from Mrs. Liddicoat's, came from between the walls of French Street, Gale noticed that it was full, that the grey water was lipping the quay-edge. A man coming out of The California, meandered in wide curves along the head of the basin. Nothing between him and deep water . . . easy for anyone, walking near the edge, to slip on the wet granite and overbalance . . . really, it was a wonder that more roysterers did not come by a liquid end.

He glanced at Pascoe, happy, and trolling a song. A few weeks ago he had been at the sea's mercy. But Pascoe could swim . . .

Curious the luck of drunkards, children, and those whom the gods loved.

Die young? Not they! They came up out of the sea, escaped the perils of earth, fire and water, and returned to rob and harass the just. Their days were long in the land; that is . . .

"You going to bed?" he asked, breaking the silence that had been maintained between them since Pascoe's seizure of the money.

"I believe so." He watched his brother turn the large key in the door lock. Queer old stick, had he come to his senses?

"I want you for a minute." He lighted the candle that stood ready on the hall table, and led the way into the parlour. "You are really going back to Jamaica?"

"I am."

"You start on Sunday?"

"That's so." He thought again of Jenifer's surprise, and a smile broadened on his brown and jolly face. "You might write and tell me how people take it when they know."

"You haven't told anybody, then?"

"Not a soul."

"And there are people in Stowe . . ."

"One or two."

"Debts?"

"No doubt they think I owe them something, but it isn't money."

Amusing to hoodwink people, so amusing that he trusted old Gale would forget his grievance and write.

Going to his desk Mr. Corlyon took out a paper. "You asked me to have the house valued."

Pascoe's smile changed, grew keen. "Who did it for us?"

"Polkinghorn. He says the place is worth about four hundred pounds."

"Four hundred? Quite that, if not more. If Stowe were to develop it would be a valuable site."

"Stowe is derelict, the Doom Bar has spoiled its chances. No shipping of any size will ever be able to get into the harbour."

"A few mammoth dredgers would make short work of the bar and this is the only harbour west side of the duchy. Still— call it four hundred."

"Having no money, I have had to take out a mortgage on the house. Here," he pushed four fifty-pounds notes across the table, "here is your share."

Pascoe picked up the notes, and after examining them, bestowed them in a wallet. "Sorry you had to do that."

Gale cleared his throat, "There is another matter," He said, his face straight and tense. "I've come to see that the money in the chest, though I saved it, does belong to you, Pascoe."

For a moment the other stared doubtfully; but the confession was in keeping with his estimate of Gale. An upright and scrupulous man. At first his love of money had been too strong for his probity; but he had slept on the matter, had come to see that he was in the wrong. After all, they were to part friends. "That's right." In return he must show his brother they were on the old footing. "Will you lend me your nag to take me to the coach, Sunday?"

"You are welcome to that one."

"Henwood can bring it back."

"Yes, surely." Mr. Corlyon unfolded the paper he had taken from his desk. "But to return to what I was saying. You have taken possession of the money and I should have a receipt for it. Best, though we are brothers, to have black upon white."

Pascoe took the paper and read it. He would make sure of the contents. The receipt would be in order, for old Gale was not the sort to try and cheat you; still, he, Pascoe, would sign nothing that he had not read.

"I, Pascoe Corlyon, about to leave Stowe to take up residence in the West Indies, hereby declare that my half-brother, Gale Corlyon, has paid over all the moneys belonging to me which were in his hands, and has paid his share of Tre-fogou, known locally as the Brown House, and I hereby give him full quittance.

"(Signed)"

Pascoe tried a quill on his nail, dropped it, and took up another. "Wonder how I shall get on in McVitie's counting house," he said. "I make a poor fist at writing."

He wrote his name in full—"Pascoe Viall Corlyon"—across the stamp of the receipt and added the date. "If you like," he said, looking up as he handed it back, "if you like I could still freight you goods on commission—tobacco, fruit, whatever I got hold of." He winked at Gale. "There is a lot more comes out of Columbia than people know of, and you've an eye for stones."

Mr. Corlyon locked the papers in his desk. "I'll think about it . . . let you know."

He had the receipt. If any questions were asked, he had it to show.

But who should ask any—why should they?

And what questions?

II

On Saturday morning, Pascoe, making purchases in the town, had noted with surprise that the shutters of the baby-linen shop were up. Catley, of Bate and Catley, the combined grocer and drapery stores, said he had seen Mrs. and Miss Liddicoat drive off in Tubby Maddicott's little old wagonnette, and as they'd a basket of food with them, he thought they would be gone for a brave little while. Astounding that Mr. Pascoe didn't know of it . . .

Pascoe was in agreement with Mr. Catley. He cast back over the talk of the previous evening, but could find nothing that would account for this expedition. Whatever the reason, it had been withheld, and this withholding made him uneasy. Did they know anything? They couldn't know, but they might suspect. Jenifer might fancy he had tried to avoid her—as he had. She might think he had not played the lover convincingly—and perhaps he hadn't. She was a pretty little woman, he couldn't run away from that; but he didn't care for her now; not a bit, he didn't, it was all Grizel with him.

Even if Jenifer suspected that he was deceiving her with his talk of marriage, what could she do? He thought uneasily of the law. But if the promises a man made when he was courting were to be considered binding . . .

He reflected with a sense of relief that men made the laws; they would not have been so foolish as to make such promises binding . . . they would know that to do so would incriminate all who ever went courting . . . all the race of men.

He was back at the Brown House in time for the mid-day dinner. Gale, who had not been out, was sitting in the armchair by the fire, and Pascoe wondered to see him with his hands idle.

"I thought you were such a busy man."

"Sometimes I work my brain."

"On other people's account?"

"I do not often need to work it on my own." He looked at Pascoe, and Pascoe had an uneasy feeling that the bright dark glance had passed beyond him, that it was focused on something at his back. He looked over his shoulder. Nothing behind him but the wall, and nothing on the wall but a few curios, nothing of any interest.

"The Liddicoats have gone driving," he said, drawing a chair to the table.

"So Mrs. Maddicott told me."

"She been here?"

"Came to consult me about an investment. She said her husband was driving them out to Springs."

"Springs?"

"Stowe get its water from Springs."

"But what should take the Liddicoats there?"

"Mrs. Liddicoat said she wanted a wart charmed." He began to cut the beef.

"'Tis late in the day for that, then."

"It has five hairs on it—that wart. I should be glad if Elizabeth Brenton could charm it away."

"But," Pascoe had thought his brother was a sceptic. If Gale believed in the power of charms, it would make a difference. He himself was by no means sure . . .

He remembered Isaiah Quinion. His eyes . . . so black and strange and piercing. People said he had ill-wished Tom Jonas's best horse, and when farmer went into his stable the following day, he had found it dead in stall. A bad man to cross, Isaiah Quinion.

If Jenifer knew that he, Pascoe, were deceiving her, would she have him ill-wished? The sea lay between him and Grizel . . .

"Do you hold with charming?" Pascoe asked.

"If the wart drops off Morwenna Liddicoat's face——"

"Aw, give me a straight answer, can't you?"

"Do I hold with charming? I suppose not, and yet . . . the truth is that queer things do happen!" His memory supplied examples, and his voice was grave, convinced. "I've known them to."

III

As Pascoe understood it, you could not ill-wish a person unless you set eyes on them. The eye had power, and if he did not see Jenifer again . . . yes, he would keep out of her way.

He would finish making his small purchases, the pretty

trifles you could not get in Kingston, the ribbons, veils, and fine stockings for Grizel, and then he would stay home. After all, only one more day.

There would be the riding through Stowe . . . but no, he would go by the lane. Horses did not often traverse it, but it was of a sufficient width. If necessary, he would lead the nag.

The lane went up behind the houses, it twisted among the gardens, and came out on the main road by Coulter's Folly. From there, nearly a straight line to Triggyveal and the Plymouth coach. He would not be quite at his ease, not quite comfortable until he were aboard ship. To-day, or next week, or next month, hitherto it had been of small consequence when he should start on a fresh voyage; now, he must not waste a day.

Grizel was waiting. Ah, but was she? He was hers, but was she equally his? If he were only sure of her.

He must get back. Nothing must be allowed to delay him, nothing . . . nobody . . .

CHAPTER VII

I

"ANYTHING special you want to do, Gale?"

Sunday morning, and the people were thronging to church and chapel, but Mr. Corlyon did not like services. For him a book, or a walk through the fogou to the sea. For one day in the week it was pleasant to put the business of Stowe from off his shoulders; indulge himself with a look at hidden treasure.

"Church . . . or is it chapel?" The place of worship Pascoe patronized was decided for him by the sweetheart of the moment, or by the wish to avoid her of yesterday.

"'Tis neither." Meet Jenifer on the streets? Not he. "I'm not going out."

Mr. Corlyon put a marker between the pages of the *Vestiges of Creation*. Before Pascoe came home he had found it an absorbing book, now his attention wandered. He read and found he had gathered nothing but words. "Well?"

"Tide's out." Pascoe glanced at the slipway, at the grey mud of the harbour, and yawned. This last day was passing slowly. If he could only have ventured into the streets, had a talk with this man and that, gathered the news. He must do something. "Believe I'd like to see the fogou again. You've the key. What do you say to going down?"

Said Mr. Corlyon in his deliberate voice: "As good a way as any of wasting time."

"Come on then." Fresh air and sea were at the end of the fogou, and that would be better than sticking in the house with nothing to do.

The brothers, Mr. Corlyon carrying the lanthorn, went single file down the stairs, through the damp and mossy cellar, into the cave. The lanthorn was half shuttered. The man who held it did not want its beam to fall on the empty chest of which he was unhappily conscious. He would keep his mind like the lanthorn. He would not think of the hours he had spent in this hollow of the rocks; of that old, now lost security; of the years, peaceful, quiet; the years that had flowed softly like a stream, flowed away and sunk into the good earth.

He might forget them, if, like the candle-beam, he threw his mind forward, if he thought of the fogou, that snake twisting into the solid hill, thrusting through into a sea-cave, into the light and colour beyond.

The brothers took the passage with feet to which the way was familiar. To the west of Stowe lay cliffs and the sea; and the fogou, yielding to the inequalities of the strata, yet contrived a westerly course. After they had traversed a few hundred yards, the blackness began to thin, and the dull booming of the sea broke into recognizable sound. They were nearing the exit, and Mr. Corlyon, thinking his secret thoughts, had almost forgotten Pascoe was at his heels when the latter spoke. "Didn't you tell me a bit's fallen in?"

The walls of the passage had suddenly slipped away on either side, and Mr. Corlyon, pushing back the lanthorn shutters, let out a roundness of light. They were in a low cavern, the floor of which was littered with debris of wreck-wood, rotting cordage, and old iron. A faint light, entering at one side, fell on the polished surface of a pool, beyond which, heaped and uneven, lay earth and quartz and broken crystal. Pascoe strode towards it, and Mr. Corlyon, swinging up the lanthorn, searched the roof. The crevice, a jagged velvet-black cut in the rock surface, was easily found.

"'Tis some wide," said Pascoe. The water filtering through the strata, filtering through unceasingly, and year after year, had washed away the soft earth, loosened the seam of quartz, the crystals. If man did not shore up the strata, more quartz, more crystals must inevitably fall, and, in the end, the rock cave in.

Mr. Corlyon pointed to the passage, not more than eighteen inches wide, that led out into the daylight. Turning sharply right, then left, it was not more than four feet long. "Two or three middling stones, and this would be walled up."

Many a little bale of goods had come into Stowe by way of the fogou. Pascoe thought of moonless nights when he had carried tobacco, wine, scent.

Never again.

He was going to settle down with Grizel, with the woman he ached for; he was going to be law-abiding, prosperous, but he would miss the moonless nights and the risks—taken as much for the fiery joy of them as for the easy money.

"Well," he said, "it don't much matter . . . now. You'll have no use for it, and it was bound to come down sooner or later."

In Mr. Corlyon's heart the new wonder moved.

Pascoe had no natural affection; he had been willing the old house should be sold, should become the abiding place of strangers, and now the fogou . . .

He must believe that to Pascoe it was not the romantic and mysterious possession, the strange secret because of which they were different from the other people in Stowe, the people of the surface . . . it was simply a passage.

Having no further use for it, he was willing the sides should cave in, the roof fall, and the fogou . . . this old human runway from the cove to the harbour . . . the fogou, should cease to be.

It made a man feel queasy! "Let us go on. I want to get out, to get into the air."

Pascoe glanced at the tall lean figure. Was Gale annoyed with him? He ought, perhaps, to have shown more interest; but he did not feel any. Feel an interest in a mouldy old passage, slippery with sea-damp, and of no further use?

"Look here," he said, good-naturedly, "it takes rather a long time for a thing to go to pieces, and when I come back, I'll help you shore up the rock." He kicked at the stones and earth heaped under the crevice. "As yet there is not enough fallen to bury a dog."

Mr. Corlyon had stepped into the narrow passage that led to the light; but, at Pascoe's words, he came back, and raising the lanthorn, peered at the crevice.

"Not enough to bury a dog," he said. "Ah, but look, there's plenty more ready to come. Oh yes . . . enough . . . "

II

"When you come back, Pascoe?"

"I shall come, you see if I don't."

"Don't make too sure."

"When a chap wants to come back, he comes."

"You think you'll want to come?"

"Certain sure I shall."

The greyness of the cavern had changed to daylight as the brothers, following the narrow passage that masked the entrance to the fogou, stepped into a little cave.

"Seeing is believing," Gale remarked. The cave, through an opening over which hung trails of green weed, gave on to a small sandy cove, landlocked, and only used by an occasional bather.

"Don't you fret. You'll see me perhaps sooner than you think."

"Well, if you come"—Gale felt his smile like a stiffness on his face, "you—you'll be welcome!"

"Not a long voyage from Jamaica."

"No . . . not from Jamaica."

The sun, now setting, shot a beam between the trails of weed, and filled the cave with reflections of dimpled and dancing waters.

A stream, trickling through the strata, spreading over the slopes of dark grey rock, had left a velvety deposit, and this deposit was coloured. In the main, it was crimson, every shade of crimson from faintest carmine to blood-red, but parts were a bright yellow, others green, others a metallic peacock. In one corner the drip had hollowed a basin, a basin lined with very pale rose, a rose that flowed over the edge, that made a broad ribbon of colour down the slope.

The sun shaft, falling on the water in this basin, water for ever troubled by the drip, had flung motes of rich light over roof and walls. Mr. Corlyon drew his breath sharply, and stood looking. He delighted in warm bright colour, and this rainbow gave him excessive, almost passionate pleasure. It was

the strange and lovely ending to the mysterious fogou, it was
his "secret heaven of flowered delight."

Curving a long slender hand, he cupped a little water in the
hollow of it and drank. A ritual that. By drinking he took
possession, every time, of this place which was his. Afterwards
he would glance at the sand to see if any had profaned its
smoothness. At high tide the cave was under water, water that
slipped through the narrow passage to freshen the black and
polished pool of the cavern, water that drowned the warm
colour, and shut out the light. When he was sitting over a book
in the brown parlour, and the tide was lipping the quayside, he
would think of the far cave at the end of the fogou, of its
renewal under the insidious creeping or storm turmoil of the
waves; he would feel that the waters guarded it for him against
intrusion, kept it secret . . . safe.

Pascoe, whistling, and without a glance for what he termed
"a parcel of muck," had walked through the rainbow cave. His
prints were clear on the ribbed sand, and Mr. Corlyon saw
them with displeasure . . . the broad, rather deep tread.

Before long the tide would turn, would flow over and dis-
solve the sharp outlines.

With Pascoe gone—like the footprints—only he, Gale,
would know of the fogou's existence.

III

Pascoe, stepping out of the cave, had walked round the great
rock which yet further masked the orifice in the cliff-face. The
tide was a sheet of silver, the westerly sun was blinding silver,
and the gulls on the sea-edge were like strung balls of dull
gleaming silver. Pascoe, looking at the home scene, reflected
that between him amd Grizel was only this gulf of waters, this
herring-pond. A few more hours, and he would have pushed
off from the shore, and with his money . . . ah, now, which
would be best—to keep it in his ditty box, or give the captain
charge of it? He knew the captain, a straight man, and of course
he, Pascoe, would have a receipt. But to hand it over would

mean an explanation, and he disliked talking about business, about his personal private business. No, on the whole, the ditty box would serve his purpose best. Pity he had not more notes; but was it? Bullion was money, but notes were only paper. He remembered that in Cartagena ten-dollar notes were worth only a few pence; and for all he knew, English bank notes might suffer a like depreciation in Jamaica. He wished he had asked McVitie about it. A shrewd man, McVitie.

Mr. Corlyon, glancing at the short thick figure, with its stare that crossed a world, felt that Pascoe's thoughts had become agonizingly easy to read. With the plunder in his sack he was waiting impatiently for the moment when he could throw it over his shoulder and be off . . .

"Dog does not eat dog"—but this dog was so vile he had turned on his own flesh and blood!

Still, there was a limit to human endurance, and Pascoe, in wronging Gale, had overstepped that limit.

No one should take from Gale that to which he had a right.

IV

The figure by the rim of silver embodied a lost illusion, and Mr. Corlyon turned from the contemplation of it. For three nights and three days he had been concentrated on the problem of Pascoe. He knew, at last, what he would do, and he was at peace; but he did not want to look at or think of him. Sufficient unto the hour . . .

Crossing the belt of sand, he stood under the Dragon Rock, looking up. The crest of the great stone had been worn by weather into a shape which, to human fancy, had suggested a beast. Shaggy with weed, it lay along the flat top, the face leaning forward, the anticipatory lips slightly apart. When the tide was high, Mr. Corlyon, sitting up-over on the cliffs, had seen a slaver of white spume drip from the jaws.

Was that what dragons had been like? Rough scaly creatures of huge dimensions? Had they lain in wait for their prey on some rock coloured like themselves, and had they leaped down . . .

Crevices in the grey stone gave the dragon an appearance of deep obliquely-set eyes. A queer enough creature . . . made, not by man, and not by God. The battering of storm, the grinding of the seas, and a rock. That was all, and from that had come, at first dimly, the monstrous outline of head, of back, of tail. With the passage of time the shape had grown more definite, until, at last, the tiny generations of man had perceived it, given it a name. It seemed almost as if, from being mere rock it had developed a sort of life, as if it had being.

Mr. Corlyon's thoughts turned to his book—to the *Vestiges of Creation*. Perhaps weather and fortuitous circumstances such as had made the dragon, were responsible for the far-off beginnings of life.

A hand on his shoulder and he started, threw it off.

"Oh, Pascoe, you? I beg your pardon."

"Time's getting on. I ought to be putting my traps together."

"We'll go back."

As they walked to the cave, Mr. Corlyon glanced back, glanced at the rock.

The dragon's face was turned towards the land, towards the green and black wall of the cliff. Long ago, fancy had suggested a connection between the fogou, the pre-historic passage which man, with astonishing assiduity, had driven through the hill, and the monstrous beast. The old thought returned. He felt that on its rock the dragon lay waiting for prey, for something coming to it by way of the fogou. It had knowledge and desire, and it would not wait in vain. Something was coming, not from the sea, but from the habitations of man . . .

CHAPTER VIII

I

THE brothers traversed the sea-cave, the long dark curves of the fogou, the slant, with man-made hand-holds—man-made, how long ago?—to the door. In the rock-cave Mr. Corlyon, crossing to a recess in the wall, had selected wine.

"The last of poor old father's bottling. It was being kept for your wedding, so it's as well to drink it now."

Pascoe had eyed the cobwebby bottles. "To wish me a safe journey from the old home to the new?" It would be jolly on his last evening to have a hideful of the best, to have his whack. He must be careful though, he mustn't risk losing the use of his legs.

"That will be it," Gale had answered sedately, and Pascoe had passed him, running up the stair.

"I'll put my traps together, and then we can have supper."

"Ah, yes, your traps." When a man went to the West Indies he took with him all that was his. You had to bear that in mind. His dunnage, heavy with another man's gold; the light packages for Grizel; his boots, cap, sailor-rig. When a man went, these things went too.

II

In the parlour, Mr. Corlyon was decanting wine. His long fine hands adjusted the funnel, he watched the dark fluid spreading over the bulge of the wine bottle. When the decanter was quite full he stoppered it.

How much would Pascoe drink? The mellow old stuff would slip down easy as milk, yes, and one glass leads to another. He must have plenty and then—the one glass more.

Mr. Corlyon took a knife out of his pocket, and tried the edge of the blade. It cut the skin of his thumb. Tut—he must be careful.

Overhead the creaking of boards. Pascoe had asked for his share of the furniture, and Gale had agreed that he should have it. It should follow him out, be forwarded by cargo boat. He was in his brother's room at the moment making a careful list of the pieces of furniture that he would have. It went without saying that he had chosen the best.

Mr. Corlyon hearkened to that careless tread. He understood that Pascoe, stripping the nest, was examining the various twigs and feathers. Money, house, ay, even the lining of the house.

He returned to his decanting. It would not do to linger. At any moment Pascoe might come down. He would come dragging that heavy dunnage, clamouring for supper, for a drink.

Gale Corlyon placed a half-emptied bottle on the sideboard, got out a small deeply-cut flagon, and turned. Before him, a darker brown than the wall paper, hung the head-hunter's spear with, above it, the quiver and bunch of pigmy arrows.

Outside help, that is to say the law, could not be invoked, for law was not justice; the spear could only be used when the odds were even, when it was a case of man to man. Mr. Corlyon took down the arrows.

If he were to steep the points in the wine of that one glass more?

It would take the poison better if it were warmed. He got out the old mulling horn, filled it, and set it in a red hollow of turf.

With the fine blade of his knife he pared the tiny points of the arrows. Almost invisible curls of dark dry wood fell into the wine. The tiny shreds floated for a moment on the bubbling turmoil, but as the wine soaked into them they sank and disappeared.

In his room, looking up the street, Pascoe was singing a chanty. He was packing and singing. Yes, though he had taken his brother's savings, the savings of a lifetime, he could sing.

No heart, nor even any bowels of compassion. Mr. Corlyon hung the bunch of pigmy arrows, quiver and arrows, on the wall over the head-hunter's spear . . . stood back to survey them. The pared edges . . . were they a lighter brown? Not much lighter, but still . . .

He took them from the nail, and as he lifted the mulling horn, dropped them into the fire. They crackled and flamed and spat, dry things but potent . . . no longer potent.

Bane for a rat.

The flames died, and a little grey ash filled the glow. Gale Corlyon would do justice, and be responsible for it to whatever—whoever—was responsible for the making of such as Pascoe. He poured the cooling fluid into the crystal flagon. Was the wine a little thick? Give it time, and the sediment would settle.

The chanty had grown louder. Pascoe, carrying his dunnage, was coming down.

"Put it out of the way—along the passage."

"I'll put it at the head of the cellar stairs."

"The cellar stairs?"

"I'm going out by the back door. I don't want to meet . . . people." He came into the parlour. "Supper ready?"

"I told Antiks to lay it in the kitchen to-night. Warmer there."

"But she——"

"Oh, she's gone. 'Tis Sunday, man."

Pascoe laughed. "To me 'tis the day I start for the West Indies. Why, hullo . . ."

He was staring at a lightness on the brown of the wall, a small pale oblong. "My curio . . . what has happened to it?"

Mr. Corlyon turning, perceived that the absence of the arrows was more noticeable than would have been those slight small marks of the knife. "That? What was it? Oh, I remember —yes—Antiks complained of it getting dirty. She was always catching her duster in it and pulling it down. I let her burn it. Do you mind?"

"Dunno as I do. A scratch from one of those pin-points, and you'd find yourself in Kingdom Come. A parcel of muck, it was best out of the way."

"I ought to have given the arrows back to you," said Mr. Corlyon, smoothly, "let you take them with you."

Pascoe looked at the other curios on the wall. "I forgot about these." he said, slowly, "or—no, I haven't room for another thing. Well, see here, Gale, they'd look as well on my wall as on yours. You might pack them in with the furniture you are freighting me."

"What you don't take with you," answered Mr. Corlyon, "I will send."

III

The brothers sat at supper in the kitchen. "'Tis pretty good wine," Pascoe said, "this all you got?"

"There's a drop more in the other room."

"When we've drinked this, we'll have it in to finish up, and then I must be going."

Mr. Corlyon was curious. Why was Pascoe going out the back way? Who was it he did not wish to meet? Hitherto, he had come and gone openly, daringly. "You are going up the back lane?"

"Best get off quickly," Pascoe said, "some women are jealous as fire."

But Stowe was full of women "jealous as fire," and hitherto Pascoe had not cared. Mr. Corlyon was puzzled. He looked thoughtfully at his brother; and Pascoe, warmed, a little bemused by the wine, felt the look as if it, and the curiosity behind it, had been tangible.

He was not going to own up that he was afraid of being ill-wished. Gale would laugh . . .

"I didn't tell Jenifer I was going."

He was through with Jenifer, yet, for some reason, was anxious not to meet her. Mr. Corlyon's mind groped for the reason. Pascoe was not scrupulous, not easily put about.

"What is Jenifer to you?"

"She isn't nothing to me."

Mr. Corlyon had an itch to know. Pascoe had made casual love to half the women in Stowe. He had flirted with Jenifer as with the others . . . a matter of course, as she was such a pretty maid. The questions, why Pascoe was afraid of Stowe streets, and whether Jenifer cared, really cared for him, clashed in Mr. Corlyon's mind. Pascoe had been away some time. What had happened before he left? The two had spent the last day at Lewhidden, blackberry picking in the quarry. Had matters come to a head then? Was there, perhaps, a promise between them?

He must know how they stood to each other, and with Pascoe half drunk it should not be difficult.

"Anyway," he said, musingly, "you have been away some time, three months gone——" He had been going to say, "gone out of this," when Pascoe took him up.

The wine was going to Pascoe's head. He had not quite followed what his brother was saying, had a bemused idea it was about Jenifer. "Three months gone?" He shivered. "Don't say that."

His eyes were lifted to his brother's. He saw on the face opposite a sudden flash . . . incredulity, horror. It struck through the fumes. Pushing his chair back, he broke into a laugh. "You mazed old rattle, why don't you say what you mean? Jenifer's no more to me than any other body. 'Tis Grizel's my maid."

Mr. Corlyon's tongue was dry. "You said three months . . ."

"I meant—Grizel."

"Well, then——"

"Oh, don't bother now," he reached for his glass. "Didn't know I'd drinked this." He glanced suspiciously at his brother surely it had been full but a moment since. And the wine-bottle was empty. Old Gale had more, yes, in the dining-room. He was hoarding it, as he had hoarded the money; and Pascoe's throat was sand dry. "Let's have in the rest."

"You've had nearly enough."

"I've a thirst on me that could drink a barrel. So come now, let us finish the wine."

The other got up slowly. "'Tis the lees and a bit thick."

"Want to keep it for yourself, eh?"

"You have had everything for which you asked; you shall have this, too." Would the wine be cool enough to pass muster? He fetched the little flagon; yes . . . nearly cold.

Leaning over the table, he filled his brother's glass, and Pascoe, lifting it, held it between his eye and the light. "Good," he said, "good! Some body in this wine."

"Take care, or you'll spill it."

"I'll spill it down my throat."

Mr. Corlyon raised his own to set stiff lips. "Here's good luck," he said.

CHAPTER IX

I

PASCOE, putting the glass to his lips, began to gulp the wine. Not much fun plucking old Gale. Feather after feather, and he made no protest. Pascoe had not thought the man was so tame. He wondered, dizzily, whether he had overlooked any bits of property—money, land—for which he might have asked.

The kitchen being at the back of the house, and its window looking down the garden, the brothers were as snug as if they had been in the fogou, with the thick hill between them and Stowe. The world outside was busy with its churches and chapels; and the earth went round, the folks on it, like maggots in their nuts, busy and self-absorbed.

In this house, at this supper table, was the sound of Pascoe drinking.

Mr. Corlyon's ears gathered the uncouth sound. His body was numb, only one sense, that of hearing, was alert in him.

Suddenly, shattering his content, pulling him back, a different sound—the rapping, the sharp rapping of knuckles on a door. He turned in swift terror. Not the door of their room . . . No, further away . . . a knocking . . . it was on the panels of the front door.

Someone was near . . .was trying to join them. His security fell about him like splintered glass. Not every person in Stowe was occupied with his own concerns, his feeding, and sweethearting, and chapel-going. The minds of some—of one, or perhaps two—were turned towards himself and Pascoe; and these minds, they would be interested, curious. Of a sudden the house-walls—walls of country stone—became to him as a curtain which at any moment might be blown aside.

These people—they might turn the knob of the door and, secure of a welcome, come shouting down the passage, "Corlyon! Corlyon!" With a friendliness that would presently change, they might blunder in on—he glanced through the firelit dusk at Pascoe, at the red-brown face, greasy with food and the heat of the room. God—they must not get in! Why had he not thought to lock the door after Antiks? Everything but that, and that would bring his plans about his ears.

Should he steal out now and turn the key? Would Pascoe notice? If he were to . . . if he asked questions? Better perhaps to leave it be.

Under the table Mr. Corlyon locked his hands together, holding on to himself, to that fierce longing to stride out, interrogate the intruders, drive them away.

A wineglass was set down clumsily. The knocking on the door-panel had reached Pascoe's brain. He looked up, startled.

"'Tis Jenifer," he said, and he leaned over the table speaking as if he thought she might hear. "She has got light of my going but," his voice was a fierce whisper, "but I won't see her. Don't you—don't you dare let her in on me."

Gale fell back in his chair. Jenifer—she—at this moment? Yet he could see the links in the chain. He had told her mother and the maid had felt she must speak with Pascoe. But, of all people in the world, Jenifer.

He passed his tongue over dry lips. "Well——"

"Aw——leave her knock."

A bell rang, rang sharply and for a long time. The iron clangour broke out on the beam over Mr. Corlyon's head; and Pascoe gaped, in quick fear, at the moving blackness. The sweat stood in beads on his hot face and yet he shivered. The woman on the other side of that frail door was urgent and her urgency was crying to him through the bell.

Mr. Corlyon knotted his hands more desperately. So difficult to sit there, to sit quietly, to look unconcerned.

"Afraid of this all day," Pascoe muttered, "She'd get me if she could." He startled his brother by breaking suddenly into a low chuckle, "but—but she can't get in."

"Can't get in?"

"I saw to it the front door was locked." The old jolly smile had come back, was curving his full mouth. After all he had bested her. Another hour and he would be gone and Jenifer would not have been able to ill-wish him.

Mr. Corlyon's grasp of himself relaxed. She could not get through a locked door.

The bell rang again, a long desperate peal. Let her ring! No lights at the front of to tell her they were in the house. She might wait a little but presently she would realize that it was hopeless. He turned from the thought of her. He was beginning to wonder . . .

If the poison should not work? The arrows had been on his wall for some time, moreover the quantity of drink Pascoe had swallowed might prevent the poison from taking effect. He might yet get up and, staggering out, pick up his dunnage . . . that heavy dunnage.

Gale's will was set that the man who had robbed him should not escape. It was not retribution but justice; and if the poison failed there would be still the head-hunter's spear. He could see it, see himself lifting it, see it shearing through flesh, bone . . . as Pascoe stooped over the dunnage.

Suddenly Pascoe spoke, and as he uttered the first word something in his voice gave Mr. Corlyon the news for which he had been waiting. He sprang up and put a light to the candle.

"Wish I hadn't drinked that last glass of wine." Pascoe was muttering He walked away from the table, dropped on to the settle. "It has made me feel queer." By the light of the candle Mr. Corlyon saw that his face was grey, pinched. He stared for a second, then, smiling, filled his lungs with the good air. Oh, sweet, sweet and good.

"I—I'm feeling awful bad," Pascoe said and looked up, looked at his brother. He was looking for help, but what he saw on Gale's face took him aback.

"You've had too much wine."

"No." Wine didn't make you feel like this—and Gale's face—that white hard look. More than hard that look. He remembered suddenly that the last glass had been thick. "You——" he cried, but he was a match for Gale—he wasn't afraid! "You've put stuff in that wine!"

He was drugged—that would be it; but why should Gale drug him? What did he stand to gain by keeping him in Stowe? God—it wasn't a mere drug. He, Pascoe, had taken the money and that devil was trying to do him in. Trying—but he wasn't dead yet—not by a long way, and he wasn't going to die. He lurched to his feet. "Jenifer!" he shouted. "Jenifer, come quick."

"You're drunk. Here—lie back and sleep it off." Mr. Corlyon caught the swaying man about the body, lifted him on to the settle.

"I'll leave the town know——" Things were growing dim and the sickness was in his limbs, paralysing him, obscuring his sight. He must get away, get help and then—Gale should pay.

Gale had thought to get the better of him—but Gale should pay.

Pascoe seemed to have shaken off the restraining hands, but his legs dragged, were growing numb. He could not feel them. No matter, he must struggle on, get to a doctor and then, yes, then he would tell the town.

His fellow men, the kindly folk of his town, they would see justice done.

An effort. Dark, but he knew the way. One step, another . . . he must be near the door.

The front door . . . then he must be in the passage and that was why it was dark. So dark. He had his hand on the door-knob but it was slipping.

Something crashed and he shouted—shouted silently into the void of death.

II

Mr. Corlyon, seizing Pascoe to prevent him from running out of the house, had expected to encounter a stout resistance. Pascoe would be desperate and having led a healthy seafaring life would be difficult to manage. But Mr. Corlyon would welcome that resistance. The irritation evoked by Jenifer's untimely call, had increased his excitement, and though he did not want to touch Pascoe he wanted to exert himself, to do something strenuous.

The sick man pushed him away, but in a fumbling inconclusive manner. The strength seemed to have ebbed from his round brawn and it was as if his gaze were fixed on something at a distance. He struggled with increasing feebleness for a few seconds, then his legs gave and he collapsed.

Mr. Corlyon, finding he held an inert body, propped it against the wooden back of the settle; but Pascoe fell over sideways and lay there, arms and legs twitching.

"Leave——the town——know——" The words were a ghostly breath, suggested rather than uttered. Throat and lips seemed to be paralysed.

Not ten minutes since he had taken the snake-poison! He had gone under very quickly ... too quickly. Mr. Corlyon could not credit it. Pascoe was foxing, was gathering his strength for a fresh effort. He must be careful ...

The fire did not give enough light—and the candle was behind on the table. He must not turn his back. A sailor carried a knife and that knife had perhaps been whipped out, in readiness. He had a sensation between his shoulder-blades—on no account would he turn.

Putting a hand behind, he groped for the candlestick. A glass went over ... no matter! His fingers were encountering food, cutlery ... ah, he had it now. Carrying the light and holding it well before him, he returned to the settle.

Pascoe lay comfortably asleep, his head on the old red cushion, the breath issuing tranquilly between parted lips. He was not ill, he was merely drunk. The snake-poison, too long exposed to the air, had lost its potency.

The candlestick shook in Mr Corlyon's hand. To have botched his job ... Drunk! In the morning Pascoe would awaken with only a headache to remind him of the previous evening's debauch ...

He might have known a man was not so easily killed!

The head-hunter's spear? He couldn't. Virtue had gone out of him. He wasn't capable of the smallest further effort.

He would go somewhere and lie down, let this tide of blackness sweep over his spirit, give himself up to it ...

Bone-tired, he was, with limbs as heavy as those of Pascoe... It would be difficult to drag himself across the room, up the stairs.

He found himself listening in his weariness to Pascoe's breathing. Why, it had changed, grown audible! The long inspirations came with a sort of doubt, almost a break.

Once more he lifted the candle. Pascoe's face was a yellowish grey, his nostrils were black and his eyes sunken. this was no drunken sleep.

Then . . . after all . . . He had known from the beginning it would be thus. Neither time nor exposure could abate the virulence of that poison. He had won. If he had had a cap he would have tossed it into the air.

He was no longer tired—he could not afford to be, for a hard night's work lay before him—but anyway he wasn't. He set the candle back on the table . . .

Was it his nerves? No, someone was really knocking on the window pane. He could see a dark outline. Good God, someone—it was Jenifer!

She had left the window, had pulled open the back door, was in the passage. He stepped quickly to the kitchen door, met her, stood there between her and the room between her and what lay on the settle.

"Oh, Mr. Corlyon, I was afraid you were out."

"We weren't out." His voice was hard, more than hard. Never before had she heard that inexorable note. It hit like a hammer, not a hammer held in a man's hand, but one driven by machinery.

"I rang and rang." She looked pleadingly at the steep chin, the thin short curve of the mouth, the whole, long, narrow face. Cold, hard . . . no kindness.

"We heard you."

"I wanted to see Pascoe."

"He knew."

"Mr. Corlyon," she took out the handkerchief, "I wanted him to have this before he went."

"I will give it to him."

"I want to give it to him myself."

"No." In his hardness and coldness he was brutal. Only a few days ago he had spoken of love . . . yes, this same frost-bound, stony, implacable man.

"Why not?"

He was silent but did not move. It almost seemed as if he had forgotten her . . . were listening . . .

"Oh, please, Mr. Corlyon, why shouldn't I?"

"He is drunk, sleeping it off." He glanced over his shoulder and Jenifer saw in the dimness a figure. She had had a doubt as to Pascoe's being in the house, but he was still there.

If only she could get past Mr. Corlyon, lay the charmed linen in the hand hanging lax over the edge of the settle.

"I would not disturb him." She tried to edge by, but Mr. Corlyon caught her arm. Only half a dozen paces between her and Pascoe. With a sudden twist she sprang forward, her hand outstretched, the small folded square between her fingers.

She would drop it on his broad chest.

"No," said Mr. Corlyon again and, seizing her, swung her round. Jenifer was a country girl, her muscles strengthened by house-work. She meant to reach that dark and now quiescent figure. She must reach it or as soon as Pascoe was sober, he would go.

The breaths to which with the very marrow of him Mr. Corlyon had been listening had checked, gone on again, checked. Pascoe still lived—did he live—did he?

The arms that closed round Jenifer had forgotten that she was a woman.

Struggling, she was thrust inexorably back and back—to the door—into the passage.

Between the straining bodies the handkerchief fell, un-noticed on to the wooden floor.

CHAPTER X

I

"BREAKFAST on the table, Maister."

Antiks' voice, but from a distance. He did not want to come back, to rouse himself. He was tired, yes and his limbs ached, and at the back of things . . .

He murmured sleepily.

"Baint 'ee very well, to-day?"

He was an early riser, fond of a cold bath, careful over his toilet. Antiks had never known him to oversleep. She came in, pulled up the blind.

"I think I have got a chill."

"What, 'av 'ee catched a cold?" A wash of pale sunlight flowed over the room. She saw that his eyes were red-rimmed, that the pale skin had darkened, was almost sallow. "Iss, you'm lookin' whisht. Shall I go get doctor for 'ee?"

"No, no, leave me alone."

"A cup of hot tea will do you good." The one weakness of his fine physique was a too great reaction to changes of temperature. "I expect your 'ead's goin' around like a top."

The kettle was on the boil. She soaked the tea, stood the pot aside for the appointed three minutes, and went on with her work of tidying the kitchen. The Maister and his brother had evidently put away a tidy drop of wine with their supper and Maister had no head for the drink. It was probably as much that as the chill.

She carried the tea upstairs, waiting on him kindly, deftly. While he drank her glance was on his round head, the hair of which, crisp and close-lying, was bedruffled, on his sinewy neck and wide shoulders. No need for him to go to a good tailor, he would look well in anything he put on. The shape of'n . . . she thought of the child that might have come to her from him. She did not want any more children; but . . . Lovely he was, and a child of his . . .

How silly when she had as many as she could do with.

"I found one of your best wine-glasses in the chimley," she said. "'Twas broke, of course."

Mr. Corlyon gave her back the cup. "Do your work, Antiks, and go home. I shall get up when I feel like it."

She went to the door. "Young Maister went off all right, I s'pose?"

"Quite all right."

"When will 'ee be comin' again?"

"He is not coming back."

"Not comin' back any moör? Gracious, you frighten me."

"He is going to marry and settle in Jamaica. No. He will not come back."

"Aw—I wouldn't believe that. This rumpy ole place is 'ome to 'im. It's bound to drag'n back."

What was it Pascoe had said? "I shall come back, you see if I don't . . . not a long voyage from Jamaica."

II

Mr. Corlyon acknowledged to stiffness, to an ache in the lifting muscles of the back; but those discomforts did not account for his remaining abed. He had slept deeply and should have awakened as fit as usual; but he felt empty, done. It was as if he could not lift his head from the pillow, as if it were too much trouble to move. He did not remember ever to have felt so slack. There was work waiting for him, but he did not think he would bother about it. He would stay where he was.

Antiks offered to bring him a book, but he only shook his head. Hold up a book? Keep his attention on the words? Take in the sense? After all the *Vestiges of Creation* was nothing but a series of guesses, while the Rhoda Broughton novel . . . he could not remember either name or theme.

As to Edwin Rabey—what did it matter if his wife had gone back to her mother? It was not Corlyon's affair. Let them settle it as they would, he had lost interest.

The black wind was blowing. It mourned in the chimney, it

drove through every crevice, thinning the blood, and darkening the winter crops. Mr. Corlyon thought it must have been blowing throughout the night. He seemed to remember . . .

III

His mind was like the ground. It lay under a blackness, a blackness of wind. It lay still and cold, perhaps dead. So exhausted was he, that he felt almost glad to lie quiescent under the numbing blackness, give himself up to it.

He remembered seeing a boy kick before him, along the ringing stones of the quay, an old tin pail. Bent, battered, and with a hole in the bottom, it was kicked noisily into the sea. He was like that, finished and at the mercy of winds out of the east and north, at the mercy of his moods.

Only momentarily though. A day's rest would put him to rights. A few hours of peace and the destroying blackness would lift. Life was as full of interests as it could hold and he knew it was. He knew it with the back of his mind, yet, in front, was a wonder how he could have bothered himself with the affairs of other people. Trivial and commonplace those affairs, yet at the time they had seemed worth while.

Nothing was except the maintenance of this dead black peace, the maintenance of it until something underneath, sonething that had been hurt, wounded, had had time to heal.

Though he wanted the peace to last, he did not think that it would. It was like a pool: water, clear still midnight water from the surface down. It was deep, but not deep as Dozmarè, and it bottomed on—what? No matter what, at least no matter as long as whatever it was did not move. He had a feeling that in those depths was a something that might presently detach itself from the sand and stones, glimmer up from the pool. He did not want to see it, he wanted it to lie there until it had rotted into nothingness.

A heavy weight of water, heavy enough to keep bones and wreckage "down among the dead men"; yet, for all that weight there was under the water a sort of stir.

It was so faint as to be hardly noticeable. If he turned his mind to something else—to Edwin Rabey's affairs—he would be able to ignore that slight creeping of the ooze.

Outside, a sailor on the old men's bench, at the head of the quay, thought to warm himself by playing an accordion.

Mr. Corlyon could not help but hear. The melancholy long-drawn notes fell on his attempted preoccupation with Edwin Rabey. In spite of himself he listened; and, listening, was caught by the emotion.

He listened and slowly, gradually, the bottom of the pool slurred. It began to move; broke, at last, into a squirm of life; into things that rose whitely, waveringly, through the water.

Tremors began to run down his spine. He was being forced by that abominable melody to see . . .

IV

He turned impatiently in his bed. Confound the fellow—would he never stop? He wanted to slip back into the quiet, which like graveyard clods had covered him: that quiet—yes, the quiet, almost, of Pascoe. A deed done was a thing that should be forgotten. He had turned his back on the events of the previous night, had concentrated on other people's affairs. At least, he had tried to but, from somewhere deep in himself, rose and continued to rise, this succession of terrible memories. He sought to keep them down but, inexorably, they pushed their way up . . . filled it. And he could not escape. His mind was a stage on which certain scenes were being enacted, scenes to which he might not shut his eyes.

The white, sun-washed bedroom had gradually become less real than the mental pictures at which he was looking, less real than the scenes in which he was taking part. He was back in the dim kitchen, with the door finally shut on Jenifer, on her despairing, incomprehensible, "Oh, it has touched wood!" He was standing by the hearth, seeing the disordered supper table, the candle, the settle. Yet he did not actually see these things, he was only aware of them.

He was too fiercely intent on something else—on those stertorous breaths. He was waiting for the catch, the threatened break. An eternity before it came. At last—a heave of the broad chest and where there had been so much sound a sudden astounding silence.

A silence and stillness that had appalled him. Only for a moment though, for what he really felt had been relief. What he had set himself to do was done. A struggle and he had won. He had planned, carried his plan into execution, and therefore could only be content.

But the stillness—it had been unnerving. Life slipped out of the body, slipped, he must suppose, into the surrounding air; at any rate it so filled the room that the only thing empty of it was the hushed figure on the settle.

He had lighted more candles. It was necessary to see the dead man's face. He must convince himself that what, a moment ago, had been full of painful life, was grown indifferent. Pascoe's spirit, if it existed, would be a flame of vindictive wrath. To have been got the better of, and by the brother he had despised, whom he had thought of as an old buffer, his rage would be extreme. But of this, on his face there was no sign. He looked entirely unconcerned.

That unconcern had made it possible for Gale to do what was necessary.

V

Though a strong man, his back and shoulders had ached before, with his burden, he got to the end of the fogou. God—how heavy! From the settle to the head of the stairs— down the stairs, slippery with weather, to the cave. The load he carried was slack, unwieldy; he had not the knack of it.

He was stumbling through darkness, he had forgotten where the passage twisted, he was bumping against an unexpected wall of rock. Interminable, the narrow black tunnel! Twisty-ways, it ran back into the hill, on and on, while what he carried was not mere dead flesh, but something bewitched with weight.

His mind had cast forward to the run of earth, the crack in the rock-roof. Would he ever make it? He must have been hours staggering and stumbling along in the dark.

The accordion on which the sailor was playing to keep himself warm, must be a good one, or it would not have affected him, Gale. That tune, people stood at the street-corners, Christmas, and sang it. He knew it well but could not remember to have been moved by it at any other time.

Scene after scene rose, passed through his mind. They came in spite of him, he saw them with a greater vividness than he had when they had taken place. At the time he had been too preoccupied to see them as horrible, doubtful if he would now had it not been for the accordion. If only the fellow would take himself off and if he, Gale Corlyon, could shut against unwelcome visions, the door of his mind. Ah—if only he need not see that limp, sprawly body that had slipped from his shoulder to the rubble; that had—settled.

Even then, he had felt sick. Staggering out through the sea-cave he had found that, after that nightmare of bitter travail, day was still in the sky. Leaning against the rock he had waited until he should be a little recovered.

Behind him, behind the wall of the sea-cave, lying there in the dark, weedy dark—Pascoe's body! He was shivering in the breeze, but he was not unnerved, he was not even cold; no, he was tired, that was it—tired.

He would have to go back; finish his—job.

If only Pascoe had fallen face under. Though Mr. Corlyon brought down on it all the loose rocks of Gudda Hill, he would still see the waxy whiteness of that face.

Not if he determined otherwise. To determine was to act. He would turn the grisly thing out of his mind and think of the sea, of the thin moon—a moon like a shred of linen—think of it rising over the cliff. Dull and white, it hung in a fair sky, a sky kept from darkening by that glow in the west.

The Dragon Rock stood black against the blood of a dead and buried sun. Against the blood—? There had been no blood and what he had done was justifiable. A man should fight for what was his, fight with what weapons he had, fight to win.

A fold of rock had made a tongue between the jaws of the Dragon, a slavering, desirous tongue; and the Dragon—it had crouched, expectant. For what was it waiting?

He had wanted to stay there, but he might not. There were still things he had to do.

VI

Lying stiffly in his bed, with the vision of that burial dark, yet clear, a vision from which he could not turn, to which he could not shut his inner sight, he found that the sweat was standing on his forehead. His shirt was clinging to his body, his fingers crisping as they had crisped on the stout pole of driftwood with which he had thrust at the loose rocks in the crevice.

On that first thrust had followed a little run of earth. The stones had fallen on that upturned face. They would cover it from sight, but no, they had rolled away. It was still there, a dim whiteness that to him was not dim. Its unconcern with this last indignity had whipped Corlyon to a fury of thrusting. Crash and roar and tumult. He was springing away, but with the dust in his throat. Coughing, he had turned to look back, but to his amazement the gleam of light, the gleam from the sea, from yellowing moon and fading sunset had vanished. He preceived that the roof caving in had blocked the fogou.

The limp loose flesh that he had dragged through passage and cavern was buried—but it had taken half Gudda to hide it. Tons of rock must have rolled out of the crack—but why did he keep harping on it? Pascoe was safely buried, and the time had come to think of something more pleasant. Why not the money? Gale had poured it back into the pigskin bags, had counted the bags, had set them in rows in the old chest. The money from the emeralds had filled another. There were now eleven bags. But a waxen face rose from under the bags and it was the face—the upturned face of Pascoe—that had substance, not the bags.

VII

Gale Corlyon sprang out of bed. Anything would be better than lying there, re-living the occurrences of the night. It was the fault of the music. Once he were in the street, the commonplace, everyday street, he would be able to give his mind to other matters.

What had he done? Usurped the law's prerogative? But the law did not do justice. The law acted in what it considered the interests of the community and that, even in the long run, was hardly justice. As to the mills of God, they ground too slowly.

To take the law into your own hands needed courage. Well, at least he had that. Even so, he must admit that he was shaken.

But only for the time being. He would be all right as soon as other events—time—was hung like dust, like mist, like a wall, between him and it.

He would walk up to the Rabeys, have a talk with Edwin about that girl at the Cornish Arms. Mrs. Rabey was partly to blame, an offish cold sort of woman, but her husband had been foolish. He would say . . . er . . . damnation, he was back in the kitchen! Clear as if time and space did not exist, that supine figure on the settle . . .

He hurried out of the house. Evergreens rose above the whitewashed wall of the garden and beyond lay the square basin of the harbour. Corlyon, if he meant to call on Rabey, should have turned to the right; but the sailor, now playing "Old Zadock," was sitting on the bench and that the events of the night were present in Corlyon's thoughts was the fault of the music. He must get away from it. Without realizing that he had done so, he turned to the left, walked towards the sea.

The tide being out, the wide, shallow estuary was a breadth of bright, hard sand. A tortuous sea-channel ran snakily from east to west. On the south, the cliffs, black-faced, were dented into coves, into bays, and the ground at their feet was "hard country." Corlyon walking rapidly was as one in a dream. Coming round a bluff, he startled a grey-blue heron and the flight of the bird, legs hanging, head up, roused him to a sense of his whereabouts. He had reached the Dragon Rock, the grey rough rock, and the overhead sun was wrapping it in white light. At least, it should have done so, but he—he saw it black against a blood-red sunset.

He must keep his thoughts from straying back. This was noon of a lovely day. He saw, as if a veil had lifted, the wintry blue of the sea, the sand dunes of the opposite shore, the island guarding the mouth of the estuary. A beautiful world—and he was alive to enjoy it!

Alive? Why could he not forget that there were others . . . one other, who was no longer alive? Pascoe had not been worthy, and he had been merely the instrument of fate in ridding the world—this lovely world—of him.

It must be dinner time. He would go home the short way, go through the fogou. He turned into the sea-cave, heard with joyous heart the drip of the water from rock to basin, from basin to the smooth blue and white pebbles, turned towards the narrow rock-walled passage.

He had forgotten. He stood, unable to believe. Yes, actually, he had forgotten.

The passage was blocked, fragments of broken rock, of quartz had fallen through into the sea-cave; but behind, solid to the roof, were stones and earth.

His glance lighted on a bit of shaped rubbish, a—was it a foot? Quickly, he stepped back. No, no—Pascoe was too far under. The black object was an old broken boot, a bit of flotsam which had drifted in on the tide, been stranded there by receding waves. Hitherto, the sea had slipped through the passage, at full tide had flowed a few yards up the fogou. It could not now. It could only beat on a wall of crushed, piled debris, tons of it. As it gradually filled the cave, rising to the rock-roof, it would beat on it more and more heavily—but it would not be able to break through.

Corlyon turned back, turned towards the basin of clear spring water. He had always drunk of it and, as usual, he would drink. He cupped his hand, but as he dipped it, the thought came that Pascoe lay behind the wall from which the water dripped. The rock held him there, and the water . . .

"Some body in this wine."

CHAPTER XI

I

"So we seen the last of Mr. Pascoe?" The smith was receipting a bill while Mr. Corlyon, leaning against the rough wall of the "shop," waited.

"I hope not."

The smith nodded sympathetically. "Reckon 'e'll come back when 'e mind to; but 'e was never the one to stay 'ome. 'E was like a rambling stone, 'ere to-day, and gone to-morrer."

"He will have to mend his ways, for he is going into partnership with friends—a business partnership."

"My Gor', if 'e 'ave to sit down and work, 'e'll mump. 'E 'edn't goin' stay in a office, surley?"

"Time he settled down. You know he is going to be married?"

"Marryin' a foreigner, 'edn' 'e?"

"Well—a Scottish maid."

"Ay a foreigner! And they'm always different from we. But you'll miss him, Mr. Corlyon, I bet; 'tis all you got, you know."

II

Every fresh person to whom he spoke talked of Pascoe.

Hitherto, the fogou had been the secret fact in his life, but that had given place to Pascoe. There was the real Pascoe, hidden under Gudda Hill, and the Pascoe on his way to Jamaica. Two Pascoes, one for the town, and put on when he went out, as he put on an overcoat; the other, a secret of the Brown House.

The overcoat was heavy, he got tired of wearing it. The hidden Pascoe was also a weariness. With Pascoe's death his anger had passed. He wanted, now, to forget that he had been wronged and had avenged himself. He would have been glad to forget that Pascoe had ever existed.

The deed being done should sink into the quicksands of time. If he were patient, waited a little, this would happen. Eventually, too, the townsfolk would find some other topic of conversation. Meanwhile, there was only one house he knew of, in which the name of Pascoe did not star the talk. Mrs. Liddicoat never spoke of him, neither did Jenifer. Jenifer, he noticed, hardly spoke of anything. She sat at her embroidery as if engrossed by it, she wore a strained unhappy look.

Poor little maid, if he could have done anything for her, he would. Strange that he should feel like that about her! Why, he would have got her lover back if possible; and that, of course, meant he did not want her himself. He did not, either. He had no longer any feeling for her.

Queer, when he had thought the world of her. But that was often the way. Hottest fire is soonest out. And Jenifer—he knew things about her, Pascoe had let the truth escape. Yet it was not that, no, it was that she brought it all back. That night— and she, trying to get to Pascoe, and Pascoe dying. Something in him, Gale, had died, too; died even more suddenly. He did not want to see her again, in fact, he would have gone out of his way to avoid her. Not that he felt aggrieved in any way, but that he had changed.

Amazing that he should have so greatly changed. His last thought at night, his first in the morning had been Jenifer, but that loveliness of corn-coloured hair, of wide blue eyes, of full red lips no longer tormented him. Pascoe's woman—but it was not that. It was simply that desire was dead. Pictures of her in the baby-linen shop, in the little old garden at the back no longer troubled his quiet of a man not young, and occupied with affairs rather than emotions. Extraordinary! He had felt so strongly, and for such a long time, and now he was like an empty cup. The fever in the blood, the craving that had been a pain—gone.

Well, he was glad. It was good to be himself again, to be at peace. From the beginning it had been hopeless, and he had known it; but, knowing it, had yet persevered. Now he was free of his obsession, could go back to the pleasant round Jenifer had disturbed—his work as an auctioneer, his friendly help given to any who needed it, his little suppers with Mrs. Liddicoat. If Jenifer had cared for him, it might have put an end to his pleasant relations with her mother, and that—no, he did not want that to happen. That was of real importance to him. During the ten years of placid friendship something in him had grown tall and broad, struck its roots deep. Every Thursday he had dropped in, to sit in the garden through the warm summer evenings and by the fire during the winter nights. He had talked or been silent, come or gone as he chose. It was not only that he was made welcome, he was made at home. The baby-linen shop, the widow's circumstances, her warm heart and sensible mind, they were as familiar to him as the rooms of the house on Quayside.

A strong, sane woman, Mrs. Liddicoat, and kind. She made a man think of the fruitful earth and the clean out-of-doors. He liked her, he more than liked her.

Her presence rested him. When he was with her, the dark recollections which the accordion player had brought to the surface of Mr. Corlyon's mind, and which, since then, had drifted in it like flotsam on the edge of a tide, disappeared. As he went about his work, the thought of her back room, the room that looked on the sunny garden, the thought of her well tended fire, of her sympathetic presence, drew him. He longed to drop in, not only on Thursdays, but every evening of the week.

Morwenna Liddicoat could be sympathetic without understanding. Words between them were unnecessary. Whatever his mood, she adapted herself. She gave him peace, she renewed his strength.

III

Mrs. Liddicoat looked up from the "toddling shoes" she was making out of cuttings of white satin, with a wild notion that the days of the week had misplaced themselves. It was not Thursday? Oh, but it must be, for here was Mr. Corlyon.

And she had nothing nice for supper.

Where could Jenifer be? She must run down to Butcher Andrew and see what he had. Why, of course, Jenifer was in the linhay, washing her traäde, and it was Monday . . . butcher would not be open.

They had been crying herrings through the town, and she had not bought any: but Mrs. Tippett had taken a score for salting-in. Nothing more toothsome than a well-fried herring, and likely Mrs. Tippett would spare her some. But there, what was she thinking of, he did not like fish. Well, then, she must fry him slices of hog's pudding, with a jam hobbin to follow— so like a man not to say he was coming.

She pushed the satin—remnants of wedding dresses which were to furnish forth the shoes of the newcomers—aside, and gave Mr. Corlyon the smile for which he was looking.

"I'm pretty an' glad to see you."

"Though I was here last Thursday, and mean to come again next?"

"You are always welcome." Her lips said it, and her eyes and the curves of her face. Her glance was more than friendly, it had warmth in it. Ten years, and she had never failed him. He spoke on an impulse. "Wennie, let us get married. I feel I can't do without you, and that's a fact."

The colour left her face; and yet, though it changed, the change was towards youth. Out of her eyes looked an intensity which was pitiful. "You don't mean that. You can't . . . you can't want me . . . "

He saw that she loved him: that she had loved him with self-denial and without hope for a long time: that she dared not believe that, at last, he had turned to her.

He stooped, gave her the kiss for which, for years, she had been waiting.

IV

Jenifer, her washing wrung out ready for the line, stepped from the low door of the linhay on to the flagged path which ran between bushes of currant and gooseberry to the wall of unequal stones at the end of the garden. Her mother would be in the kitchen sewing white satin uppers to kid soles. She must tell her she had finished, that as soon as she had hung out her traäde she would be ready for tea. As she passed the window, she bent to look in.

Her mother and Mr. Corlyon! That look in his unusually bright eyes, why—it was the look he had had for her, Jenifer. No mistaking it. She moved away, began, mechanically, to hang the clothes on the line. A week or two back, and he had said it was she he loved, now it was her mother. Ah, they were brothers, Pascoe and he.

Love, men talked to you of love, and appeared to be dreadfully in earnest: they not only seemed, they were; they felt so strongly that you pitied them, and then—all in a moment—it was over. They did mean what they said and implied, you could not doubt it. But they meant it only while they were speaking, only while they were in that particular mood.

To think she should have been so foolish as to believe a man's love could last! Love . . . with marriage to follow? It should have been the other way round. Oh—that she should have been so green! Only three months away, yet he had forgotten. As quickly as that! And he had begged of her, how he had begged! She burned with shame at her recollections—that she should have been so easily won!

"Jenifer!"

She did not hear, and the man looking over the wall at the end repeated her name. Rousing at that, she saw it was Denny Manhire, the groom from Caer, the kind boy who was always doing little things to give her pleasure. The sight of him eased the pain at her heart, was a salve to wounded vanity. Here was somebody who thought the world of her. He did, but would he if he knew? She went on with her work, and Denny, his arms on the wall, waited.

She was like that, she kept him waiting, yet in the end she came. He did not mind, for he had the evening before him, and it was not often he was able to stand and look at her.

Her sleeves were rolled high. To keep it free of dust, she had covered her glintly hair with a white kerchief. Over her blue cotton frock she wore an apron, an apron which, in spite of the hours she had spent at the washing tray, was still snowy. Raising dimpled arms, she fixed garment after garment on the line, and the mild breeze set them a-dance. At last, she turned, and Denny tried to encourage himself with the thought of those four rooms over the stables at Caer, but he only remembered their emptiness, and that it was for Jenifer to say whether or no they must remain empty.

"I bin wantin' to ride over for more than a week."

"For Mrs. Pendragon's traäde?"

He put a hand over to take hers, but she showed him fingers crinkled from the water and shook her head.

"My hand is all clibby."

She would not even give him her hand! That tottering confidence of his—his confidence in the rooms, limewashed by himself, and looking over the busy stable yard and back premises of Caer—fell with a crash. She wanted neither him nor his rooms, and he might have saved himself the trouble of riding in.

He had his back to the sun, but the light was on Jenifer, on roses that had been nipped by some wind of trouble. Denny saw that she looked tired. All day at the washing—it might be that.

"Why Jenifer, you'm lookin' whisht, what you been doin' to yourself?"

The colour rushed into the girl's cheeks. "If that is all you got to say . . . "

"Aw, don't fetch your spite out on me, lovey. I'm sick and sorry to see it."

Gawky, scant-haired, yet kind! Some men took all they could get and gave nothing in return, but there were others. It might be Denny was one of the others, and she wanted kindness. It was a bad old world, that it was.

"I'm out of heart with everything."

"What?" Denny had hoped for himself; had feared Pascoe; deep down had known Pascoe was Jenifer's fancy. "Is â gone?" Caer was five miles from Stowe, and news was sometimes lame-footed. He had not heard Pascoe had left, and it would account for the alteration in Jenifer's looks.

"What is that to do with you?"

He had known, hoping he was mistaken, hoping—until she spoke. Dreariness, like a wash of dirty water, spread over his soul. In the same boat, he and she. Poor Jenifer! But the rascal Pascoe had cared for her! *Had*—they all knew what Pascoe was!

"What worry you, dear life, worry me."

She glanced at him thoughtfully for a moment, then shook her head. "My worries be my own."

She was such a young soft little thing. The sight of her in trouble made his heart ache. "Let me share'n."

The incongruous suggestion made her laugh, and the laughter brought back old ease and friendliness. Denny had always been good to her; perhaps, even if he did know . . .

Anyhow, what did it matter?

"Share them? My lor', you can't do that!"

The laughter was encouraging. "Jenifer, you been funny with me lately, and after us being such good friends . . . "

"I can't help it if I be." She gave him a quick look. "Pascoe is goin' marry some black woman out there."

"Then you can't have him." He could sympathize, but under the sympathy, his heart was full of gladness.

"No-o," her eyes, wide-set and darkly blue, were bright with tears. They spilled over, big flashing drops, they fell on the crazy pattern of the wall. "But, Denny, I—I been playin' the fool."

The meaning of her words leapt at him, and he stood in a momentary confusion. It was as if he were being hit in many places at once. She, Jenifer, she had played the fool—yes, and with Pascoe Corlyon. She—his, Denny's maid.

Well, he hated her for it, the bitch.

This came of putting faith in a woman. He knew what maidens were, none better; but Jenifer . . .

While he, the silly ass, was trusting her with all his heart, she was carrying on with Pascoe—Pascoe, who was everybody's larbut. The blood gathered behind his eyes. He wanted to kill. She was his, and she had let him down.

The sun shone on a falling teardrop. Jenifer had treated him badly, yes, but she had had, was having, a rotten time. She was having the same sort of time as he.

Gor'—the same sort of time! And she need not have told him. Why had she? She wanted to make use of him! Ah—she wanted him now. Well, she might want. He was not going to father another man's brat, not he. See her in hell, first!

See her in hell? Jenifer? No, no. They were both unhappy, but he could help, and he wanted to. Why, when she was a little maid she had always run to him, Denny, when the others teased her. They were not at school now, but it was the same thing, pretty much.

"It don't make no odds," he began, and was surprised at the difficulty he found in speaking. He could not get the words up his dry throat. "'Tis you—" he and Jenifer, they were more than sweethearts.

His words checked the flow of tears. She gazed at him, doubting, unable to believe, and he made a quick movement, a little gesture of pity and protection. His maid, his poor little maid.

"Oh," she said, "oh, Denny!"

A little shakily he asked her, "What be goin' do?

For a fortmight, ay, and longer, she had been asking herself that question. It was a fortnight since Pascoe had left Stowe, but ever since she had known for certain how it was with her she had wondered what she should do if he did not marry her. "Emma told me—there's a women can help you—time like this. They say Rebecca French—"

Manhire put his arm over the wall, took a hand that was no longer refused him, took it in a warm, heartening clasp. "Now don't, my dear, don't think of such a thing."

The wall was low with a round coping stone. She let him draw her up to it, was glad to be so drawn. It was good after months of fear, after a fortnight of more than fear, to be able to open your heart. "I don't want to do it, Denny, but—"

"Do Pascoe knaw?"

"He didn't ask, and I didn't say. I reckon he guessed, but didn't want to know."

"He shen't, then, not ever." The child should be his, Denny's Manhire's. To think of it thus, eased his heart of pain.

"Last minute, I thought I must tell him . . . and I went down to the house. They would not open the door, but I could not be kept out. I went in back door, and he was on settle, foxin'."

"Foxin'?"

"Aw—I could tell he was not asleep. He was not snoring natural, and his breath caught as if he was listening to us. You see, Mr. Corlyon would not let me pass."

"Why wouldn't he?"

"Don't know for why exactly. Perhaps he did not want me to marry Pascoe."

"Why not?"

"Well—men's funny." He had not wanted her to marry Pascoe because he had wanted her himself. He had, then; and it was such a little while ago, yet now; he wanted her mother!

Denny saw she was not going to answer his question.

"Then, what about your mother?"

Jenifer's fingers, hitherto lying slackly in his clasp, suddenly took hold. "Mammy?" Even Mammy had her own life, and other people's troubles, Jenifer's were outside it. "She'm more taken up with Mr. Corlyon than she is with me. I believe they'll marry."

Pascoe gone, her mother occupied with her own concerns—life was, indeed, a desert! She felt that she stood alone, friendless except for little Denny Manhire . . . and he was looking at her so kindly.

"Jenifer," he said, "don't you do nothing you will live to repent. Let your baby come out to the light."

She looked at him wistfully. "'Tis what I should like to do." She could feel it warm in her arms, and she did not belong to have it, but, oh yes, she must, "The li'l darling, I do dearly love——" she must not say that she had played with the thought of hers, loving it and longing for it, but always afraid . . . "I do dearly love babies."

He, too, he loved them. A home without children? Why, 'twas the children made it home. He let his thoughts turn to the future—there would be the little one that was coming, and then others, his and hers. The rooms over the stable would be full of jolly noise. Trust him, the first little chap should be made welcome, should have his share.

"Your mother may be vexed about it when she do knaw, but she'll stand by you, and we'll get married at once, and all will be for the best."

He was for shouldering her burden. A brave, jonik little chap, but she must not take advantage of him. People had not treated her well—at least, one person had not, but that was no reason for behaving badly to Denny.

For a moment she stood, pulling herself together. Somehow, the hand that had clasped hers was round her waist. She drew herself away. "I don't want for you to marry me out of pity. There's more boys in the world that 'ud have me, even if I have got a child. Don't think I can't manage without you."

He pulled her back. "Maybe there's more boys for you, Jenifer, but there's no other maid for me."

CHAPTER XII

I

MR. CORLYON raised his hat, which had a little more curl to the brim than that of other men, and Mrs. Liddicoat watched him walk away down the street, saw him look back when the street became Quayside, saw him enter by the discreet gate in the whitewashed wall. She thought that faintly, above the swishing of the sea-water in the harbour basin, she heard the closing of a door.

Her heart went with him into the Brown House, and up the stairs, and into the room where he would sleep; where, presently, she too would sleep. She was possessed by tingling excitement and, under that, lay a deep warmth.

He had said: "Till Pascoe went, till he left me for good and all, I had not realized I was a lonely man." And later: "I want someone in the house with me; someone to come back to of an evening."

Not lover-like, but he did love her. He had put his arms round her, roughly and clumsily, in proper man's fashion, and had hugged her. Again and again. He had given her lover's kisses, and the simple hearty kisses of affection.

Behind her in the house, she heard Jenifer locking doors and windows, but she did not stir. It was not often in her busy life that she could spare a moment; but to-night, when happiness had come to her, she could not go in, not yet.

The inequalities of the opposite roofs were dark against a silver sky, and she looked past these familiar outlines, lifting up her heart. To have thought life was over as far as love went! Why, the love she had had for her young sweethearts, for her husband, had been, compared with this, as lamps in a street, small things at best. Yes, small bright things, but now that the sky had lightened for her, no longer bright. Those early loves—she looked back, seeing them at last with understanding. They had been sweet and worth while, they had had to do with

babies, with home-making, with the business of living. A
mixture of emotions, that early loving, but this late-come
feeling was different, being the love of one human creature for
another. She thought of the tide in the harbour. The tide, the
tide of life, had flowed over and hidden her real self. On its
bosom had rocked a strange medley of craft, and she, under the
surface bustle, the passage of the ships, she had slept. Now the
tide had ebbed, and ebbing had carried the flotsam seaward.
She had been left free of foreign craft; and to her had come the
soft wind and the downshining stars, and the enfolding night.
He had come, the man whom she might love through the quiet
years, the years that remained. She had slept till his kiss had
awakened her.

But—could she accept what offered? Did she dare? She was
middle-aged, her body had been given her to use, and she had
put it to its natural uses. How she wished she had again her
virginal breast. His head, the weight of that precious head on a
breast worthy of it! No, she had not that to give.

Falteringly, she had spoken to him about her age. The words
had been difficult to say. Her cheeks had grown hot, as hot as if
she had been blushing. But he—oh, the dear of'n—it was as if
he did not see the white in her hair and the lines; he had looked
through them at—was it at her?

"I know how old you are," he had said. Of course he knew.
His life and her life, every year of them, had been spent in
Stowe, near Stowe.

"I know how old you are, and it does not matter."

He never uttered other than the truth. Not, of course, the
real truth, but the truth as he saw it. She could depend on his
sincerity. To him, then, strange as it might seem, the lines and
the silver threads were of no importance.

Wonderful that, for Mr. Corlyon was held to be an appreci-
ator of beauty, of soft, frail beauty. So stiff himself, he had
been attracted by weakness. He had not married, but he might
have. Yes, there had always been women.

That sort of woman.

Morwenna Liddicoat had not thought he had it in him to
love, not really love. Any man could make love—seed thrown

by the wayside which would spring up, throw a gaudy blossom, and wither away!

But—love.

Deep, warm, big, filling you as a vessel is filled, making you feel as you felt sometimes in church. The love of God . . .

She was to give up the baby-linen shop. He wanted her to go to him, and she would. He had only to fix the date. She was ready—now.

She had lived for many years on the edge of the street. The river of Stowe life had splashed her drexel. She had had the amusement of its constant variety, but the time had come to put up the shutters. She laughed at herself—at the itch in her fingers to have those shutters up!

He had said she might have a maid to help her with the work of the house. She! He did not realize—the dear—how already, though his love-making was only the hour old, she was looking forward to the day when she would cook his meals, sweep up the mud his boots brought into their house—*their*—scold him a little so that he should be made to see that she was there, yes, there, and, working for him, loving him.

She could cook—none to beat her in Stowe—and she would give him tasty meals, and have the joy of seeing him eat what she had got ready. She knew what he liked. The Thursday night suppers had taught her.

The thinking out, the getting ready of that meal had been the chief pleasure of her week. Now she would have it, not once a week, but every day. She would go out to buy the food, to buy it with his money, with the money he made, that he spent the day making, that he made for her.

As to her money—Jenifer could have what had come from Peter, and she would hand over the rest, the farm her father left her, to Gale.

She, Morwenna Liddicoat, wanted to be dependent on her man, to go to him, and say, "Give me so much for the marketing." She thought of him counting the shillings into her hand, thought of the joy it would be to bargain with them, spend with grudging care, spend as little as possible. Those shillings, because he had earned them, they would have a special value.

"Mammy, Mammy, bain't you never coming to bed?"

The lap-lapping of the tide made an accompaniment to her dreams. He would be asleep by now, asleep in the room that looked over the water towards the east. The sound of his laugh, rough with a sort of catch, was still in her ear. Or was it in her heart? She stepped back. Really, she must not stay there wasting her time.

When she came to turn the key in the front door, she hesitated. Lock him out? Put a bolt between them? No, never again. She had slept all locked up inside herself until he roused her to answer him, to open.

If she were to leave the door on the latch? But how about tramps—a tramp? Well—not many in Stowe, and besides, how was a tramp to guess that one of the respectable doors of the street was on the latch?

Not that Gale would want to come at any odd hour. Only, she felt she could not turn that key. Day and night, never again should there be between them bolt or bar.

II

"Mammy, I been waitin' for you."

"Have 'ee, my dear?"

Mrs. Liddicoat had taken but a little time to slip out of her clothes and into bed. She would go back to her dreaming, and so sleep.

"I got something to tell you."

Must Jenifer break in with uninteresting outside talk? Her mother did not want the thread of her thoughts snapped, her attention diverted. "I be tired."

"O—Mammy!"

An arresting note in the child's voice. Mrs. Liddicoat turned on the pillow. "What is it, dear?"

"I got to get married."

Ah!

But she had guessed—half guessed it. She had not quite believed it. Her Jenifer! Other women's maids, but not hers.

"You—got—to—get—married?" She was saying to herself that a forced "put" was no choice.

"Mammy!" Jenifer sat up, clasping her knees. "When you was young—"

Mrs. Liddicoat's thoughts flew to old sweethearts, to the love-making of what seemed only yesterday.

"Honest men make honest women. You was born in wedlock."

"Mightn't have been."

Heavens! what would the child say next? And if she had listened to Willy Hosken; even if—but this was profitless.

"And my child'll be born in wedlock."

"Who's goin' father it for 'ee then?"

"You don't know?"

"Aw, I can guess," and because it would be Pascoe's child she was partly reconciled.

"I fixed it up to-night wi'—wi' Denny Manhire."

Denny Manhire? A good little workchap. Jenifer might have done worse. No happiness for any maid with come-and-go Pascoe; and—she would have his child.

Mrs. Liddicoat was conscious of confused longing—his child! She might never look to hold a child of Gale's against her bosom. They were past that. A good thing, and yet—ah, well, there would be this little one, his brother's child. It might be like him . . .

"You was so taken up with Mr. Corlyon you didn't see us in the garden."

The wall at the end was low, and Denny not the first of Jenifer's lovers to have vaulted it. But it was to be Denny in the end, well, well!

"'Tis all right then?" Jenifer would marry, and she would miss her, but—because of her love for Mr. Corlyon, her personal happiness—not so very much.

Jenifer turned away, drew the clothes over her, hunched a shoulder. "'Tedn't all right," she said, with a sort of violence. "but 'tis the best I can do."

III

"Let us go out for a bit."

Mrs. Liddicoat's back room was the most comfortable place Mr. Corlyon knew, and yet—. He glanced at Jenifer sitting on the other side of the table. It was impossible to talk before her, also . . . well, he could not stand that continual reminder. To see her for a few minutes, even sit with her through a meal, yes, that was all right. It was afterwards, when she got out her work and sat with it under the shower of lamplight, that in the dark pool of his mind the ooze began to crawl with life.

It rose to the surface, and he could not help himself, he had to relive the scenes through which he had passed that night. They rose, they detached themselves, they passed in procession. Vivid against the blackness, sharp, clear . . . so much more vivid than when he had been living them. Then he had been ignorant of what would happen next; had been living in the moment. He knew, now, what must come.

He had struggled with himself before he spoke. His boasted self-control, where was it? He would think of nothing but the game of cards that he was playing, he would forget Jenifer was in the room! He looked at his hand, but beyond it shone the bright hair. He moved his seat, but could not forget that it was behind his shoulder. The effort to forget only made the memories more insistent. He was back in the kitchen of the Brown House. His body grew tense, he was struggling with Pascoe, ah, Jenifer's face at the window . . . What had she seen? To this day he did not know.

The sound of those slowing, difficult breaths—and Jenifer trying to pass, to get to Pascoe. God, if she did not go he would kill her, he could not stand it, no, not a moment longer. His hand twitched . . . a knife on the supper-table.

"One for his nob," Mrs. Liddicoat had said, recalling him to the present.

Blinking, he came back to the little room, and her kindly presence, to the fingers scoring a point on the cribbage board.

Thank goodness, Jenifer was to be married as soon as the

banns had been called. Meanwhile, how could he sit in the room with her? "Let us go out for a bit?"

If a little surprised, Mrs. Liddicoat was willing—oh, more than willing. He was anything but a restless man, yet he might feel he wanted her to himself. She thrilled with the hope of kisses, of more than kisses.

"We'll go up to Coulter's Folly," he said as they stepped into the mirk of the street. They would go up the little lane behind the houses, the lane in which Stowe folk had courted before ever the mud cabins of the first comers had changed from cob to country stone.

The dark figures turned by the garden of the Brown House on Quayside, turned up between the white walls and over-topping shrubs. Very few people were abroad that evening, possibly because a droll-teller had gathered them in Nancarrow's barn.

"We will go slowly," said he, warm in his coat, "and we will keep in the shadow of the tamarisk. It is lovely to be out here and by ourselves."

Venturing greatly, she took his arm. He pressed her hand to his side; then, shifting, put his arm round her shoulders and bent his head. "I want you all to myself," he murmured.

"You can't want it so much as I."

She lifted her face in happy, thrilled expectancy. His lips closed on hers, on warm strong lips which were yet soft, and into him passed a sense of healing. This love which was about him like an atmosphere was giving him something of which he stood in need.

She had pushed evil memories, the trouble and sickness of them, out of his mind. Alone with her he was himself again, his old strong self, the self that went about calmly, peacefully. He had been solitary, but happy. Now after a time of discomfort, of obsession, he was once more happy. And it was in some deep way due to her.

They climbed the hill slowly and as they walked he leaned over her, kissing her again and again, kissing her with a passion new to her experience.

The night was about them and Morwenna's face was turned

to him. She was learning that the night had been made for lovers, that she, even she, who for ten years had been lonely— nay, who all her life had been lonely, that she loved and was loved. Above in the dark heavens, flowed the silver of the Milky Way, behind them in the little houses was the drama of life. They came to the verge of Coulter's Folly, to the top of the ancient earth, and felt that they were alive because they loved.

Leaning against him in the shadow of the tamarisk she gave herself to his passionate hands. "Say you love me," she whispered.

CHAPTER XIII

I

LEAVING his papers for the night, Mr. Corlyon went to his armchair. He was cramped by sitting at his desk. He had spent the morning at a sale, the afternoon stooping over deeds, and it was good to lean back, stretch his long legs across the rug.

His eyes ached. He would take it easy for a little.

His mind was still running on the deeds. It was a case of property changing hands, property that had an old mortgage on it. For all that the Pendragons were so well known, he would not be content without a release. He must see their agent. Perhaps, to-morrow . . .

When land changed hands, there was money in the transaction, a bit for everybody concerned; and, seeing that Pascoe had helped himself to his, Gale's savings . . .

But Pascoe hadn't. The pigskin bags in the old chest were as fat as ever. He knew although he had not been into the cave since that night.

Oh, damn—he did not want to think of the dark rows, replete, covered with the holland. To act a part you must believe in the actuality of what you were saying and doing. Pascoe was gone to Jamaica, he had laid greedy violent hands on Gale's money and Gale was now a poor man. The chest was empty of everything but flat leathern bags and a piece of holland. As Gale had no longer any savings there was no need to padlock the iron bands, the low black door.

But they happened to be fastened—very well, let them stay as they were.

At any rate there was nothing behind that door which interested him sufficiently to take him down the slippery stairs and across the cellar. A few bottles of wine and—ah—in the corner—

He had forgotten Pascoe's dunnage. He should have carried it through the fogou, buried it; yes, he should have done it that night. Now it lay behind the forty-gallon cask—a ditty-box, clothes. Nonsense, he had the keys in his pocket, and Pascoe was on his way to the West Indies, clothes and all. Only that morning Antiks had asked him if he thought "young Maister's" ship had reached Kingston.

He had studied the shipping list, told her Pascoe must have arrived, that by now he was probably married. They must not expect letters, not yet awhile. He would be too busy to write.

He believed it, he was acting up to his belief . . . it was the only safe thing to do.

II

Though his eyes ached they did not close. After his day's work he ought to have been ready for a snooze before he took his supper. Odd that he was not, for he had not been sleeping well. Dreams, broken slumbers, long hours of restlessness!

He was, nowadays, too wide awake, too much alive and it was tiring. A good deal could be said in favour of dullness! A certain comfort in spending your days working, eating, sleeping, in spending them temperately. Temperance in living meant a continual sense of well-being. He had awakened to it of a morning after quiet sleep. He had taken it with him through the full, but not over-full, hours of daylight. It had been with him not only all day but every day.

He was conscious of an unwelcome change. He, hitherto so quiet and self-contained, had grown eager, excitable. All day long he was doing things, all night he was thinking of more things to do. He seemed to think at a great rate, to be fevered with thought. It was strange and also it was distressing. Only when he was with Morwenna Liddicoat did the peace to which he was accustomed re-enter his soul; but as he stooped to her doorway, he found that his mind, continually bubbling, grew calm; and as she talked to him, caressing him with her words, creating an atmosphere of passionate affection, the unrest gradually sank. He was like a kettle of boiling water that has been taken off the fire. The fierce tumult slackened, died and he went from her in the old pleasant quietude; and he took the thought of her with him like a flower, he slept with the scent of it in his nostrils. Those nights he did not dream.

"Have you noticed my mole is gone?" she had asked him, and he remembered that once upon a time she had had a mole, a mole with hairs. He had thought it repulsive.

"I had forgotten you had one."

"I went to the teller and had it charmed and last week it dropped off."

She showed him her cheek, smooth, unscarred.

He thought that if she had had fifty moles, he would hardly have seen them, and that he supposed was love. He had never felt for a woman what he felt for Morwenna. Always he had had an eye for the pretty maids . . . for their intriguing ankles! He would have liked to kiss this one, go yet further with that.

He found that since he had known he loved Morwenna, he no longer looked after strangers with desire.

III

He felt unusually tired. He had been busy, so busy he had not seen Morwenna for three days. Perhaps it was that. The remedy was simple, he would go over that evening.

Jenifer was to be married the following week and after that Morwenna would come to him. She, too, had been busy. Apparently when a maid married many things had to be bought and made. Morwenna had not neglected him, but she had been—well, just a little too much occupied with her daughter. Thank goodness, Jenifer was going to live at Caer. Five miles away! She could not be running in every day, taking up her mother's time. He wanted Morwenna to himself.

The consequence of her being occupied with preparations for the wedding meant that he had been left to his own devices; and he had thrown himself too heavily into his work. He had thought of nothing else.

Had he not?

Well, he had tried to avoid thinking of certain things, and to do so had thrust not merely a finger into other people's concerns.

He was used up, tired out and yet restless. He had overdone it. Perhaps if he were to take a glass of wine—

He glanced at the sideboard, but the broad mahogany counter ran, smoothly polished, from the sharp edge to the foliated back. He thought it did and yet—

Had he, within the last hour or so, fetched wine from the cave, decanted it, left it on the sideboard, left it . . . ready?

A trick of memory—oh, those ghastly tricks! He had not got up any wine since . . . since . . . damn it all, he had had no wine since he decanted the bottles for Pascoe. There could not be any on the sideboard. Well, then—that faint glitter as of glass— what was it? Had Antiks left a tumbler?

But he remembered that when he had crossed to his desk early in the afternoon, the slab of polished wood had been bare. Yet, on the sideboard, dim, hardly visible—

He sat up, straining his eyes to see through the blue dusk, through the flicker of the uncertain firelight. A shudder ran down his spine and it became all at once necessary—in some vitally important way necessary—that he should prove himself mistaken. The jutting wings of the sideboard threw an even darkness across the counter and in that gloom was, he felt sure there was— nothing.

A faintly bright outline? Nonsense! And yet—but he wanted to think it was not there. It could not be.

He had watched Antiks set his two decanters on the shelf in the china cupboard. Afterwards he had locked the door, taken the key.

No use denying that he saw a dim shape, a shape reflecting tiny rainbow gleams. A pricking sensation caught his neck, a tingle as of rising hairs. He was not seeing a decanter, but a small cut-glass flagon.

The flagon had been washed and put away. It was standing on the shelf in the china cupboard.

He recognized it, admitted to himself the fact, and his heart seemed to turn over, he felt sick. Leaning his head on his hands, he shut his eyes. It was there, the little flagon, actually there.

For a long time he sat quite still. He was faint and he must wait till he grew better. The shadows thickened. Outside, the lamplighter, trolling an old song, went up the street. He would go up French Street, past the baby-linen shop, he would see—

Ah, if he, Gale, could have seen Morwenna, if he could have laid his head on that kind bosom. She would have cherished him, obliterated this dread. He would have drawn from her the help he needed at the moment, the strength to face this thing. Acknowledging its existence, he must try to understand, so that he could deal with it.

Getting out of his chair, he walked to the sideboard, stared through the mocking shadows.

Faint, clear, the red-brown of the mahogany showing through its upper half, the flagon stood upright on the counter —a little flagon of cut glass!

The room heaved about him—for the flagon was half-full of thick red wine.

IV

He had put out a twitching hand, but his fingers had passed through the appearance, had touched the mahogany at the back. Once more he shut his eyes, but this time it was in the hope of destroying an illusion. It had been a fancy, had sprung from overwrought nerves, it was not really a something on his sideboard. When he looked again it would have vanished and he would laugh. To have imagined such a thing, he, of all people, he who had kept his mind free of the country beliefs, who was of all Stowe the most sceptical!

He opened his eyes and it was still there, a film of glass, of wine.

A figment? He swept his hand across the board. If he could he would push the flagon off, hear it crash on the planching, see it in fragments . . .

His hand felt cold. It was as if a dank air had been breathed on it—but the appearance persisted, the wraith of a little flagon which held a wine-glassful of liquor. It stood on his sideboard, as it had stood in substantial fact the night that Pascoe—went.

It was, of course, an hallucination; and hallucinations were a matter of health. He turned away, made up the fire, lighted the lamp Antiks had placed in readiness on the table, stood for quite five minutes with his back to the sideboard, occupied the five minutes thinking of the deeds, the mortgage on the property—

Turning—he saw the sideboard in the full light of the lamp, came to it with a mind refreshed. It would be bare, he knew it would. There was nothing on it, nothing . . . Oh, but, wait a moment! Not the glitter of cut glass and yet . . .

White, misty, a mere outline, the frailest of appearances, but—he struck the board with his clenched hand—but it was there.

V

This came of not keeping a tight rein on his fancies. It stood to reason that what he saw so clearly with his mental vision he might come to think was tangible—that is, if he allowed himself to dwell on it.

Undoubtedly the flagon was an illusion. That he must admit, but what he could not understand was why, if he must have illusions, they should take this form. He had not been thinking of the flagon. Until that night he had forgotten the part it had played. A sequence of scenes had crossed and recrossed the stage of his mind—Pascoe lifting his glass that last time and so on, but no thought of the flagon. Yet the appearance must—he would not admit the doubt—it must have come from his mind.

It could not be a thing in itself.

It had sprung from his mind, could consequently only be seen by him. It was not actually there, an object visible, however dimly, to other people.

He rested a hand on the mahongany and for a moment his body shook with sharp foreboding . . . visible, that flagon half-full of wine, visible to other people! Tales of hauntings— the white hare that he had maintained was an effect of moonlight, the patter, patter as you came back from the crouched burials at Harlyn, the presence on the stair at Trevone, the H'ant in the Little Wood. People had spoken to him of these, of Susie and Edgar "piskie-led'n" from Caer to Vorrick, of appearances on the sea-commons, of what danced on the road up at Church Town. They had told and he had listened, but he had been incredulous. He had said: "Till I see these things for myself I cannot believe in them."

He had thought people invented the tales. Imagination, twilight, a windy stir, and the white hanging became a ghost!

Now he wondered, did not feel quite so certain. They had said they saw, was he seeing . . . ?

He sat down on the nearest chair. His glance travelled about the room, came back to the sideboard. How if the appearance should be a wraith, not a figment of his mind, but an actual, intangible yet visible, wraith?

The wraith of a flagon, perhaps of more than a flagon . . .

He got up and went quickly into the kitchen.

VI

The cover-fire stood by the wall. According to domestic usage the master would adjust it over sod and ember the last thing before going to bed. In the morning when it was lifted away, the turf would be still burning.

Mr. Corlyon, walking quickly through the dark, touched it accidentally, and the piece of cumbrous copper clattered on to the level. Though he had himself in hand the noise so startled him that a hot flush ran over his body.

He stood stockstill, holding on to himself. It was only the old cover-fire!

The kitchen, facing west, was lighter than the parlour had been. The red of sunset glittered on the panes, filled the room with a warm glow. Mr. Corlyon looked about, looked searchingly, looked with an unacknowledged suspicion. He told himself that he must look in every corner. He would rather not have scanned certain parts, but he forced himself to be thorough.

The table by the outer wall was laid for supper, the settle stood to the left of the hearth. On the red cushion of the settle—no. For a moment he had fancied . . .

VII

As soon as he had eaten his supper, he would walk up to the baby-linen shop. He would like to go in, stay. Morwenna was a sure refuge; her sanity put ridiculous ideas to flight.

A chair was drawn to the table, but he did not take it. He could not sit where he had sat that night. He could not sit opposite to—not opposite to Pascoe! But what nonsense . . .

It was not that Pascoe would be opposite, but that behind would be the settle. Rubbish, it was not the settle! He could not sit with his back to a hot fire. He had never been able to, and besides the master's place was at the end of the table. Yes, but not the window end. If he sat there he would know a white face was looking in . . . ah, but he could pull down the blind.

What had come to him? The settle, the face at the window! He was "bevvering." It was because of the appearance in the parlour. That little flagon, it had been a shock to his nerves; but he would pull himself together. He must, or there was no knowing . . .

He would have supper—not that he was hungry. After such an experience how could he be? And the meat was tough. He must speak to Antiks about it, tell her to hang it longer, she always thought it should be eaten as soon as it was killed. Pah! he did not want to eat, but he must or it would look strange. He must be careful not to do anything that would arouse suspicion.

Tough meat and absolutely no appetite—it was like eating sawdust, but he must get it down.

He leaned his head on his hands, disordered, uneasy . . .

What had happened to him? He had killed Pascoe because such a man was better out of the world than in, because he, Gale Corlyon, had felt that he must. It had been he or Pascoe, and he had won. That was all there was to it, and Pascoe's burial in the fogou should have ended the matter.

It had ended it, but he was out of sorts and, as a consequence, his imagination had run away with him. Only natural that it should.

That cut-glass flagon—he knew it was safe in the china cupboard, but he would make sure of it. He unlocked the door, and, of course—there it was! It stood in its immemorial place beside the decanters, a little deeply-cut vessel of old glass. That on the sideboard had been an illusion. He put his hand on the flagon. Good to feel the sharp edges, the weight of it!

He must try and forget that other. He would stroll up the road, go at once; and he would not so much as glance into the parlour as he passed. When he came back—perhaps. He took up his hat, set it on with a defiant cock. When he came back he would be a different man.

VIII

"Where is Jenifer?"

"She's out with her chap and we've got the place to ourselves." Very soon Jenifer would be gone and Morwenna would have him altogether, but even this was better than nothing. She smiled on her surroundings—the small cosy room with the horsehair sofa against the wall, the bright new-fangled grate, the closed doors that led into shop and linhay. The room was theirs, walls that had been set about the bits of furniture to shut him and her off from the rest of the world.

"That is good." He went to the sofa, sat down, called her to him. "Come over here."

She had been glad to see him. She had felt she could not be more glad, but at his deepened voice, at the look in his eyes, her heart swelled. She walked across the intervening space as if drawn by irresistible force. Yet she felt shy, felt she must speak of some trivial matter, must take refuge in that way from her too great happiness.

"My dear life, you'm looking like anybody bewitched.

Have you had a bothering day?"

He pulled her down beside him. "Never mind about that." He must be careful what he said, yes, even to her.

It would not be difficult, for he was always careful . . . yet for once in his self-contained life he would have been glad to talk.

"Not unless it comfort you," she said, making, as usual, no claim.

It would have comforted him. Another mind to have shared with his this bewildering knowledge, would have lightened the burthen . . . but he dare not trust her.

"Words don't help." He did not mind her knowing that he was troubled.

"They don't," but loving did, the outward signs of it.

Close to him, leaning against his broad chest, she looked up. His eyes were not as dark as they belonged to be, as they were when he was thinking of her; and the arm about her, though it lay warmly in place, was not drawn tight. "I've often thought," she murmured, "when I been sitting facing you, playing cribbage—"

His mind came back from its secret places, came back to her. "Well?"

"I've thought I should like—"

"What did you think—all that time ago?" He was smiling down at her, glad to forget his worries, inclined to tease.

But she was serious. "That I should like—to put my arms round your neck and kiss you—I ought to been ashamed of myself!

His smiled deepened. "You would not have had to wait long if I had known," and he bent his head.

"No," she said, evading him, "'tisn't that. I want to kiss your face by myself, to kiss it, all of it, and you do nothing."

He laughed at that, laughed in an amused content. Leaning back, his head on the rolled end of the sofa, he let her have her way. Morwenna was still perfectly serious. She had often thought how wonderful it would be to touch that clear pale skin, and now she might, he had given her leave. Almost reverently she kissed his temples where the crisp hair was receding, kissed his smooth cheeks, his soft eyelids. She crooned over him as she kissed, murmuring of the long hard chin, the hidden eyes. "And I do like it that your moustache is so crisp and stiff. If it were let to grow curly, 'twould be curly as a sheep's back."

For years she had looked at this dear face from what had seemed an insuperable distance. "I'm like the nigger," she said. "When he was asked what the world stood on, he say 'Ah, it stand on a tortoise; and de tortoise stand on a emmet; and de emmet on a rock; and—and—oh, it be rock all de way down.' I'm loving you all de way down." She had kissed his dear face from brow to chin. Now she looked at his lips. She longed to press them, but she did not dare. She knew, too, that he was waiting for that last deep caress. The stir in her blood told her that he was, but no, she could not.

"I don't know what makes you care for me." She would have to pay for her boldness. How could she have offered to kiss him? She had done it because, poor chap, he looked so whisht; but she had not meant to—to make him feel like that.

She felt ashamed of herself, would have liked to get up and run away and hide.

"I don't know either." His eyes were open, they had the dark and shining look that made her heart behave so oddly. "Kiss me!"

She could not run away, she could not even refuse, she did not want to. Her blood, moving hotly, brought her lips to his.

"You look handsomer to-night than I've seen you," he murmured. "Women always look handsomer when I am loving them."

IX

Not till Mr. Corlyon was locking the door of the Brown House did he remember the apparition. The air of the passage seemed to him, after the warmth of Morwenna's kitchen, after the freshness of the sea-breeze, clammy, stagnant. Before him, within the house, lay the dark, and the dark was peopled.

He thought of Morwenna. If only he could have brought her back with him. She would have come. She would have done anything he asked of her. She was—he held his head higher—she was his woman. Absolutely, in every fibre of her, his.

Her presence in the house would, like a destroying flame, have crumbled his vision into the grey nothing of ashes. Her movements would have blown them away. He saw her suddenly as a plump broom. Saw her busy in the old rooms, busy creating the clouds of dust which, with housewifely women, were the precursors of a new order. Walking along the passage, he smiled at the thought. He smiled until he saw a line of light under the parlour door.

He must have left the lamp burning.

He could not let it burn itself out. Yet—he did not want to go into that room.

He pulled himself together—put a hand to the door-knob. He would turn the lamp out without looking at the sideboard.

But once in the room, in spite of himself, his glance strayed to it. He had to look.

His heart sank away; the sensation of nausea rose in his throat . . .

The little flagon was there.

CHAPTER XIV

I

MR. CORLYON woke with a start. Though it was still dark, movements on Quayside told him day had begun.

His experiences of the previous night had made him anxious with regard to Antiks. He must be down before she came; and he woke to a fear lest he had overslept. The noises that he heard—were they outside the house, or in? Antiks had a key to the back door . . .

She could let herself in; and, once in, she would go round the house, drawing back curtains, opening windows. Suppose that, on going into the parlour, she had caught sight of the flagon?

The sweat broke out on his body, and jumping up, he ran down the stairs.

Thank heaven . . . he drew a long breath . . . thank heavens, he had been mistaken. Antiks was not yet come. In the cold dark house, so like a large grave, was no sound, not so much as the chirp of a cricket.

Was the flagon still a faint film of glass and wine standing on the sideboard? He went into the parlour, into a blackness so intense that you fell over familiar pieces of furniture. He barked his shins on the wood-basket, cursed, but went on to the window. Drawing back the dark red curtains, he looked over the wire blind and down the length of the garden. Lights on the Lowestoft boats, a rattle of anchor chains, trawlers going out.

The out-of-doors was busy with its own affairs; it was in no way concerned with him.

The window faced east, and the sky was lightening over Brown Willhay and Rowtor, the parlour was no longer a mere pocket of darkness. Mr. Corlyon, turning his back on the tide, waited till the black shapes of the furniture had drawn themselves clear of the night, till he could distinguish the stretch of polished wood that lay between the carven wings of the sideboard.

His heart leapt with relief and joy. The sideboard was bare, was most beautifully bare. Its smooth surface stretched uninterruptedly from front to back, from side to side. With a step grown young, he crossed the room, scrutinized the wooden slab, shut his eyes to look again—looked at the same admirable smoothness of mahogany.

He had left the flagon there overnight, and during the dark hours it had vanished. People said "Gone for good"—it was the fitting phrase! The flagon had been a figment of his imagination, due to weariness and overstrain. He must be more careful; must diet himself, take it easy. After all, he was getting on.

Ah, but if the apparition were to return? He must bear in mind that it might. It would, of course, be something only he could see, still . . .

He stood, staring at the sideboard, cogitating. He stood there till he knew how he would contrive that the flagon should not appear.

II

When Antiks came, she found Mr. Corlyon dressed and busy. "Whatever be 'ee doin', draggin' all that cloam out o' cupboard, Maister?"

"I"—he must give her an explanation that would be convincing—"I want the place nice. Mrs. Liddicoat say 'tis looking bare."

Antiks' morning mood darkened. If Mrs. Liddicoat was to have a voice in household matters her time to shift must be come . . . and she did not want to go. "Where be goin' put they putchers to?"

"On the sideboard."

"Leave'n stay, and I'll wash'n a bit for yer."

He glanced at the selection he had made. No denying that the jugs and dishes were dusty. Stored away since the death of his stepmother, they were likely to be. All the same, it annoyed him that he must wait; that he could not carry them into the parlour, set them in place, do it that very moment.

Stowe believed him to be easy tempered, a man who heard a story through without growing impatient, who was willing to sit, smoking, listening; who, when he had heard all, gave good common-sense advice. No one had ever seen him ruffled.

He choked back the irritation that was rising from that new overstrung self of his.

"They'm lookin' rather mucky," Antiks said. He had taken them from the wall cupboard, stacked them on the table among the supper dishes, till, as she expressed it, "kitchen was dancing like Launceston jail." "My dear life, Maister, do 'ee go in an' set down, or you'll be hollerin' 'Marblew' for breakfast and I'll have nothing ready."

"All right." He walked away. He would turn his attention to something else. Ah, yes, that mortgage! It was for the benefit of the younger children of each fresh generation of Pendragons. A clever family, clever, that is, in a certain way. Once they got their claws on to a bit of land, they knew how to keep it. Generation after generation, unbegotten, even unimagined, yet with a claim . . .

※　　　※　　　※

What a time Antiks was, washing "they putchers." He had thought of her as quick, but she was no quicker than others.

※　　　※　　　※

He must make his client insist on having a release from the mortgage. These people, they trusted the Pendragons, yet it was only last year that Mr. Llyr Pendragon had refused to grant any more building leases on the score that he preferred green fields to houses. Stowe could not expand while the Pendragons owned it. He was in favour of State ownership—Norway had it, why not his country?

Was Antiks never coming with that china? Ah—at last.

She had pushed open the door with her foot, because she was carrying a tray. Now he could set to work.

But on the tray was only his breakfast!

He went to the table, sat down.

"'Aven't ate more'n a sparrow since Maister Pascoe went," said Antiks.

"Never mind me, go on with your work."

Although so keenly impatient he must eat. Already the fact that he had not much appetite had caught Antiks' attention. He wished people were not so noticing, but he must remember that they were. He must remember, in particular, that Antiks was.

What was the matter with him? Why had he no appetite? Thick slices of fried hog's pudding! It should have been delicious, yet it had no flavour. Was it true, as he said, that he had eaten no more than a sparrow of late? That he had had no appetite since Pascoe . . .

It had, of course, been a shock to discover that Pascoe was dishonest, a callous brute; to find yourself regarded as a money-bag—squeeze, and a bit of gold falls out! It was more than a shock, it was shattering. Something in him seemed to have given way, and that something had been like the iron that held together the staves of a barrel.

"All the king's horses and all the king's men
Couldn't put Humpty-Dumpty together again."

—not even Morwenna would be able to mend what Pascoe had broken. She soothed and rested her lover, but the band—the iron band—was lost.

When Antiks came in with a big tray, he was walking up and down the room, working off his impatience.

"'Twill make a lot of dustin' for I," she said, planting it on the table.

"I'll see to that."

"You'll dust they putchers?" She laughed at him. "I should like to see yer doin' of it! Never dusted nought in your born days, and I'm sure you bain't goin' do it whiles I'm doin' for 'ee. No," she took a cloth from the sideboard drawer, "an' you bain't goin' put'n on the bare boards, Maister, or they'll scratch'n."

He stood back, let her have her way. "At any rate, I'll set them out."

With Antiks watching, he chose a grey beer-jug, stood it on the spot which had yielded that rainbow gleam a few hours earlier. By it he placed some pewter, a square bottle of hollands, some old lustre ware. It stood to reason that when a space was filled by one object, it could not be taken possession of by another. He looked at the beer-jug, at the raised figures of drinking riotous folk on its sides. A fine old crock, and solid. The diaphanous film which had occupied that spot would never worry him again.

"Now that be looking 'ansome,' Antiks said, and for all her sweetness she was a little envious. So he was after Mrs. Liddicoat, was he? Well, she did not blame the man. With young Maister gone not to return, he must find it dull here in the evenings, and she herself could not expect—er—more than she got. As men went, Maister had treated her pretty well, better than some. A pity that she liked him. Jimmy Old wanted her, but she could not take so much as a kiss from him without thinking on Maister. At her age, too, and with all she knew! "Be you goin' in the town, Maister? I 'aven't streaked the room out to-day—"

"Never mind the room."

"Mucky ole place 'tis."

"You can clean it to-morrow."

He must know whether the illusion would return. He did not see how it could, but he must make sure. He would give it a day, and during that day neither business nor Antiks should drag him out of the parlour.

"I have work to do here," and he seated himself at the high desk.

"Well," she said, only anxious to please, "it don't matter, for I've the bread to bake, and it 'aven't plummed yet."

To Mr. Corlyon the day dragged by on leaden feet. Antiks brought in the mid-day meal, brought wood and peat. "When the wind come in at kitchen winder fire never go well," she said. "But what I've made'll last 'ee till the beginning of the week."

"Have you finished then?"

"I'm off now."

As the door closed behind her, he gave up pretence of work. The relief of being alone in the house! He made up the fire, and sinking into the deep chair by the hearth, closed his eyes. It was yet early in the afternoon, but he had a feeling of release from strain. He might relax tired limbs, a tired brain.

When he opened his eyes, it was to find he had slept a couple of hours. The day was darkening, the peat was low in the fire-basket. Half asleep, he had a little feeling of expectation. There was something, he could not quite remember what, something for which he must be on the look-out. He sat up, remembering fully. He looked across the shadows at the dark bulk of the sideboard. A satisfactory array of delft and lustre-ware! That had been a fine idea of his.

In the half-light it was difficult to distinguish china from pewter.

Not difficult at all to see a faint clear glitter—to distinguish a shape, half filled with wine.

III

During the three days Pascoe had been at home, Mr. Corlyon had lived with an intensity hitherto unknown to him. His thoughts had been so ardent they had been almost alive. Almost? Could a man's thoughts take shape, come alive? a thought was expressed in action, but the thoughts themselves, the vehement, vigorous thoughts? Were they—nothing? The idea that they might not be was new to him. Was it possible that, during those hours in which he had been learning what manner of man lay under the veneer of Pascoe's sailor heartiness, that his mind had given off films of thought? Feeling so strongly, had he been able to endow his emotions, his thoughts, with substance? A substance that was exceedingly tenuous, but visible? Had thought a delicate material body, so fine it seemed intangible? Good heavens, if one's thoughts should have a separate existence, should be mental children! If once generated, they lived on by themselves!

Or without granting that a thought had substance, might it not be a sort of force? Flung violently into the surrounding air, it might remain there, vividly impressed on—yes, but on what? Not on the air, for that was continually being blown about. On space, perhaps, the space on which is air, light, heat. In one way it was like the darkness, for when the night fell, the beer-jug and other objects on the sideboard could not be seen. The thought-film—if that it was—of the little flagon also tended to obliterate them.

The idea that emotions, thoughts, might have a life of their own was a matter of the sharpest interest. It might be a fact. Yes, but even if it were it did not prove that the appearance on his sideboard was a force, or had substance. Though the appearance might be a wraith, it was, he thought, more likely due to some disorder of the mind.

An illusion could be ignored. Existing in your mind, it was as exclusively yours as an opinion.

But a wraith, or a thought that had impressed itself visibly and immovably on space? That—it might reveal the secrets of man's life.

IV

Mr. Corlyon passed the night in his big chair. He would find out how long the little flagon—transparent as rain—stood dominantly among the other objects on the sideboard. It came with the decline of daylight, so much he had established. When did it go?

He sat by the fire, nodding off at intervals, and waking in fear. His first glance was for the sideboard, for the iridescent gleam. As the night deepened, it seemed to him that the array of china was hardly solid, that the little flagon was the one outstanding object on a vaguely plenished surface.

If he had not known, he might have mistaken the figment for the real.

He sat up in the chair, opened the *Vestiges of Creation*. He would lose himself in these surmises. A strange mind, that of the writer. He had not feared to question, to hold the old beliefs up to the light. Mr. Corlyon had found the book profoundly interesting; ah, but that was before . . .

The apparition could not be in any way connected with Pascoe?

Pascoe was dead.

When a man lay under Gudda Hill, with a thousand tons of rock between him and the sunshine, he had done with life. Ah, and you had done with it when you died in your bed. Dust you were. The dust eddying in the unswept street was the dust of dead men. Millions had been born, and had died. They were gone, they were scattered, a bit here, a bit there—dust. The spirit of life animating that dust had been spilt by the breaking apart of the vessel. If men had been ghosts clad with flesh, if when the flesh fell away the ghosts had been left—the earth would have been filled with them, a host past numbering.

You might as well believe that after death a woman would meet her untimely fruit. He smiled to himself. The thing was absurd, farcical.

Pascoe dead was Pascoe destroyed.

Yet he, Mr. Corlyon, must grant that thought could print itself on space. The flagon had been born, if not of the events of that night, at least of the mind which had brought those events to pass. It was an emanation from his mind.

Or—or Pascoe's.

If thoughts and emotions had a separate existence, they might persist after their originator were under sod. Pascoe's feelings when he realized that his brother had poisoned him, his anger, his will to repay might have persisted as an emanation. The air grows foul with the breath of drunken men, remains foul after the men have passed.

Mr. Corlyon was seeing Pascoe's fury and longing for revenge, as things with which he might have to reckon.

Between the rep curtains, the tide of returning day was slipping, wave upon pale wave, into the room. As the light grew, he perceived that the flagon became less distinct. He watched, anxious to make sure. Yes, it was fading. He could hardly see it—mistiness, nothing . . .

His night's vigil had taught him that the wraith came with the night, and with the night it went.

CHAPTER XV

I

"Seems strange," Antiks said, "you stickin' indoors so. Don't give me a chance to streak the room out. A mucky ole place 'tes, too. The floor has tracks all over."

"I am going out now." His business called for attention, and it was humiliating to be kept in the house by a ghostly flagon. It looked as if he were afraid of the thing—he! The truth was haunts, bogies, apparitions, they affected him no more than pieces of furniture. If they were there, well, they were. What did they matter? Ah, but they did. If seen by other people, they might affect a man's future. Though he were in the right, a haunt might make it appear as if he had committed a crime. An innocent man might be found guilty!

Mr. Corlyon saw that he must be cautious, take care no one but himself knew of the flagon. He wished that he felt certain it would not return till night, not until after Antiks had gone home to her children. Some days now since he had decided to stay indoors in order to learn when the flagon appeared, and how long it remained. He wanted to convince himself that it was only visible during the night; and he was nearly certain, but no quite . . . no . . .

He must go out. He must chance the reappearance of that iridescent gleam among the cloam on the sideboard. After all, Antiks had her work; she would not be on the lookout for flagons that had been put away in the china cupboard. What a person expected to see they very often saw. That, now he came to think of it, might be the reason he saw the flagon! No, no the thing was real. He saw it, saw it more plainly than he saw the grey beer-jug. It was actually there, a squat square-sided glass vessel—at least, it was there during the night.

He went over to the Estate Office. The agent had seen Mr. Pendragon about the mortgage and the release had been made out, but it was evident they considered Mr. Corlyon was making an unnecessary fuss. He was a flint on the smooth

county road, an awkwardness. His brain—so shrewd a brain—
was at the service of the workers, was for ever scheming for
them. Llyr Pendragon, when he heard the auctioneer's name
always growled and sometimes his growl grew thunderous, but
he could do nothing; and Corlyon went on with his work,
snipping at this bit of power, that so-called right.

He was for Stowe. He thought a man should own his house;
or, if not, that the community should. Taking the grudged
release he smiled at the agent. Once more he had got the better
of the incubus. As he walked out of the office, however, he
forgot the burning question of the land and its ownership. His
thoughts had fled down the street. Antiks was cleaning the
parlour! How, if while she were dusting, the flagon should
have become visible? Nonsense! He must not let fear run away
with common sense.

He turned into the Farmer's Arms. Mrs. Maddicott had
asked him to find her a profitable investment for some money
she had saved; and the Dick Jackas would borrow it to build a
house. They were hardworking people and would pay well for
the accommodation.

She wanted to speak to him about something else. Rebecca
French, "who they call the witch, was trying to buy her cottage
and landlord were askin' too much for't. Would Mr. Corlyon
speak for her? Her rent bein' only a shilling a week, landlord
didn' belong to ask so much. 'Twas fulish of'n, seein' she could
witch'n if she like."

Mr. Corlyon found himself declaring that he was too busy to
attend to the matter. He caught the look of surprise on Mrs.
Maddicott's face. He, who had always been willing to forward
anybody's wishes—what had come to him? Pulling himself up,
he temporized. He had had a cold and that had made him extra
busy, but, of course, anything he could do; she knew he was
only too glad to be of use. Who was the landlord? Biddick? He
would be sure to run across him market-day, would make a
point of it. And now Mrs. Maddicott must excuse him; oh yes,
more business.

He swung rapidly along the street. Before him, halfway
down the slope, lay the baby-linen shop. He would get a

glimpse of its keeper, and a mere glimpse was better than nothing. The dear, warm woman, she was like a fire on the hearth. A man could hold his hands to it, sit by it, grow warm all through.

With Pascoe gone, his was a lonely sort of existence. There was nothing now to which he could look forward, not even an occasional letter. All Stowe was his friend, but that meant he had no intimates. A cold life and, lately, a troubled one. But when Morwenna came to him he would have the best of company. With her on the other side of the table he would be able to forget that thin glitter of glass on the sideboard—and if he did not think of it, perhaps, it would not be there. Was that too much to hope for?

He strode on, paused. The shutters of the baby-linen shop were up, the door was fastened. Mr. Corlyon felt as if he had been cut by a friend! Where could Morwenna be? When he wanted her, she had no right to be out.

Perhaps she had gone to ask her sister over for their wedding. She might have told him she was going. Not long now before she would be at the Brown House, and then, every minute of the day, he would know where she was and what she was doing.

He went on towards the harbour, but the blankness of the shop face had depressed him. His mind returned to its problems, slipped past them to the fear lest Antiks . . . Letting himself into the house, he trod quietly along the passage, appeared at the parlour door.

Antiks was at the sideboard.

In blind confused anger, a flurry of fear, he stepped up to her. What had happened, what had she seen, what did she think? "Antiks!"

She turned, her face pale. "O, my lor', Maister!"

"What are you doing?" As he spoke, he saw that she was frightened of him, was frightened because he had taken her by surprise. The flagon was there, he could see it, the faintest possible glitter; but he did not think it was visible to her. Not yet . . .

Why, then, was she frightened? His glance passed her,

rested on the bottle of hollands.

"Spirits?" he said.

"I felt all fainty and queer-like."

"You were all right when I went out. What is the matter?" What had occurred to upset her? If one queer thing happened, another might.

"Dunno, I'm sure." She came a step nearer. After all he did not belong to be terrible vexed. She had not taken much. "See 'ow goosey-flesh my arms be!" She held a plump dimpled arm for his inspection with a smile which would grow or die according to his mood.

It died, for his face was without kindness, his eyes coldly brilliant, his lips thin and set. "If you take to spirits, my maid, you'll go all to pieces. Let me catch you at it again and out you go, neck and crop."

He went to his desk. Above it, on the wall, hung a calender, big black letters on a white ground. As he put back the lid, his glance rose to it. Good heavens, it was Jenifer's wedding-day. That, of course, was why the shop shutters had been up. To think he should have forgotten!

II

Antiks went back to the kitchen. A month ago Maister would have kissed the arm and forgiven her; but that Mrs. Liddicoat had him now, and he was sour as a whiggin.

Some people had the luck and others the children. Do her justice though, Mrs. Liddicoat wasn't like some, she didn' go scandlin', nor she didn' throw it up to people what they done. After all why should she? Had had one man and now wanted another. She'd got'n, too. Not that Antiks put confidence in men. She had had experience.

If a woman was good enough for one thing, she was good enough for another. So far as that went though, she, Antiks, didn't want to be married. The same man all the time? She liked a change, she did. Well, mostly, but—the Maister . . .

Nobody's like'n in Stowe. Lovely built man, great square

shoulders and slantin' body and long legs! 'Twas hard luck as he'd gone after Mrs. Liddicoat who was so thick as she was long, and old; and who'd turn her, Antiks, to doörs. A really covechous woman, the more she got, the more she want.

Antiks began to prepare the dinner. Maister had been stiff as an old tree to her, but give'n good bellyful and praps he'd bend a bit.

III

Mr. Corlyon sat before his desk with a yellowish parchment open on the thin green leather. He was not reading the deed, had forgotten that it lay there. His mind was entirely occupied with the little flagon.

To begin with, it had only appeared during the hours of darkness. Now, though the noon light was resting on the tangle of grey roofs, if stood plain to see. The bottle of hollands, the cloam and pewter, showed dim beside its brightness of polished glass. So shadowy were they that Mr. Corlyon wondered how Antiks could have managed to help herself. He was sure it would have been impossible for him to have distinguished between shadow and substance.

The haunt, or whatever it was, was growing from day to day more noticeable. As yet Antiks had not perceived it—she would not have helped herself to the spirits if she had! His lips twitched at the idea of Antiks helping herself from that vague bottle if she had known that a ghostly flagon was touching her hand. Helped herself? She would have screamed and run away and talked—how she would have talked! No, she had not seen it yet, but she would. And Morwenna—

Well, and if they did, what matter? The house would get a reputation, would be looked on as haunted; but the haunt was a very mild one. It told nothing, showed nothing; and what more natural than that a decanter of wine should stand on a man's sideboard?

It was an odd thing that the haunt should be confined to the little flagon.

If it were.

He had been conscious, during the last few days, of a dim sensation, a—it was rather more than a suspicion. Of an evening when he went for supper into the warm half-lit kitchen, he experienced a certain discomfort, a discomfort for which he could not account. He wanted to believe it due to his leaving one room for another. But that pricking and tingling of the skin across his shoulders! He could not put it down, altogether, to his having walked from one room into another. Always, as he crossed the threshold of the kitchen, a shudder ran down his spine. Why? He was beginning to find it required an effort for him to go at night into that room. He had to take himself to task before he could induce himself to leave the parlour. Yet it was the parlour that had developed a haunt, not the kitchen.

He told himself that he was puzzled. Why should the kitchen make him feel queer? It was in that room Pascoe had died, but in so old a house, there must be hardly a room which had not witnessed death. Certainly there had been one difference between Pascoe's death and that of the others. Pascoe had been killed and he had known it. At the time, Gale had been glad that he should know. What would be the use of killing if the killed lay down in an eternal ignorance? Pascoe had died beaten at his own game and aware of it. Baffled, furious, his last breath would be a longing for vengeance, the vengeance that was for ever out of his reach. Was it possible that when life drained out of his body, that longing, set free, had become a something in itself?

Whatever the reason, Mr. Corlyon must admit that the atmosphere of the kitchen was no longer friendly. Instinctively he seated himself back to the wall, ate hurriedly yet watchfully, felt relieved when, supper finished, he could return to the parlour. He had begun to expect—to go back in thought—to imagine he could see—

＊　　＊　　＊

No good came of trying to put off an evil moment. He must go into the kitchen and eat as usual or Antiks would notice, would talk. The deed crackled as folding it he pushed it indifferently under the row of pigeon-holes. He found that he was growing impatient of other people's business. It was impossible to keep his thoughts on their concerns long enough to do any satisfactory work. Nor did he feel the old keen interest, the sense of power. Mrs. Maddicott's savings, the Dick Jackas' mortgage, Rebecca French's cottage—trivial. What did these things matter to him? His mind was occupied with his own affairs.

If he could only decide which of the explanations that had occurred to him was correct. Was the little flagon that haunted his sideboard an illusion which troubled him because he was out of health? Or was it real, a thought-form sprung from his mind, impressed by it on space? Or could it be an expression of dead Pascoe's undying animosity?

Pushing back his chair, he went into the kitchen. Flame had broken through the sods, the lime-washed walls were bright with its reflection, on the disordered table . . .

But the table should have been set for supper!

IV

He was looking at dirty plates and glasses, at a stain on the cloth. The light was shining on decanters—and none had been in use since . . .

He stood staring. Another illusion! That splash of spilt wine was not there. He saw it, and yet he could not really see it, for it was not real. He was only remembering.

He could see through the litter of broken meats, of china, could see that the table had not really been laid for two but only one. Bright silver, clean cutlery, the uncut loaf—they were certainly there, but faint, as if seen through mist.

He was not startled, for he had known for some time that there was more in the kitchen than he saw. He had known, but had hoped whatever it was would remain invisible, would not develop.

No knowing now what might happen. He felt a deep depression, a sinking of the heart. Would this appearance persist?

Would he have to sit, night after night at this unclean table, eat and drink amid this unremovable dirt? Oh, impossible.

And was this disorder of the table all? He knew that it was not. He knew that if he looked . . . and he wanted, he longed to look; but, no, he would not turn his head.

The settle, the old settle that stood at right angles to the hearth, was shadowed by the high mantelshelf. If he turned he would see that shadow of the shelf.

He forced himself to sit at the unseemly table, to eat and drink. No matter what he saw, what he heard, what he felt, he would not give away. He was Gale Corlyon and he was not afraid.

Yet it was difficult to keep his thoughts from that—that shadow of the shelf.

He must bear in mind that when you expected to see a definite thing, the odds were in favour of your seeing it.

Sometimes, however, you knew without looking. For instance, he knew that on the settle was—not only that shadow of the shelf.

On the seat lay a red cushion. Pascoe's mother had made it the year she died. She was a clever needle-woman and always busy. Mr. Corlyon thought of the pride she had felt in the well-fitting cushion. If she could have known that her child was to lie on it at the last . . . to lie there . . .

For some time Mr. Corlyon had fancied he could hear a sound as of someone who breathed—who breathed with difficulty. It seemed to him that those slow breaths were coming more slowly, that they must soon cease. On the settle, as he knew, lay a figure . . .

He could not help remembering that he had lifted that slack heavy figure from the settle, had carried it through the cellar into the fogou, had pulled down on it the impending hill.

Memory . . . it was nothing more! There was no figure lying on the red cushion, the settle was a mere blank piece of furniture. To look was to show that he doubted, and therefore he would not look. No—and then he looked.

Oh, yes, he had known. The settle was dark with the outline of a man's body.

V

Mr. Corlyon, staring at that black shape, was filled with exasperation. He left his seat at the table, came to the settle, studied the apparition with a sense of fierce repugnance. Dim, but recognizable, it stretched from end to end of the seat. It dulled the red of the cushion as if it had been, in truth, a shadow, yet it had substance. Yes, to a certain extent, substance.

Pascoe, sure enough. Hair curly as a spaniel dog, the full lips that had been old Tom Corlyon's, the hooked nose. Short, broad, rarely strong . . . Pascoe.

But Mr. Corlyon had seen the rock fall on, crush that body. This could not be Pascoe. The rascal lay some hundreds of feet away, lay in the rocky clasp of Gudda. Though dead and buried, that sailor rig, the white disk of that face, might yet be seen by people, might yet bring disgrace upon the family.

No, but it should not. A black bitterness shook Mr. Corlyon. He thrust his hand into the shadow and it went through. It seemed to pass through a layer of cold air, but at last it rested on the cushion. Furious he dragged the cushion away, but all that happened was a red strip of wholesome cushion lying on the floor, while on the settle the wraith of Pascoe lay on the wraith of a cushion. Still more exasperated he tried to move the settle but it was fixed to the wall.

That at least he could deal with. The settle was worm-eaten and of little use. He would break it up, burn it.

The axe was hanging to the wall. Lifting it from the nail, he set to work with a vigour, savage in its intensity. The wood being dry, split easily and he chopped off legs, back, seat, as if he were destroying an enemy, as if the settle were alive. He felt, indeed, as if it were in league with Pascoe, as if it were part of the appearance. Certainly, if there were no settle Pascoe could not lie on it.

The flames roared up the ancient chimney, the wood withered, shrank together, vanished. The settle was a pile of feathery flakes. Mr. Corlyon's wrath passed with the fluttering ash. It was as if he had been hungry and now was filled. He looked about the kitchen. The very atmosphere had changed. The air was no longer charged with heavy emotion. He had purged it by sacrificing the old bench.

Returning to the parlour, he settled himself in the big chair and, once there, realized that he was shivering. his teeth were chattering, his knees knocked together. It must be that he was unduly excited, but why should he be? He had done a sensible thing in destroying the settle, had got the better this time of Pascoe.

Though his exertions had made him sweat, his feet were cold. They were always cold, but to-night painfully so—he must change his boots.

A little unfortunate that his house-shoes should be in the kitchen.

He hesitated a moment, then laughed at himself. Of what was he afraid. The kitchen had been cleansed by fire of its oppressive atmosphere. Having dealt with the haunt or whatever it was, he could go in knowing he had nothing to fear. To fear? He had meant that it contained nothing unpleasant, that there was no longer any likelihood of his seeing the wraith of Pascoe.

His shoes were kept by the wood-basket under the window; and, while he was about it, he might as well adjust the cover-fire.

But—what was that shadow at right angles to the hearth? For a moment he felt dizzy, confused. He had burnt the settle and yet that—that shadow. Putting a hand to his brow, he stood for a second with his eyes shut. He must get the thought of the old bench out of his mind, then he would see that it was not there.

A line of darkness jutting from the wall! He saw it clearly, the wood bright from years and years of rubbing, the glow of a red cushion and . . . on the cushion . . .

God! but he had destroyed the settle, had chopped it into slivers, thrown the wood bit by bit on to the fire, had watched it burn.

It had gone up the wide chimney in pale feathery ash, had been blown away by the sea-wind, scattered over the world. It was incredible that it should be in its year-long, generation-long place by the fire, that it should be still a settle, still haunted.

Incredible, yet . . . the horror of it was, that its reappearance was not, altogether, a surprise. He had destroyed in a raging fury, but as his passion died, satiate, he had suspected that what he had done would be unavailing. No, he had hardly suspected, and yet when he saw the settle he had not felt any sharp surprise. Below his mind had lain a covered, hidden expectation.

He had not been able to burn the settle, and the sight of it no longer angered him. His excitement had passed and he was tired; empty, too, empty of resource. He would fetch the shoes—go to bed. He crossed the kitchen and so real was the wooden foot, gripping the floor below the settle, that he made to step round it. As he did so he felt a qualm of the old annoyance. The foot was not there—not really there. He put out his hand . . .

Nothing—though the settle rose before him, polished, dark —nothing.

Not quite that.

He had seemed to plunge his hand into cold air.

VI

Unable to sleep, Mr. Corlyon lay watching the flickers of yellow light that danced on his wall. the flickers were glints from the riding lights of the trawlers. As the sea swayed the vessels, the glints swung up and down the wall, tiny flecks that had been familiar to him since childhood; that he had thought were star-gleams, until his mother, coming to his bedside one night to kiss him, had told him to look out of the window, see for himself.

The flickers were a part of the old comfortable routine of life, the routine that was giving place to a new order. He lay watching them, lay quietly and thought.

It had come to this. He could not destroy the haunt. He had

proved that. It remained to see whether in any way he could deal with it. Meanwhile he must admit that it affected him. To-night, for instance, it had made him yield to anger. He prided himself on his self-control, but the sight of that figure on the settle had proved too much for it, and he had let himself go. The burning of the settle had been an orgy. The passions that underlay a man's everyday behaviour had been released. He had slashed and smashed in a destroying fury and, strangely enough, felt the better for it. In wrecking the old bench he had poured out the lees of himself, a black toxic energy that had been fermenting at the bottom of his—not mind, exactly— perhaps of his consciousness. Tired though he was, he yet felt more his old self, better able to consider this inexplicable pseudo-ghostly appearance—to consider also its effect on himself.

He had to deal with the appearances; had, if it were possible, to circumvent them. First, though, he had to decide whether he were the man he had thought himself, or whether there were in him deep-lying unimagined possibilities. How was it that he, so self-contained, had flung himself in destructive fury on that tainted bench? What was it that of late had been let loose in him? Before Pascoe came home, he had had none of these sudden rages; now at a thought, a vision, they rose, breaking through. He had, of course, known what it was to be angry, oh, terribly angry; but his wrath had come upon him slowly, had come because of some proven injustice or cruelty, and it had stimulated him to make carefully considered war on the oppressor. His anger had been impersonal, a clean thing, but these rages—

Were there two Gale Corlyons? Had he an underlying self that fell into blind mad rages, that was fundamentally unstable? Did it manifest itself in his preoccupation with the little flagon, with the scenes of Pascoe's death, with what might be seen in the kitchen? He, Gale, had no superstitious feelings about death. A dead man or a dead pig—what was the difference? But the new Gale, the Gale that clamoured in the dark places, that Gale had hours when he was shaken with a sort of panic. The apparitions sent shivers down his spine, the hairs of his body rose, he felt that he must draw back, flee "from the wrath to come." That was it! He must flee from the unknown, an unknown that was sweeping down on him and which was hostile, sinister. At these times he could not reason, he could only suffer. At these times he was not—himself.

And the self that was violent, unstable, and over which he had only a slight hold? It must always have lain under the reasonable, courageous self, must have lain there, a coiled and sleeping force. He had been unaware of it—ah, but not altogether unaware. He had known that he was capable of sudden, and strong action; that he would dare what other men feared to attempt. This secret knowledge had given him poise, had set him above other people, had enabled him to war successfully with those in high places.

He had sat in judgement, knowing himself capable of carrying out a decision however tremendous. The necessity to do so had come upon him with the discovery that Pascoe, his beloved and cherished brother, was vile. He had acted, then, as he had known he could. He had condemned and he had done justice. His reasonable self approved, yes, and in spite of the haunt continued to approve.

He approved the action, but was surprised to see that it had cast a shadow. The haunt of the little flagon, the oppressive atmosphere of the house, the illusion of the settle and of what lay on the settle, were shadows that had become visible because the feelings that had prompted and carried through his action had been intense.

The shadow of a deed!

Was it only that?

If only a shadow, why did it not remain as it was at first? From day to day it—yes, it altered. The flagon had at first been almost imperceptible. Now it stood out definite, recognizable, an actual glass vessel; stood on the red and white cloth with which Antiks had covered the sideboard. Mr. Corlyon felt that no one looking in that direction could fail to see it. Moreover, at the beginning it had come with the dusk, glimmered through the hours of darkness, vanished at dawn. It was now always to be seen amid the array of ware, only it was more distinct than cloam or pewter; while, as to the grey beer-jug, that had become a shadow of its rotund, opaque self. It was the same with the appearances in the kitchen. At first they had seemed not so much actually in the room as at the back of his mind. Gradually they had come forward, become faintly visible; now . . .

What would happen next? He had the feeling that he knew; yet, when he tried to look at his knowledge, it was not there. But, shadows? They were more than that . . .

His glance followed the glints which danced in a faint glow, a glow of lighted water, but he hardly saw them. He was wondering whether the haunt had not a sort of life.

It grew and it developed. It seemed to him not so much a shadow as a fungus. He had heard of houses being attacked by a fungus, by monstrous growths that sprouted from walls and floor, fleshy yellow hands that grew and grew. The apparitions were a sort of ghostly fungus, which had invaded his home. What could he do to rid himself of it? He did not know.

Meanwhile he must take certain measures. If Antiks had seen the flagon, no particular harm would have ensued. The settle was a different matter. If she caught sight of what lay on it, though she promised not to talk, she would not be able to help herself. It would become known that the Brown House was haunted, not by some old-time ghost, but by "young maister."

His hands went to his throat. They could not prove it! Oh, but they could—the dunnage in the cave, the cairn of fallen rocks at the end of the fogou. They would not rest, once they got scent of the matter, till they had dug down . . .

He had done righteously, he was passionately convinced that he had, yet the thought of the popular outcry, of the dark prison, the rope . . .

So far, Antiks had gone about in her usual cheery fashion Had she? Once or twice lately, he had caught her looking at him—a sort of questioning look. You felt before you saw! Was she beginning to realize how oppressive was the air of the kitchen?

He dare not ask her. And he did not dare chance it.

VII

"Whatever 'av 'ee done with the settle, Maister?"

"I've got rid of that."

She was clearing the breakfast-table. "Nothing but ole traipsy traäde, anyhow."

"I am going to put—er—a glass cupboard against that wall."

"'Twill come in very handy."

"And—Antiks—"

She paused, the breakfast-tray on her hip. He thought how sweet and morning-fresh was her face. A pity she must go; still, he did not dare risk it.

"Now that my brother has gone to live in Jamaica, I have decided to make a change." He glanced away, he did not want to see her face change, her eyes . . . After all, she did not seem to have noticed that little wraith that stood out so valiantly among the fading delft and pewter. Must he? "I—"

She waited, guessing that her time had come, feeling her heart sink.

"I am going to marry Mrs. Liddicoat."

Antiks' heart sank and sank. She thought she must be going to faint. "I jaloused it." Her hands shook so much she had to put the tray down.

At last Mr. Corlyon looked . . . that piteous face! He felt sorry, but his mind was made up. "She won't want you, my dear."

Her glance was submissive, but it asked a favour. As well have asked it of the cobbles in the street. "You want for me to do for 'ee till she do come, won't you?"

"No—better not."

Her surprise spoke. "What be goin' do, then?"

"I can manage for myself."

"My dear life, in a day or two the house 'ud be walin' from dure to dure."

"I can't help it."

She could not accept her fate without making an effort to

escape. Her eyes besought him. "Must I go sir?"

"You can have your money to-day."

"Oh, Maister, 'tis hard lines."

"When a thing has to be done, it is no use wasting words."

The tears were rolling over her cheeks, but there was no more to be said. She took up the tray, was going out.

"Antiks . . . "

From the doorway she looked back at him aflush. "That old settle. I don't suppose you ever noticed anything—er—anything—"

The flush died away, and her voice had a dull sound. "What do 'ee mane?"

"Well, anything about it, anything strange?"

"Iss, I 'av then." She paused, but he did not speak. "I didn' think of sayin' anything about it."

"What did you see?"

"'Twadn't what I see, but what I heered."

In Mr. Corlyon's ear was the sound of a breathing that caught, that started again. "What—what did you hear?"

"I heered the tickin', the sign o' death. God's truth, I did."

Mr. Corlyon sank back in his chair. "Oh, that!" His relief was so great he could have laughed. "That is only an insect gnawing the wood; nothing in that, Antiks."

CHAPTER XVI

Morwenna

I

ANTIKS was gone.

Mr. Corlyon need not fear that what happened in the Brown House would sift through Stowe.

Often, people neither saw nor heard things, only felt them with what lay behind the senses. He wondered what it might be? Instinct? Dogs, cats, horses, they were able to recognize the—he supposed he must call it the uncanny. He had seen animals looking at, shrinking from what, well, what was not there—at any rate, not visibly there. He had known a horse start, grow damp with terror in a wide and apparently clear road. He remembered the story of Balaam's ass—that was the sort of thing.

But Antiks did not appear to have this instinct. At least, she had not noticed that anything was the matter with him, of his house. She had gone unwillingly, but had not carried with her a suspicion of wraiths and hauntings.

He was glad she was gone. With the haunt showing signs of further development, in another day of two she might have begun to notice. He felt that he had settled with that menace. At all costs, the appearances must be kept a secret. As long as he was the only person who knew of them, they were of no importance, could not do him any harm. As long as other people . . .

Gazing steadily at the flagon, puzzling over the gleams of the prismatic glass—gleams in a thing that was not really there—he asked himself how people could let their nerves be affected by a thing so harmless. A haunt was as useless as an ornament, and of no more account. An ornament? He smiled at the thought of housewives saying, "Our little ghost? Yes, it is in the shape of an old Greek statue. A handsome object to have about the house. Oh, no, we would not be without it. A house without a ghost suggests that one had been overlooked by Father Time."

If everybody saw the haunts that lived with them! The trouble was that as only certain apparitions were visible, people made a fuss about those they could perceive. A fuss? They behaved like children.

The haunt itself was of no importance, what mattered was its effect on others. He must contrive that the existence of his should not be known. He must not let anyone guess that the Brown House was in any way different from the other houses set higgledy-piggledy along the ancient street.

II

Mr. Corlyon, with the threads of Stowe life running through his hands, had yet found time to turn a considering eye on the women, busy with their sweeping and scouring. He thought much of it a waste of time. He could boil a kettle! Yes, and cook eggs, and even potatoes, so he would not starve; but as to turning out a room! If his bedroom grew fusty he would move into another—plenty of rooms in the house. Women dilly-dallied about their work. Why turn out one room a day when you might have them all cleaned at once? If household work were properly organized, the bulk of it would be done on one day of the week. Still—after all, not only women pottered.

He would miss Antiks, but he could manage, and it would not be for long. Morwenna would be troubled when she discovered he was by himself in the house. She would want to come to him.

And he needed her! Not for the bodily comfort, though that was what she would think, and it was as well she should; but—

He had tried to convince himself he did not object to the presence on his sideboard of the little glass flagon. Nor when he had slept well and was morning fresh, when the day was bright, and his mood cheerful, did he mind it. But there were times . . . yes, as night drew on things looked different.

As the sun sank below Gudda, and the blue of the sky and of

the shadows deepened, a man's point of view changed. The dark was full of incomprehensible sound. You listened, trying to account for this little pregnant noise, for that. You heard the stairs creak as when Pascoe had carried down his dunnage; you heard steps that had been long familiar, steps that no longer walked the house— at least by day.

If Morwenna were in the Brown House, he would not hear those significant sounds. He would be listening to her quiet talk.

All day, while transacting his business in the town, he would have in his mind the good thought that he was going back to her, to that warm smile. When night was folded black about the house, her figure would come between his eye and the glitter of insubstantial glass, between him and the settle which he had so ineffectually burnt.

His new self, the self he had learnt to fear as full of untoward possibilities, would sink into the background, would fall asleep. His old, stable self would take control. She, Morwenna, was a simple soul, robust, of all women the one for him. They would be married as soon as possible. He would bring her . . .

Did he dare?

If he brought her to the Brown House, she might, in time, become aware of the haunt. It was possible. It was more than that—it was likely, in fact, how could he doubt that it would happen? The wraiths grew out of nothing; were, first a feeling, then an inexplicable fear, then a shape.

If only in some violent way he could have destroyed them. The tremendous satisfaction of it! But he could think of no way . . .

III

Could he endure to look on, see the vague doubt, the unpreventable strengthening of that doubt, the final certitude? That certitude! That she should know he had killed Pascoe!

And she would.

The thought was agony. He had done righteously. Oh, yes,

he had. He was convinced of it, but she . . . she might not be able to see eye to eye with him. And if she could not? He might explain, tell her everything, and it might not make any difference. "A woman convinced against her will . . . " It was necessary that she should be with him, necessary for his happiness, for more than his happiness. She must uphold him, his actions, his point of view. Ah, but would she? Could he trust her? His brother . . . How would she take the knowledge? Would she sit in judgement, would she—condemn? Even if he explained, could he trust her to think as he thought? He was assured she loved him—at the moment. But love—

He had been sure that Pascoe loved him. Pascoe's love! Why should he imagine that Morwenna's was of more sterling quality? Once bit . . . After all, love, what was it but another name for desire? And desire passed. Once it was satisfied it passed.

Man slaked his thirst at a stream, then wandered on. No sort of permanence, but a long road starred with lamps. Under each of them he paused for a moment; but, in the end, always, he went on, uphill when he was young, downhill when he was old. Somewhere on the road he paused to rest, to sleep—perhaps between two of the stars.

Morwenna might think differently of love; but then, she was a woman. She would see it as a fire on the hearth, a moderate flame hedged round with the respectability of home walls. To her, love would not be so much passion as affection.

Yet, when she looked at him, there had been a kindling in the grey eyes, an emotion he could not fathom. It was a look that had thrilled him, to which something in the depths of him had responded. He wanted her to go on looking at him like that.

Ah, but—the emotion of a middle-aged woman! It could not burn white-hot for long. He must be prepared for a damping down of the fires, for the mere glow of companionship.

He wanted that rapturous, adoring surrender to go on and on. It was like the darkly red and darkly brown fields. They yielded to the ploughman's will with a tremendous giving of corn, yet underneath was their unchanging stability. Morwenna's love was to be like the ground under his feet;

"rock all de way down," as she had said. Pascoe's conduct had proved human affection to be slight and shallow, yet Gale still hoped. The world had shaken under him, had snared his foot; and he was trying to escape from it on to "hard country." He longed to believe Morwenna capable of a deep and abiding love; and yet, how could he? Love o' woman! He had experienced it. It passed, it always passed. six months, or at the outside a year, and it was over. Why should Mowenna be different? How could she be? Yet he needed a love that understood and would endure; he wanted her to bring him such a love.

If she were to find out that he had killed his brother, he might give up hope of it. No quiet, civilized woman could make such a discovery—and not be overwhelmed with horror. If he brought Morwenna to the Brown House, he must be prepared to watch the tide of knowledge flow over her love, drowning it as the tide in the estuary drowned the yellow sands.

He would not be able to endure that gradual passing of love, the dying of it, the change from absolute trust to suspicion, to knowledge, perhaps to fear.

To a fear of him—oh, no, no.

Sunk in the great chair, he sat with his head between his hands, shivering. Morwenna's face as it was now, that dear, open, love-lighted face was clear in memory. He saw it changing, losing its doubt, its eagerness, growing blank. She would still smile, but behind her smile—

She was the sort of woman who, in her relations with people, would keep up appearances. He could imagine her hanging a curtain between their souls. Her civil speech would be the shaking of the curtain, she would pretend he had her confidence, her unabated love; but he would know, he would not be able to help knowing.

Each little sign, he would see it! It would be torture.

He would be helpless, unable to get away. He would have to watch Morwenna's soul grow furtive, peer at him secretly. She would be afraid; yes, in the end, she would be afraid for herself.

IV

He knew, knew with searing conviction, that he could not bring her to the Brown House.

He was strong, strong-bodied, and with a sceptical hard-fibred brain. About him like a tangible thing lay the loneliness of his life, but he had hitherto been able to put up with it. What he had done he could do again. A man had to be strong, not for his own sake, but to satisfy a demand which had grown with and was at the core of humanity, to satisfy the spirit of man.

At the last, a man died, but he did not give in; he could not let himself—break.

It was Thursday. The evening he was in the habit of spending in the room behind the baby-linen shop. Morwenna would be waiting. She would have prepared supper, thought out a tasty dish, cooked it—and she would be alone.

Jenifer was married and gone. He would have had Morwenna to himself.

But he must not go.

She would be at the half-door that gave on the street. She would be looking out for him.

She would wait; and in the Brown House he also would wait . . .

CHAPTER XVII

I

A NEW thought falling into his mind filled it with joy . . . Why should he not shut up the Brown House and live with Morwenna in the baby-linen shop?

He was amazed that such a simple way out of the difficulty had not already occurred to him. An easy way! His desk could be put by the window in the back room. He could see his clients there—and Morwenna was the kind of woman who knew how to make herself scarce. She seemed to have an instinct about it. Dear woman, she was really wonderful . . .

He sat back, smiling!

Thursday! Of course, it was Thursday! He must not keep her waiting. His hat! Christ—how keen and jolly and alive he felt.

II

To her lover Morwenna had made no secret of the reason which had induced Jenifer to marry Denny Manhire. "She was straight with'n, and he would not let it make any difference. No such woman in the world, he say, as Jenifer. She don't care for'n now, but she'll come to it. He've treated her jonik, and that is more than the other did. In time a maid learns to take what is offered."

Mr. Corlyon could feel sorry for Jenifer. Submission where there was no love must be nauseating. "Who was it?"

"Aw, you do knaw who 'twas," and Mrs. Liddicoat's face broke into that smile of the eyes, that smile behind the eyes that he had learned to look for. With other women, Corlyon had watched their lips, with Morwenna, the full firm lips curving up were less expressive than the glow in the eyes.

"Pascoe?" he said, his mouth a line. The treacherous hound had behaved ill to everybody with whom he came into contact.

He stole a glance at Morwenna. If she knew—she should be glad that Jenifer was avenged, that Pascoe would not do more harm!

"Yes, 'twas Pascoe." she murmured, and her expression was inward, as if she were seeing something which as yet only existed in her dreams. "I don't belong to be glad, but I be."

"Glad?"

"'Twill be like as if 'twas yours." She was seeing Jenifer's children. Little steps, curly nobs and pigtails, with, at the head of them, a splendid boy, a boy like Gale.

"Lord, no. You must not say that. Pascoe's child won't take after me!"

He was lying along the sofa, his head in her lap. The feel, under her hand, of the crisp hair was sending, thrills of fire up her arm, and because she felt so strongly the fact that Jenifer, her child, was bearing a son to Pascoe seemed to medicine something that ached a little. He had said that Pascoe's child would not take after him. Why should it not? "I'm hoping it will then."

Pascoe's child! It would be Pascoe over again. It would remind him . . . but no matter, he could look it in the face. "He was only my half-brother, he was not like me."

"But they do say you are your father over again. The li'l chap may take after's Grandfer."

Like himself or Pascoe, however, the coming child was to Gale unwelcome. "I like children, who doesn't? But I had sooner my nephew was not a bastard."

Morwenna's hand left off stroking. "Well," she said, "if no one else is glad of'n, I am." She thought of the women with whom at one time or another, Gale's name had been coupled— pretty and nothing else, or pretty and easy. As she put it— "very tawdry." Not the sort to have given him sons like himself. Ah-h, to think none should have given him a son! The silly bits of things, not to have known it did not matter whether a child had its father's name, if only 'twas made in his image— him not finished with when he came to die, but going on.

Her glance rested on the dear head, relaxed in peace against her soft fullness. To have had Gale's eyes look from a babe's face, from the babe at your breast—that any woman who loved him should have been able to forgo that!

She leaned back against the sofa dreaming. Her sons, Edgar and Tristram, were fine men, the both of them. But if she had been Gale's wife, what splendid sons she would have had. Poor old Peter, but—well, he was dead; and she, heart and body of her, she belonged to Gale. It seemed as if she always had. The other life was like a vision, grey, half-forgotten—yes, though she had the children to show for it.

"Go on stroking my hair." He was postponing the discussion of their future, enjoying the calm, the quiet. He had solved his difficulties, and he had only to tell the dear woman what he intended to do. She would be glad to have him. Pleasanter for her to stay where she was, all her odds and ends to hand, than move; and he, too, would be glad of the change. He had never thought to leave the Brown House. Nor would he now, if it had not been for Pascoe.

The serene atmosphere of the kitchen was pleasant, homely. He longed to stay on, not return to the living death on Quayside, but that might not be. Already, he was faintly conscious of a pull, as if he were needed in his own house, were being called back.

Must he go? Perhaps, if Morwenna continued to smooth his hair, it would make him forget the little pull, enable him to stay. "Go on."

She was glad her touch gave him pleasure. He should not have mis-called the child, poor little innocent, and if he had been a woman, and had had the bearing of children he would have known better. Still, men, poor creatures, they were like that, they never really understood. She went on, drawing her fingers over the hard hairs. She liked that he was, in essential matters, so ignorant.

III

"I don't know that I ever wanted children," he said, meaning that he did not want them now.

Morwenna thought it only natural. A middle-aged man! She gave him her view of the matter. "No, but I'd like for you to have had a boy, a boy as 'ud have been you over again."

"I don't know. Better not, perhaps." In the new grate the embers fell from the fire-spot with a little tinkle. Mr. Corlyon's glance rested on that comfortable stir. It was like Morwenna to be the one person with the pluck to try something new, the one person in Stowe. A forthcoming, eager, genial woman—would she be able to help him? Well, if anyone could, she might. After they were married he might venture to tell her; yes, when their interests were the same. Ah, but no. Now, or not at all. He would treat her as fairly as she had treated him.

He could not utter the words. He would do anything but tell her, and yet, if he only could . . .

Morwenna's glance brooded. She was looking down on the features that were always a surprise, an enchantment.

The comeliness of them drew her irresistibly. That he should love her. Stooping, she let her lips rest on his forehead. It was warm because he was alive, and the warmth came from his quietly beating heart. The tears rose in her eyes—she was so happy.

"No," he said, "I shall be all right as long as I have you."

As he spoke he turned from the fire to the woman who had kindled it; and at his look, she thrilled from her lips down. The thrill was only bearable because he was near, because she might lose herself in it. He wanted her—not children—just her. She glowed, stirring a little. She could not come any nearer, but she was flowering towards him, offering all she had, all she was.

In the muteness of ecstasy she sat very still, her cheek against his. She had the human warmth of that cheek, the thrill of his skin on hers. He was the most darling man in all the world, the most wonderful.

She was not to do her woman's duty and give that strength and beauty back to life. Perhaps she did not want to, not altogether, not very much. It would have been an effort, taken a long time, and as you grew older you got so quickly tired. Besides, a child would have taken up her time, and Gale did not want to have only bits of her, but the whole. And, in the same way, she wanted him. As his mother had had him when he was young, so Morwenna wanted to enfold and cherish him now.

Their life together, it was going to be perfect! Her pleasure to work for him, to make him happy. He had been lonely, hers to show him what companionship could mean. She would be to him what the nail is to the finger, the eyelash to the eye.

IV

The need for haste has come upon Mr. Corlyon. He was conscious of a noisy undertow which, against his will, was dragging him from this place of peace. As long as Morwenna's hand had moved over his hair, stroking, he had been able to ignore the steady strain on his will. It was more than a strain, it was a sound, sounds, broken, and yet significant sounds. It was invading his mind and, if he wanted to talk to Morwenna of the future, he must make haste. The sounds were filling his mind, preventing him. They were an outcry of words, jumbled, and they came in like a tide.

"Sooner'n you think for! You'll see me . . . not far . . . come back . . . you will see me sooner than you think for! When a chap wants to come back . . . "

He turned to Morwenna. Ah, surely she could silence the voice?

"What is it, love?"

He must not tell her. He had trusted Pascoe, and Pascoe had betrayed him. His secret must be kept from everyone; even from Morwenna. All his life he had kept secrets, made no bones about it. Why should he even think of taking Morwenna into his confidence? He knew why. It was because if he told this, shared it, he would halve the burthen of it. He had a feeling that if he were able to tell it, not only half, but all his trouble would vanish. But no, he must not tell. Besides, he did not think he could.

Half sentences, recollected words, a voice. He was being called away, back to the Brown House. He did not want to go.

If Morwenna, with the weak, unbreakable chain of her arms would only prevent him!

"Sooner than you think for." The nonsense of it! See dead and buried Pascoe? But he did see him. He saw him on the settle. No denying that Pascoe was in the house. There and visible. He realized strongly that on no account must he let anyone into it. Best, then, not to let Morwenna know Antiks was gone. Why, good heavens, she might insist on coming over! Might want to get his breakfast, or some woman's foolery. Yet he had to discuss his change of plan . . .

Hesitatingly, he began to talk. The Brown House, being down on Quayside, was a bit out of the way. How—if instead of her coming to him, it were to be the other way about? If he lived at the baby-linen shop, his clients going through the town would be able to pop in any time. He got up from the sofa, began to walk up and down.

Only by walking about could he keep under his impulse to go. Something was pulling at him, something he would not be able, much longer, to resist. He was away from the Brown House, and anything might be happening. But it was not that, not only that. The something came from his underlying self, impelling him powerfully, yes, irresistibly.

Morwenna saw the new plan as sensible. Her house was on a main street, you passed through it coming from the coast villages, going to the fish market, the warehouses. Also, it was large enough—shop, kitchen, and the big room overstairs. What more did they want?

"Turn the shop into an office for you?"

He had not thought of that; but yes, it was a good idea. He did not want her to work—except for him.

"I'll get rid of my stuff, and of the counter and shelves," she planned; "and you can bring your desk over, soon as you've a mind to."

"Then that is settled!" His walking to and fro had quickened, he was showing a restlessness that puzzled her. When he arrived, she would have thought, so glad was he to be with her, that he would be sorry when the time came for him to go. But he was evidently in a hurry.

The voice in Mr. Corlyon's mind was reiterating its monotonous:—"When a chap wants—" The voice was so loud, the impulse to go so strong, that he hardly heard of saw Morwenna.

He struggled into his thick coat, and, at the last, his thoughts came back for a moment to the woman. Flinging his arm clumsily across her shoulders, he kissed her, and the kiss was hearty like a boy's. He was fond of her, but—he must go.

CHAPTER XVIII

I

Mr. Corlyon stood in the passage between the rooms. Nothing in the passage. A quiet place, and dark. He stood there thinking. In the parlour the little flagon dominated the array of ware, in the kitchen was that disordered supper-table. He no longer had his meals at it. Sometimes, when he caught sight of it unexpectedly, his gorge rose and he longed to deal with it as he had with the settle.

No use trying to destroy it. You might burn the wood, and yet something would remain—a semblance. The wave of irritation receded, leaving a black residue. What could he do? As he stood with his hands on the lintel of either door he felt sick, hunted. The haunt had grown—was growing. At first it had been confined to the sitting-room. Before long it had spread to the kitchen, and Mr. Corlyon was expectant of further developments, expectant and troubled. Night always brought that sense of trouble, of dim reaching out to knowledge.

Pascoe lay on the settle—he would not always lie there.

Up to the present, the shadows that had taken possesssion of the Brown House had not moved, but they might.

He knew that, in time, they would.

What he did not know, what he could not imagine, was what they would do.

Pascoe's design was to let people know what had happened to him. How would he set about it?

Mr. Corlyon, unable to guess, felt that he must be on the look-out and ready. That night he had left the house, locking the door behind him, had trusted to luck. He must not do it again. Certainly, as far as he could see, nothing had happened. It was what might that would keep him on the spot He could not leave Pascoe to do as he would.

How peaceful it had been in the baby-linen shop! While there, he had felt safe, at least, he had at first. Later . . .

It was not only that during his absence things of dread and

horror might be shaping. It was the feeling that he must be in the midst of those happenings, that he must know. In Morwenna's back room, in its calm, good, restful atmosphere, he had been unable to keep his thoughts from straying to Quayside. What was happening behind his own locked door, in the rooms he knew as he knew his own body? He had been obliged to go and see.

The haunt had drawn him back, and what had happened once might happen again. If he were living at the baby-linen shop he might—would—be uneasy, would perhaps be unable to stop. The shop was a refuge, but how if he were unable to avail himself of it?

Standing between the doors, his body swayed a little, swayed with his mind. He could not bring Morwenna to the Brown House, he was not able to leave it.

It was nothing to him that a shadow lay on the settle, that it was black, and the blackness cold as winter. He could go further and say it was nothing to him that the shadow might move, but . . .

He must be there to see it move.

It was exacted of him that he should be there. He would have escaped to Morwenna; but he was like a dog on a chain, and it pulled him back.

That very evening he had put it to the test.

His hands dropped from the lintels, he sank in on himself. The outlook was black, and there was no star in the sky. He could not have Morwenna on any terms.

II

The night was to Mr. Corlyon the right setting for his mood. Hitherto a man of transitory affections, he had realized that this late-come love was as necessary to him as light and air. He would not give it up. He would find a way of arranging matters so that he might keep it. He must, or life would gradually become impossible.

He sought desperately, sought through the night, and every

now and then the figure of Morwenna rose, vivid in memory. When this happened, his seeking mind would fall asleep, give place to sheer longing. His woman! He had a vision of her with thick hair, new-washed and flying in an August wind under an August sky, a soft cloud of hair that robbed her of her years, and her firm mouth, and her definiteness. Between the waves of loose hair he had seen only her eyes, eyes that worshipped and adored.

That long tender glance! Could it be that he was a sick man with fancies, fancies which that glance of hers, making him good and keeping him man, was able to drive away?

Fancies? Was it possible the haunting was a disordered fancy, nothing more?

He straightened the sheet below his chin, straightened his limbs in the bed. Ah, if . . .

But no, he could not think it! The apparitions did not come from his mind, they were nothing to do with him. He could not believe they were an illusion and, right or wrong, a man acted on his beliefs.

His mind swung between thought-films indelibly stamped on space, and a survival. Pascoe—the Pascoe who had loved Grizel and broken his promise to Jenifer, was at the heart of Gudda. His body was changing, disintegrating, becoming one with the earth. But something of him might have survived death.

What were the ghosts his neighbours saw? Hitherto, he had accounted for them in one way or another; he had not believed them to be actually visible, things which had an existence outside the imaginations of mankind: but he had been shown cause to reconsider his verdict.

Pascoe, under a jovial surface, had been a fierce, primitive creature. At the moment of death a man might find himself possessed of undreamed-of powers. The stories of appearances at a distance of people who were at that moment dying suggested that this was so. A phantasm might be a thing in itself, might have a tenuous, yet material body. He could not deny that haunted houses made you feel as if you were watched; as if something lurked in the shadows, and waited behind the doors.

He had said—"imagination," or that "people were out of sorts!" He no longer thought that explanation covered the ground.

Pascoe's furious disappointment, his rage, his lust of vengeance—these things might have survived his death. They might have taken a certain shape, might be animated by a living principle. That principle, Mr. Corlyon could see, would be Pascoe's hatred of himself, his indestructible will to get the better of him.

What had survived was not Pascoe, but the evil of him. It was that with which Mr. Corlyon had to reckon—an incarnate (or discarnate) menace.

"I'll leave the town know." That was what he meant to do. Not Pascoe, no, but what remained of him. But how would it—what—?

Granted the existence of this evilly-disposed entity, you did not know what were its powers, its limitations.

He turned restlessly. The thing was no illusion. He saw what he thought he saw, and presently he might hear, might do more than hear—the possibilities were unending. To another man they might have been overwhelming; but Gale clenched his teeth and, above his steep chin, his lips were a line, iron-hard. He had beaten Pascoe once: he would beat him again.

Even if it cost him Morwenna.

Morwenna, and his sanity, and his life.

He would stay in the Brown House, deal with each fresh development as it came. So far, he had not been conspicuously successful in getting the better of the haunt; but if he put his back—meaning his brain—into it, he stood a chance.

But—Morwenna! That soft breast. It offered itself to a man's hand, rounded under it. And her kiss . . . the swooning sweetness of it.

His eyeballs ached with the tears he might not shed. In distressful longing, he flung himself from side to side. His throat, his chest, his whole body ached. A life of stern denial! Oh, impossible! Day after day, with the knowledge that she lived up the street, to stay in his own place! How could he know her there—so near—and not go . . . ?

III

If you had once made up your mind to do a thing, there was no turning back. Whatever the cost, you went on—pig-headedly. You accepted the results, allowed nothing short of death to turn you back.

From Thursday to Thursday Mr. Corlyon stayed as far as possible within the house. Though he kept appointments already made, when it was a matter of fresh business, he proved elusive. He went out early and late, but not in the broad daylight; went by way of the side streets and back lanes. Always a quick walker, he went, now, like wind-driven dust. If people spoke to him, he excused himself on the score of being late for an appointment. If they came to the house, he let them ring and ring. He would be in the parlour, behind the screen of the wire blind, waiting. When, finally, they gave up the attempt to see him, he would draw a deep breath. He did not want their business. At odds with himself, how could he give these trivial matters his attention? Later, perhaps—

Hithterto, Thursday had stood out from the other days of the week as promising a time of quiet enjoyment. Some people's weeks are punctuated by pay-day, others by the rest and quiet of Sunday; but for years, Thursday had been the good day of Gale Corlyon's week. It came this week, as it had all those others . . .

He could not eat; if he were to go out he would go straight to the baby-linen shop. For hours he had walked to and fro in his haunted house—no longer seeing the wraiths! At last he sat down, sat himself on an uneasy chair behind the brown wire blind, held himself there with hands clenched on his knees.

From the road came the clop, clop of hoofs, the roll of wheels, the voices of men. The timber wagons were dragging lumber from the Norwegian vessels to the ship-building yards. They would go, the three brown horses, the carter, the baulks, up French Street.

All week he had avoided the hilly street. It would be impossible to go past the shop. Now it seemed intolerable that others, the wagons, the men, should be travelling along that road, while he . . .

But he had made up his mind, and he would not budge. Under the window, his strongly-knit whipcord figure remained as motionless as a statue; and, like the work of a great artist, though petrified, it was full of life. This was the first Thursday. To win through the next would be easier; and the next, and the next, till he was, like the very old, indifferent.

He could look forward to that. The agony of living would be at an end, but not yet—not for a long, oh, an impossibly long time.

God—could he sit there, holding himself down till passing hours made it too late for him to go to Morwenna? How much longer? The palms of his hands were unaccountably sore—he had clenched them until the nails cut the skin.

Hours more of it . . .

And Morwenna, up the street, so—so damnably near. He had only to take down his hat, open the door.

She would be so glad. Waiting, she would have grown anxious. He could see the questioning look, the extreme relief, the joy.

At that very moment she would be looking towards him, wondering. Ah-h—what did it matter? He must not think of her, he must remember only that, come what might, he must not—he would not go.

CHAPTER XIX

I

MRS. LIDDICOAT withheld from a fairly contented Jenifer the shocking fact that, though she was middle-aged and, by unamiable people, might be described as stout, she was the happiest woman in the town of Stowe.

He—her man—he was coming to live in her house—but she did not mention that to Jenifer, over for the day, and full of Caer news! He was going to leave that ramshackle old place of his and live with her, cosily, in the slim little, trim little house on the street. She was no gossip, not she, but she did like to know all that was happening in the town. Quayside was at the end of the world. Nothing beyond it but the sea.

Besides, in a compact place like hers you had everything to hand. Her cupboards—

What would he do with the accumulations of the Brown House? Sell them? No, people kept their old rubbish "till death did them part." In her little house, though, there would not be room for his traäde—at least, only what he belonged to have, his clothes, and so on. Her eyes smiled—why, she would have to make room for his clothes! Her wardrobe was a licking great piece of furniture, shelves and drawers, and a hanging cupboard. She must pack her things close so that his trousers might be laid out, full length, one pair on the top of the next. He was a peculiarly clean-looking man. That, of course, was due to his skin, that pale fine skin. But his clothes became the handsome figure of him, were always neat, fresh, well-cut. During the long years of their friendship she had set many a stitch for him, now she would mend and make for him as a right. Love gave you the right to do things for people; and the doing of these things was a pleasure, almost the greatest you could have. He wanted a new pair of thick stockings, the dear of'n, and she would begin them at once . . .

There was the shop, too. He had not said what day he was coming, had not, perhaps, made up his mind. Her business to get on with the arrangements, be ready for him.

She knew it would be soon; and though she had been too much excited to fall, at once, into the sound sleep of middle-age, she was early afoot. Rebecca French had said, observing her methods, that for anyone who would take trouble there was a fortune in the little shop. Very well, then, she might have the business and see what she could do with it. As she lived on the opposite side of the street, it would not be far to move the goods.

Going blithely into the fresh morning, Mrs. Liddicoat crossed the road. Rebecca would not be able to pay money down. The Lord only knew how the woman lived, though there were tales, maids slipping in after dark, and so on; but if she paid so much on the takings every week that would be jonik. Morwenna did not want to drive a hard bargain, too happy for that; besides, best to keep on the right side of Rebecca.

The witch slept late. She came from her bed to open the door, and the black ringlets hung disordered on either side of her olive-tinted face. "You'm early afoot," she said. "Mornin' isn't aired yet."

"Wanted to see you on business my dear."

In the dusk of the shuttered room the other's eyes glittered like new-broken coal. "Should have sent Jenifer over to me months ago."

Mrs. Liddicoat came in and shut the door. "'Tisn't that, then."

"That is what they do all say to begin with." Throwing back the shutters, she thrust sticks into the smoulder of turf. "Love and life, my dear soul, love and death."

Mrs. Liddicoat's curiosity was aroused. "Do a-many come to see you, Rebecca."

"A braäve few! For though there's some are too frightened, there's more that daren't stay away." She opened the door into her tiny garden, and stooping. picked up a toad. "My 'andsome," she said, and coming back with it in her hand, sat down on a stool by the hearth. "I'm ready for you now."

Morwenna leaned forward, smiling. What she had to say

would be a surprise for Rebecca. "You've told me time and again you'd like a little shop of your own, and now's your chance."

The other leaned against the wall for a moment, her dark face grey. "What do 'ee mane?"

Mrs. Liddicoat explained, and gradually the woman's face lost it unhealthy hue. She had shut her eyes, and, for a moment, she kept them shut. The suddenness of the offer had made her feel as if she were in a place that was all open doors.

"Suit me all right to have a li'l shop of me own." Her earnings were precarious, and she was getting up in years. Of late, she had spent anxious moments wondering how to manage, seeing herself cold and hungry, and—and old! She had no near relatives, no friends, not a soul to care what happened to her.

But if she were to take over the baby-linen shop with its assured custom she would be able to earn enough, more than enough; moreover, she would be a person of importance in the town, a shopkeeper. She knew, at once, that she would accept Morwenna's offer, knew that she was glad of it.

"Suit me to have the shop, and suit you to get rid of it, eh?" She must not let Morwenna realize it was a godsend. Sitting up on the small black cricket, she considered the possibilities of her one room. "How about a counter? And—" her glance ran like a small live thing about floor and walls, "And I shall want shelves."

"Edgar Rabey could bring over mine and fix them for you."

"Thought it all out, haven't you?" Morwenna, who had sat by her at school, had made a good thing of life, and how had she deserved it more than others? First, Peter Liddicoat, now Gale Corlyon! "So you've got'n at last? Well, you have waited long enough." Her eyes were scornful. "Whyever women tie theirselves up to men is more'n I can think."

"'Tis nature."

"'Tis askin' for trouble, addin' fuel to fire. Never had a man myself, never wanted one."

"Yet you was a pretty maid."

Rebecca touched the toad, now making an ungainly effort to

crawl out of her lap. "These li'l chaps be company enough for me, and they don't cost I nothing but love."

Morwenna rose to go. "Love?"

"Love for this, or love for that, 'tis all the same."

"Oh, no."

"Two kinds o' love, is there? This that cost I nothing, and yourn as is all tangled up with life and death?"

"Don't 'ee, Becky."

Rebecca followed her to the door. "People want for it to be only life; but, more often, many times more often, 'tis tangled up with death."

II

Old stock and new, rolls, bales and cardboard boxes, the contents of the shop—greater in quantity than you would have expected—were carried over by the women. Edgar Rabey, as good a little work-chap as could be found in Stowe, shifted shelves and counter, and as Morwenna shut the door on him and his last load of wooden fittings, she looked over the gutted shop with a feeling which was half eager pleasure yet half regret. She had enjoyed having a business and meeting the travellers for the wholesale; enjoyed using her mother-wit— getting cheap lines, job lots, and slightly flawed goods, getting them because she knew how to smile at and interest the men! Very pleasant while it lasted, but she was going to do what would be still more pleasant. She did not regret selling to Rebecca. Oh, no not really.

In the dirty littered room she saw possibilities of a comfortable new order. She would wash the walls with colour, primrose, she thought, as the room was low and faced the sunset! Then she would fetch down the carpet Loveday had given her when they moved into the Ring o' Bells. It would look handsome on the good boarded floor. She was glad now she had had the boards laid. A stone floor was cold to the feet and, tender soul, his feet were so often cold. She was almost glad that they were.

He was so strong, it was heartening to think he had a weakness
—any—

No fireplace in the room! That could be easily remedied.
This time of year mason didn't belong to be busy. A fire as well
as a carpet for those cold feet.

The desk would be best between fireplace and window, so
that the light could fall directly on to his papers.

A thin curtain of muslin across the lower panes—he would
have light, warmth, the place to himself and, if he wanted
anything more, he had only to ask. He need not even do that.
Trust her to find out what he wanted, and give it to him.
Somewhere in the Bible it said—"to the half of my Kingdom."
The half, only the half? Some people were poor givers!

The curtain would prevent him from being overlooked.
Able to see out, to mark who passed, he would be unseen. The
people who came on business, they too must feel they were not
spied on, that they were alone with him.

She took the top of a packing-case, nailed it over the glass
hatch between kitchen and shop.

III

The roses of the flowered carpet lay brightly on the boards, a
fire blazed behind the bars of the new grate, and fine muslin
shut out the world.

"Look empty it do," Mrs. Liddicoat thought, glancing
about her, at the pale primrose of the walls, at the space that
had been crowded with cardboard boxes and paper packages,
and stock. "But if the dear brings his desk—his desk and a chair
or two—"

Thursday—and in the kitchen a fowl was boiling, half an
hour more, and she would take it out of the liquor, set it on
potatoes in the baking dish, and put it in the oven. On the table
ready for the sauce stood milk, crumbled bread, and muslin
bag with clove and onion. As everything was ready, she might
go up and change her dress.

Overstairs the room was in some disorder—not time to do

everything! Once he was come it would be different, but she had been busy getting ready; and while she was alone what did it matter?

By the back window stood an old chest—open. Her mother's chest, and she kept in it the two pairs of linen sheets her mother had left her, the two damask cloths, the pair of white blankets, the patchwork quilt.

When the darling came, he should have a bed fit for a king. Fit for? He was a king, and he should sleep in fine linen, lie under the bright silks and satins and velvets of Grandmother's quilt.

She regretted that she had not found time to open the bed-tie, pick over the lumps. Very little lumps, hardly noticeable— after all, the tie was stuffed with goose feathers. She had bought them from Sarah Martyn, over to Saint Ryn, and Sarah, whatever else might be said about her, was honest. She never mixed duck and fowl feathers with the goose down! Still, in the king's bed there must not be the suspicion of a lump. Give her one day more, and she would pick them over.

One day more? Put off his coming yet another day? Oh, no! It had been a busy week, and she had been absorbed in her preparations, yet every hour had held the hope that he might come, that she might glance up from her work to see him looking at her. Those whimsical eyes! They made fun of her scrubbings and scouring. She was to do as she liked, but he saw no need for stirring up of dust and shifting of furniture. With half the disturbance he would have been quite as comfortable. Dearie dear, the foolishness, the enchanting foolishness of men!

Mrs. Liddicoat lifted from a peg in her hanging cupboard a long linen bag. within, uncreased, yet preserved from moth and dust, hung the purple gown. The ruches at sleeve and throat were fresh. She would add the French lace collar, the gold chain . . .

She wore her hair loosened a little at the sides and fastened in a seemly knot at the back. So many women had curls, curls in a bunch, or short ringlets hanging from a centre parting, but she must have neatness. If you were the sort for curls, that was all right; but if a woman like herself wore them it would look foolish. And he—he had never said what he liked. a smooth head, or waves, or ringlets, she did not know. Hilde Fone had had a single fat curl that she tossed over her shoulder; Emmie Rosevear had had an unruly mop, no less. Thinking over the maids that Morwenna had seen him with, she was unable to come to a conclusion. All sorts! Perhaps that was it. He liked this, and that, and the other, but she need not worry for, if he had never spoken of her hair, when it came to marriage, it was she whom he had chosen.

From a box where it lay folded in tissue paper she took the lace collar. It had come to the town on a woman fleeing from religious persecution, and had been handed down from mother to daughter, a bit of decency. Rebecca French envied her the collar, said she had an equal right to it, seeing the woman it came from had been her great-granny too. True, they were some sort of cousin, she and Becky, but then, most people were if they only knew. Morwenna had the collar because her side the family had been saving, while Becky's father—a proper dragon of a fellow! Why, they said 'twas he changed the white stones on the edge of the cliffs so that Exciseman Tonkin fell over in the dark and broke his neck. It was not brought home to Jacob French, but in the whole place no such a daredevil as he.

The collar was of fine lace. When her mother gave it her, it had been yellow with age, but she had washed and bleached and mended it. It looked well on the bright purple of her gown, and Gale had said he "loved" her in it.

If only the neck about which it lay had been firm of skin, firm as it was full. She looked at her reflection. Her throat was white, but the skin under the chin was baggy. Once, and not long ago, either, she had had the fairest neck—or so they said—in Stowe. She cupped her face in her hand and, stooping to the mirror, considered the result. Her fingers, gathering in the loosened skin, revealed a soft round chin, the chin that goes with an eager and a vital spirit; revealed, too, the white column of a neck once beautiful, and still fair.

Morwenna had always been aware of her good points, had

thought her duty done when she saw them again in her children. Not till the hope of Gale Corlyon's love bloomed in her heart had she regarded her looks from a personal point of view. What had she to give? Not beauty . . .

She wished she were not so ignorant of rouge pots and the like; that young hussy, Jenifer, knew more of such matters than she. Yet it was she to whom the knowledge might have been useful.

If only she could have ironed the creases from her face as she ironed the clothes when she had made them water-sweet! Not many wrinkles, but more than enough. Thank goodness, her skin was still soft, soft as silk.

If she had done differently during the careless years, would she now have had a firm smooth skin, and no grey in her hair? A good head of hair, but for colour it was like a sea-mist. It had been yellow as a daffy. It had darkened to brown, it had dimmed to this cloudy grey.

A slack skin, and wrinkles, and grey hair! Yet he, who might have had the pick of the parish, he wanted her.

She was not worthy, not in her body, only in her love.

IV

The fowl was roasted to a turn, the sauce made, the jam hobbin ready, and yet the step that would have been so welcome had not swung up the lamp-lit street, and over the drexel.

Mrs. Liddicoat stacked plates and dishes in the warm oven and, closing behind her the kitchen door, shutting in lamp and firelight, went through the outer room to the street. She had intended to give Mr. Corlyon a surprise, to let him in, and then fetching a candle, show him what had kept her busy. He would be delighted with the freshy-limed walls and the gay carpet. Liked bright colours he did, and jollity, and things of good repute. Well, he should have all the brightness she could bring into his life—a man who spent all his spare time doing kindnesses for folk! A Bible phrase came into her head: "He saved others, himself he cannot save." Yes, indeed, he saved others, oh, in lots of ways, but he was going to be happy, he himself. She would see to it that he was.

She stood at the door, looking into deepening night. the Brown House was in darkness. That might mean either that he was just setting out or that he had gone into the town on business, was coming on to her from some unpaid errand.

"That you, Mrs. Liddicoat?"

A voice from across the street. Morwenna had thought she was sufficiently in the shadow not to be seen. She tuned her throat to an amiable greeting. "Making your fortune, Rebecca?"

The light of the little low room, now transformed with goods, outlined Rebecca's spare figure. She was stroking a small, dark something she held in her hand and her sharp glances raked the street. "The business has made one bit of difference to me," she said. "I used to be sorry for the maidens that got theirselves nabbed, but now 'tis the artful ones I 'aven't got no patience with."

As she spoke a woman, carrying a covered basket, stepped out of the Farmer's Arms. She crossed the road, coming down on Mrs. Liddicoat's side, but she need not have hoped to escape recognition. Rebecca looked from the woman to her basket—"Good evenin', Mrs. Maddicott. A fine bakin' day, wind's in the right direction."

Though Dusha Maddicott returned the greeting she did not stop; and Rebecca's darkling glance followed her down the street.

"She'm going to they Spargos, that's where she's going," she cried, as Mrs. Maddicott turned east across the head of the quay. "She's always bakin' pasties and 'obbins for they."

Morwenna heard without heeding. The little jealousies of the street, what did they matter? What did anything matter but that time was passing and there was no sign of Gale?

A hot supper did not improve by keeping. Unwillingly she went back to the kitchen, He would not come any the quicker because she idled away her time. At her waist, fastened to a wad of straw, was the stocking she had begun, and when she had slaked the fire with fine coal and sand, she went on with the three plain, three purl. Jenifer's stockings, her own, and now Gale's. Hers and Jenifer's as a matter of course, but every stitch she put on to the needles for him gave her pleasure. Stockings for those narrow feet, feet like the quality had; but, then, he was quality—at least his mother had been!

Morwenna, knitting and yet listening, was disturbed by a clash of voices. Trouble had broken out in the street and now she would not be able to hear his step. An excuse to go back to the door! Little she cared for the women's quarrels. Some trifle or other. Why it was Mrs. Maddicott—of all people, Mrs. Maddicott! Looking so untidy, too. Where was her bonnet? Morwenna had never seen her on the street without it, but now she stood in Rebecca's doorway, with her fire-red hair a rumpled mass.

"What is it? What is the matter?" Up and down the street women were at their doors, and Morwenna turned to a neighbour for information.

"She do think she been ill-wished and that Rebecca done it. She be tellin' her of it."

The procedure was time honoured. Only by confronting the ill-wisher could you get her to remove the spell.

"When I got in," cried Mrs. Maddicott furiously, "I was fair boilin' with lice."

Rebecca, a small dark figure on the threshold of her house, stared coldly. "Comes of going into Spargo's dirty place."

The defence being reasonable one or two of the on-lookers smiled, but not Mrs. Maddicott. "'Tis not the Spargos and don't you miscall them, or you'll have they to reckon with. 'Tis you—and I know why you done it! You jaloused I was taking a loaf to the old man and you thought I belonged to give you one. You, with your new shop! Why should I bake for you? And now I'm lousy as a pig; but if you don't take the charm off me, I'll—" she lifted her hand threateningly, "I'll cork you up."

The women glanced at each other. It was the approved method of releasing a person who had been witched. A brave woman, Mrs. Maddicott, not many of them would have dared threaten the witch.

"You can't," was all Rebecca said, but her eyes were venomous and Mrs. Liddicoat, shuddery cold inside the purple dress, was thankful she had always been on good terms with the possessor of those eyes. No doubt about it, Rebecca could ill-wish you if she had a mind to.

"And why can't I then?"

"You don't know the words."

"Don't I then? Betsey Rosevear told me all about it."

Corking up was no light matter and Rebecca, although she had never experienced it, had heard tales. The menace in her eyes turned to an aloof dignity.

"You think you'm lousy," she said, "but you're mistook. Go home now, and as your foot cross the drexel you'll find you are clean as ever."

She stepped back shutting her door in the other's face. Young Mrs. Spargo was a higgler and chicken are lousy; but chicken-lice cannot live on a human being. Her prophecy would come true—at any rate before morning.

Meanwhile the tale that she, Rebecca French, had ill-wished Mrs. Maddicott would travel abroad, bringing her more and more after-dark visitors, people who believed she could help as well as harm, people who were in trouble of one sort and another.

The women faded into the obscurity of doorway and passage, and Morwenna found herself alone on the cobbles of the sidewalk. a wind out of the north, cold and with a suggestion of frost, was sweeping up from the harbour. Looking through the blackness, she shivered a little, recalled by the passing of the teacup storm to a dreary fact. He was not come.

V

When Mrs. Liddicoat sank into her down bed that night, she felt as if she were sinking through it into nothingness. In actual fact, she soon came to the "hard country" of her mattress, but her heart continued to sink until it was floating in a night that was black and cold and still.

When he had parted from her, a week ago, it had been with love on his lips. The fact that he had not been near her since—it might mean . . . A leisurely place, Stowe, no one so busy but he could spare time for a craik; and he would want to see her, just as she wanted to see him. Not a morning but when she woke she had thought, "I shall see him before night," and night had found her disappointed but not discouraged. "I shall see him to-morrow—" and always she had known, for sure, that Thursday would bring him.

Yet he had not been in. Not once had he looked over the half-door. And now, even Thursday was past and he had not come. She lay in the dark, crying.

VI

A clear, bright day called her from shallow dream-troubled sleep, and called her early.

It might not have been the day that called her; but the uncertainty, her fear. From the rounded window of her bedroom, she could see the Brown House, its front caressed by the sun, it panes shining in the dawn light. Antiks Hellyar "did" for Mr. Corlyon and Morwenna would watch her go in. It might be he was ill.

Antiks would go down the lane at the side, over the stepping-stones in the wall, and in at the back-door.

Mrs. Liddicoat, putting on her blue woollen dressing-gown, sat down by the window. On those opposite, the sun glittered; at the back of them, Gudda Hill was yellow with light and also with kissing flowers—bushes and bushes of them.

The day brightened and warmed, but no Antiks. Smoke rose from the kitchen chimney—Morwenna knew those chimneys better than her own—a window was raised.

It was Pascoe's window and she had long sight. Though Gale was in shadow, for the room looking south was a pit of darkness, something in her knew that he had opened it, that he was there looking out, looking towards her. She was as certain as if she could see into his mind that he was thinking of her; and her body tingled and glowed. She lost the sense of personal being, was no longer Morwenna Liddicoat but a something that throbbed towards him, that was part of his life.

He stood for some time at the window and absorbed, utterly happy, she waited. He was alive, he was well, he was thinking of her—what more did she want?

In the course of the day, he would let her know why, the previous evening, he had failed to come. She would be at work in the house and, some blessed moment, would lift her eyes to see the face and figure always in her thoughts. Or she would be in the garden and would hear a voice, his voice; would hear it so gladly that for a second she would turn faint. Before she could run in she would have to lay her hand on her heart, pull herself together.

He did not like a fuss, so as she ran, she would have to steady herself, conceal her too great joy. When she reached him she would have to smile as if he had not been ages absent, give him a good everyday welcome! "Well, you are come then? Glad to see you, always glad. Come on into the kitchen and set down."

CHAPTER XX

I

THE hours of Friday dragged a painful course. Mrs. Liddicoat could not settle to any work. The lumps in the feather-tie? What? Run down to him when he came with her hair all fluffs? No—the bed could wait. Dig in the manure her son-in-law had brought her from Caer when he was fetching coal? She was not in the mood for it, not in the mood for any work that took her out of the primrose room or away from the rounded window overstairs. Why did not Gale come? He had stood in Pascoe's room, looking up the street, yet the slow minutes fell away and there was neither sign nor sight of him. What had happened, what was the matter? The strain kept her moving restlessly about. She began a job but left it half finished. She went from one room to the other; did a little washing, a little ironing, but eventually pushed trough and iron impatiently aside. The work was of no importance, nothing was, nothing but the fact that he did not come. Night closing down she could only think miserably that perhaps to-morrow . . .

If he did not come to-morrow she would do something desperate! Uncertainty was wearing, was more than wearing. If she knew what was the matter she would be able somehow to adapt herself. Nothing was more difficult to endure than this not knowing where you were and what was going to happen. No, no, it was not that. She was unhappy because he did not come. If he stood before her in the flesh, she would be able to endure anything.

On Saturday she caught a glimpse of him. He had come out of his house and was walking swiftly—so swiftly he almost seemed to run—down his garden. Her heart fluttered with excitement, with hope, but in a moment he had crossed the road and was out of sight. Evidently he was gone out on business, and was late. When he came home, though, he would not be in such a hurry. She might expect to see him in an hour or two. She sat down behind the muslin curtain, waited an hour, another, but—he did not come.

Sunday, Monday, Tuesday, Wednesday—

At night her heart fell into the void of an accepted dis-appointment. All day long she had hoped, every hour, every minute, but the stroke of ten meant that she must hope no more. He had not come. That day he would not come.

She had to live through the hours of blackness before she might begin again—hours, minutes, every second of the day.

If only she understood. Had she done anything he did not like, was he annoyed, angry with her? She remembered the figure at the window. He had stood there for a long time, motionless, looking towards her, thinking of her. She could not doubt that he had been thinking of her. Well, then, he could not be angry . . .

Thursday morning! A day of wind and racing cloud and sharp scurries of rain. She went across to the butcher's and bought a sweetbread.

At any rate she would pretend to herself that he was coming. As she walked through the primrose room, the walls echoed her step, the grate stared through a menace of black bars. Empty . . .

Her plans, her preparations—she put the sweetbread on the kitchen table, leaned her face on her arms and sat motionless. If she only knew why—

For what seemed to her a moment but was in reality a long time, she sat by the table, seeking the reason. He could not cast her off without a word. Suddenly, too. Something must have happened, something of which she was in ignorance. Her mind traversed straight roads and winding but to no purpose. She had no clue, was in a maze; but it was unbearable this going round and round, this uncertainty. Hours, days and the ache of longing, why, oh why? He who was kind to the whole of Stowe, to whom those in trouble turned as a matter of course, he could not be unkind to her. It was not possible. His caresses burned on her lips, on more than her lips. He could not have kissed her—like that—if he had not loved her. And yet, if he had in his breast the ache of longing that was in hers, he could not—simply could not—have stayed away.

He had been able to stay away, therefore he could not love her as much as she him.

Perhaps men did not love like women. How was she with her one experience and that so commonplace, how was she to know?

Gathering up her parcels, she tried to find in work an antidote to pain.

II

To Morwenna, sitting hands folded, in her kitchen while the hours of Thursday evening dropped slowly away, those fruitless moments were the last turn of the screw. When she could bear the tightening no longer she went to her room, and threw herself, face down, on the bed. She lay there wrestling with the longing to go, to go at once and ask her lover why he was torturing her.

Absence, silence. . .

All evening she had hardly dared to breathe. The clock in the church tower had cried the hours, and her spirit crossing the "land between" had pleaded for her with that other spirit. He had proved inexorable. All the wiles she knew and yet she could not prevail!

How had she contrived to vex him? Never a cross word between them. She admired him as a man, and he had seemed to admire her management of her cottage property, of her shop, of her little home. If he had wanted her to be different in any way, yes, any way at all, she would have been willing. She would have felt that she was doing it for him. She wanted to fill her life with the doing of things for him, then every moment would be a joy. Already she had given up the shop. . .

He knew how utterly she was his, so it was not that. Well, then, what could it be?

She lay, in the bravery of her purple gown, her face against the pillow. What matter the reason? He was not come and she could not, oh, she could not bear it.

The night was very still. She was lapped in a stillness of

misery, in darkness and bewilderment; and under it all was the
old craving. If she could only see him, ask . . . Well, and why
not? What was to prevent her going to him? She had gone in
spirit, why should she not go in the flesh. It would be more
satisfactory and, surely, he wouldn't mind.

Before she fell asleep, she had decided to see him, question
him. What he told her would be the truth. On this resolve she
slept and slept well; and it helped her through the following
day. Fixed in her decision she set to work on jobs that she had
left half-finished. Now that she knew what she would do, she
could possess her soul in patience.

III

For days a swell with following winds, had ground the coast.
The fishermen of Stowe, watching askance, had made ready for
flooded kitchens and cellars; but, during the night the sea had
fallen silent. When Morwenna Liddicoat came out of crooked,
narrow French Street, into the space and light of the harbour
she looked on water that was summer-blue and still.

The latch of the little iron gate clicked under her hand and
her heart began to beat heavily. How would he take her coming
to him in this way? Would he be annoyed or would he look up
from whatever he was doing with a surprise that brightened,
that became joy? She only knew that she was afraid, yes,
horribly.

Smoke was rising from the kitchen chimney, but not from
that of the parlour. She had heard that Antiks Hellyar was no
longer "doing" for Mr. Corlyon, and at first she had been
pleased. It looked as if he, too, were beginning his preparations.
then, why . . . what was the hitch?

Would he be in? Oh, yes, she knew he was. She had the
feeling in her bones, that he was not only in but near. Strange,
but she could almost see him.

If he had a fire in the kitchen, he would be sitting there.
Being such a chilly mortal he would not sit in the cold parlour,
yet she felt as if he were nearer than the kitchen. She almost, she

quite saw him, saw him with the eyes of her mind. Ah, and she
knew for certain sure that in a moment more she would see
him, himself.

Her fear had changed to eagerness, a wave of sensation
tingled through her body. So near! Stepping off the gravel on
to the strip of lawn, she looked over the wire blind of the
window. . . .

Met his eyes.

For a moment she was too tumultuously glad to realize
anything but that she was seeing him. She stood, her heart in
the look she gave him; but the face turned to her, the face
looking out of the gloomy room, was white and hard. It did
not reflect either her gladness or her surprise. He must, she
thought, have watched her walk up the path; must have understood. She looked into his eyes, the eyes that had softened to
her such a little while ago, but they were a flint grey. No
warmth, no gold in them and the set of his jaw, grim. she had
seen a snapped-to rabbit-trap. The iron teeth—Gale's jaw—

Her knees shook and for a moment she wished she had left ill
alone, that she had not come. Then she rallied. He did not
belong to look at her like that. The tumult of her spirit, its love,
its longing, stilled. She was afraid, but not of Gale. His
absence had been grievous, but what he might do now might be
worse, for he might wound love itself. She realized suddenly
that she did not matter, but love—yes.

She knew now that she was sorry she had come. Nevertheless she was there and must take what he gave. She bent
towards the window and in a voice she tried to keep steady,
said: "'Tis the prettiest day we've had for a long time. Won't
you come out for a walk, dear life?"

Usually he spoke slowly, as if considering his words, but
to-day he had them ready. "I can't come."

The unfamiliar readiness took her aback. Not only that but a
quality in the voice. Never had she heard tones so stone-cold,
so hard. "Why can't you?"

"I have made up my mind."

The voice might have come from between the lips of a statue.
The words were like lumps of marble, dropping, dropping, on

to Morwenna's heart and each stone, harsh and jagged, cut into the soft flesh. "Aren't you comin' any more?"

"No."

Although he saw the blood drain from her face, his remained set and cold. To-day she was suffering, yesterday it had been he.

"What have I done?" The glass of the window was between them—but he heard. Her fear, her grief—they were, in a way, comforting. He had felt, too, and at bottom all feeling is the same.

"I don't know that you have done anything."

"Then can't I—can't I make it right?"

"No."

She sought desperately, in crazy haste, for an argument, something that would wipe that look off his face. His voice was not only hard, it was final, the end? Oh, no, not that, anything but that.

"You don't—" He must deny it, there was a mistake some-where, and she must manage to break through, get past this stranger, get at the real Gale. "You don't want me?"

He did not answer. The truth lay behind his grimly-set lips. If he opened them it might slip out. Want her? She was sanctuary, salvation . . . want her?

Yet even this was better than sitting alone, thinking. Here was a fight and it was a relief to hit out, to hurt as he had been hurt; yes, and to know that his unhappiness was shared.

She waited, searching his face for a kindness she felt must be there. Ten years of friendship, a month of loving, surely they had bred in him some sort of affection for her? But no, not a hint of it. The set face, the eyes!

Hard as grey ice, those eyes.

They told her what she had known all along. It had not been possible that a man as splendid as he, should love—her.

"Is it because I am—" her vanity boggled over 'old,' "because I am not young?"

A flicker in the hard eyes. She was a poor thing to fight, laid herself open. You had only to strike! If she had been a better fighter it would have been easier to strike, but he must go on.

He had killed Pascoe, now he must kill—one thing grew out of another—he must kill this.

He bent his head. He could not lie with his lips, but—in love and war . . .

Seeing, she grew yet more grey and he thought for an angry moment that she was going to faint. "Because I am old?" she cried, no longer boggling over the word. What did vanity matter, now? "Oh, I knew it, I knew it."

The death-blow! No woman could stand that! He had a feeling of release. Those clinging arms, they were gone, and he was free.

If she would only go.

His eyes stared unseeingly. He was near, so very near the end of endurance. That humble acceptance by her of his knock-out blow as natural, expected, beat on his self-control. If she did not hurry away he might . . . he would . . .

She must go and quickly, or he would tell her . . . tell her the truth.

Why did she not go? He could not stand it, not a moment longer. Oh . . .

She was looking at him, as the damned look on the face of God. Cast out of heaven she might not see him again. At last—ah, yes, at last she was turning away.

He heard her feet on the crisp gravel of the path. She was gone.

He sat like a man who has been changed from living flesh to stone. The receding footsteps dragged. Morwenna went heavily as if she were indeed old.

The gate at the end of the path shut between them with the fall of iron latch into iron socket.

CHAPTER XXI

MORWENNA

I

WHEN it came to bread-baking, meat-roasting, Mr. Corlyon
found himself at a loss. Simple things presented no difficulties,
and he had found food in the larder. He could make coffee,
cook eggs and had a ham in cut. Amazing though, how quickly,
even if he only used one plate at a meal, the cloam accumulated
in the dish-pan. Also very surprising in what a short time the
cupboard grew bare. He did not know how to replenish it.

He did not want to go out and buy. A neighbour or some
man on business might come while he was out. Getting no
answer when they rang, they might look over the wire blind,
they too.

There was no knowing what people might not do. The door
on the garden wall was locked but it was easy to come over by
the stones. Antiks had come that way, Jenifer. He thought of
somebody peering into the firelit kitchen, seeing . . .

The settle he had burnt was conspicuously there, the settle
and its occupant. No one could help seeing it.

He passed a hand over his forehead. Nowadays his brain
seemed full of woolly cloud. Other people—why, of course,
other people might not be able to see the settle.

Or they might, he could not be sure. Antiks had not seen it.
He felt pretty certain, now, that she had been quite unaware of
its existence. Ah, but that was because the haunt was a thing
that grew on you. . . It was at first only a feeling. It took a long
time to become visible. In the end though it was so over-
whelmingly real that material objects grew insubstantial beside
it.

That had been his experience and, naturally, would be the
experience of others. Antiks, anyone in the house, must in time
become aware of it; faintly aware, then more so, and at last,

unable to think of anything else. Yes, he must keep everyone out and in order to do so he must be on the spot.

Pascoe should not succeed in letting the town know that he had been put away—justly, oh yes, justly! He would come, in time, to see it was hopeless. Gale could be as dogged as he was patient. They were, after all, brothers, two of a kind, and he had always taken the lead. Pascoe had often had to give in and now again . . . but this was not Pascoe, not really Pascoe!

The spirit of vengeance! A spirit that Pascoe, dying, had released. He was dead and by now rotten. It was not he who lay, with circumstance, on the settle; who—

No, he had not moved. It was the flicker of the flames.

Gale, heating water for a necessary washing of plates and dishes, began to clear the table. Hardly conscious of the act, he tried to put aside a wineglass the bottom of which was black with sediment. Long since, he had made a hole in the turf fire, dropped in that glass and left it to melt, yet it still stood on the table. He was afraid lest, by accident, he might pick it up, drink those dregs. Nonsense, of course, but nowadays he had absurd ideas.

He put the plates and knives and forks in the dish-pan. His fingers were numb, so numb that it was difficult to realize the water was hot.

II

A bare larder! Though the store cupboard contained rows of last year's jam, a man cannot live on jam. He had known plenty of fellows who managed for themselves; ah, but how? Where did they get their food? He could not but think that somewhere in the shadows, there must have been a woman. They had not admitted it, had been proud of being able to do without help, and he had believed them. But he was grown dubious.

The larder must be replenished. Not that he was hungry, but that in order to keep well he must eat, and in order to eat must have cooked food. Well? He wondered if he were. He supposed so, but he was never hungry—the fault, perhaps, of the food—and he slept badly. Yes, very badly and his dreams! Such dreams, full of tumult and violence and, once or twice, of grief. In those last he had been a little boy and his mother was dead. All those years dead, yet he grieved as he had the evening they came to tell him of the accident that had killed her.

When he woke, his chest was heaving and a band seemed to be fastened tightly round his head. Generally there, when he woke, that band. After he had eaten breakfast it loosened and as the morning passed he would forget he had been troubled with it. To him, night brought, not sleep, but hours of thought, during which he swung from one explanation of the haunt to another. When at last he dropped off, he was whirled about, unrestfully, by the dreams. It was, he thought, little wonder that he woke to that tightness about his temples.

If he could only fix his mind on something outside himself and his affairs! If he could leave off worrying about the haunt and its potentialities, think of—why not of his neglected business?

The people of Stowe, their concerns, their troubles, felt curiously far away and unimportant. He saw them through a cloud of dust that some wind out of clear skies had blown across his path. They were as large, as vital, as compelling as ever, it was the dust.

He must not allow it to affect him, he must pull himself together, force an interest. If he did, he might hope presently to feel the old keen wish to be of use. Meanwhile there was still that affair of the Rabeys—Carrie at home with her mother and he carrying on with the girl at the Cornish Arms. Poor Carrie, she was consumptive, before long she would be out of the way and Rabey would be able to marry the other woman. The marriage vow was till "death us do part." It was horrible to think of them waiting for—that. Mr. Corlyon had been asked to have a talk with Rabey, see what could be done; but someone with less sentiment than he was attending to the matter. So often the way . . . things arranged themselves! Yet sometimes one could help—which reminded him that Mrs. Rosewarne of Crug had asked him to meet her at the market and that it was Saturday. She wanted his advice with regard to selling that field on the edge of the town.

The fresh air might be good for his head. Ah, but he had forgotten the house—the possible visitors! Saturday—on a Saturday everybody was busy! If he were to hurry there and hurry back . . .

The glare of day, the glitter of dancing water, hurt his eyes and he pulled his hat forward. For weeks he had lived in the half-dark of the house and it was pleasant to be out. Mechanically he took note of the weather. The wind had gone back into rainy country, but for the moment the day was pretty enough.

Treading his way between the stalls, greeting the farmers' wives, Mrs. Prin of Ludgian Veal, Phillipa Old of Bosence, young Mrs. Rodda, his glance fell idly on the wares displayed. Why—here was food, the cooked food of which he stood in need. Fresh bread and cake for hussies who were too lazy to bake their own, pasties, butter, eggs, cream. Bate and Catley had ordered a boiled and bread-crumbed ham from Mrs. Old, but she was willing to let Mr. Corlyon buy it. She liked the handsome face of him, would as soon he had it.

"Be 'ee goin' to carr' it in with 'ee?"

He had not thought of that. "I suppose I am."

"Or shall I send it?"

That would not do at all. "I'll take it, thank you."

"Better 'ave a frail. Gipsy Lee at the other end got a plenty."

Mr. Corlyon, with some of the old graciousness, raised his hat. He would buy the basket and, after he had had the arranged-for talk with Mrs. Rosewarne, would hurry home. Already he repented the impulse that had brought him out. Who knew what might not be happening within doors?

He avoided French Street. If he were to go down it he would not have the strength to pass the baby-linen shop. Something would draw him over the drexel, into the house. At the back of his mind was a shadowy feeling that, at the worst, Morwenna might in some way resolve his difficulties, save him from—not himself, but—oh, the whole thing.

Absurd, that idea, for he was going to save himself. He did not quite know how, had not thought it out, had only made a beginning. the weekly market had solved the difficulty of food, the fresh air had relieved his headache. He could think of that growing developing haunt with a better heart.

That growing, developing haunt. . . .

In spite of himself, he almost ran up the path from gate to door.

III

The market, the gossip he had heard, the change of scene, had stirred him to a defiance of Pascoe. That evening he resolved to have his supper as usual in the kitchen. Setting the ham on the table—that table which, however defiant he might feel, he could not clear—he flanked it with the crusty bread, the yellow butter. A better supper than he had had since Antiks left! It looked so good that he could almost believe he was hungry. At any rate, he would be able to eat.

He cut the ham—no matter that the plate had been insufficiently rinsed, that the knives were darkly iridescent and the forks dull. He broke a crust off the loaf and was spreading it thick with the butter—

Surely he was not alone in the room? A movement . . .

It must be the fire. A fire made noises, threw shadows. You did not live by yourself in a house without knowing how—er—companionable a fire was. Not daunting, no, companionable.

He turned back to his supper, put food into his mouth, but that suspicion of movement . . .

The thick shadow of Pascoe lay on the settle. It lay there day and night. It lay as the dead lie. The dead do not move and yet—Mr. Corlyon's knife slipped from his hand, rattled on to the plate. If Pascoe—

The top layer of peat had hollowed gradually now, breaking, it let out a flame. Shadows sprang up the wall, a shadow was rising from the settle.

Pascoe!

It rose, it came over to the table, it sat where Pascoe had sat. Mr. Corlyon drew back. He was not afraid, no . . . but . . .

He did not want it touch him!

If it were to put out a hand, brush his, oh, just accidentally, something in him might give way. He was, he felt, on the edge—yet he had known that this would happen. He ought not to feel so surprised, so startled. A moment—he would be all right in a moment.

He sat back in his chair, sat as far as he could from the dark semblance of Pascoe. He fixed his eyes on that thick but not solid blackness. It was actually there, and it would not go away; it was there like the decanter in the parlour, like the settle. It would be eternally there. He, living with it, would have to accustom himself to the change. He would, too, but he must have time.

Yes, time. Even now he no longer felt afraid. Nonsense, he had not been afraid. What—afraid of a shadow?

The figure stretched a hand and a shudder shook Mr. Corlyon, but the hand was stretched to something on the table. Heavens—it had picked up the glass, the wineglass with that black sediment.

Mr. Corlyon pushed back his chair. This was more than he could stand. A ghost moved, yes, he had known they did; but he had not known they could move with a settled purpose. If this figure were to re-enact what was done and finished with, it would make of the past an undying present.

That must be what Pascoe intended! His vengeance on Gale would be to let everyone know, everyone who came into the house. Gale had countered that by shutting his doors to all the world. He could endure the sight of Pascoe—of this thing that was not Pascoe but made in his image—could live with it. Yes, it should not get the better of him. There was nothing he could not, would not, endure, nothing.

He went into the parlour. there at least he would be alone. As long as he had some corner of the house to himself, he would be all right. He lifted the edge of the peat, let out flames and heat. Ah, that was better! He settled down in his chair, began to read—but he found his thoughts straying. While he was absent, what was the apparition doing? He did not want to know, but he must. It flashed upon him that if the thing could move about the kitchen, take up a glass . . .

Why there was no knowing where it might not go, what it might not do.

IV

Another wakeful night, but he had got something out of it. How if he were to destroy the house and its unseemly inmates? A leak of oil here and there and a match, the place was old and full of dry wood; it would burn like carpenters' shavings. How about Pascoe and his vengeance, then?

Not being insured, he was free to do as he liked. He would wrong no man if he let the place go up in flames, and he would be rid of the haunt—

To be rid of it would be worth his home, his so-called comfort, even the savings in the pigskin bags—worth the world! With him it had come to that! Anything to be rid of this ghastly obsession, and fire was cleansing. The house had been attacked by a disease against which limewashing, spring-cleaning, was of no avail. Drastic measures, then.

Arson? Nonsense, a man had the right to burn his own house. Mr. Corlyon would be careful to choose a still day—he did not want to endanger the warehouses at the end of the road! It would go up, the old house, like a burnt offering, a spire of flame rising into the blue.

Only after he had eaten his breakfast did it occur to him that once before he had burnt something—ah, yes, the settle. And though he had seen it crumble into white ash it was still there.

He might set fire to the house but could he destroy it? The flames might eat wood and plaster, might blacken the stone foundations, but could they touch the spirit of the house? When the burning was at an end might not a frail outline persist, walls which though dim as if seen through mist would yet be visible, walls through whose transparency the story of Pascoe might be played in the sight of Stowe?

He was assured it would be so played—trust Pascoe for that. "I'll leave the town know." They would not know what of black-heartedness on Pascoe's part had brought it about. They would see only what Pascoe wanted them to see.

The burning of the settle had marked a stage in the development of the haunt. He might have thought it had released a force—forces. If he were to meddle again—oh, better not.

V

On thing at least was certain. Never again would he try to sit down to his meals in the kitchen. Pascoe should have the place to himself. A dirty place it was, too, but he could not help that. He must not have anyone in to clean it. . . .

As Antiks would have said, the room was "walkin' from doör to doör." Good old Antiks, how comfortable she had made him; how he wished he could have her back, hear her moving about—but he heard someone in the kitchen, oh, impossible, a wraith does not make a sound! But—someone was there—

He must bear it in mind that what moved about the kitchen was not Pascoe. All that had been human of his brother was dead. Utterly and for ever dead. The haunt was not a man, it was not even a spirit. He thought of it as having a sort of life, a life that was malignant, that could not hurt him yet, but which might, later on.

If only he knew how to deal with . . . er . . . whatever it was. Clergymen existed—there was one at the Lizard—who declared that they could exorcise haunts. They did it for five guineas and it was cheap at that. He had not hitherto had much use for parsons; but if they could effectually banish ghosts they had their uses.

How if he were to ask the Rev. Paul Bodrugan to come over?

If he did, he would have to explain the apparition. It would then be Mr. Bodrugan's duty to hand him over to the police. He linked his hands, clasped them round his neck, tightened them slowly. It would mean—that.

He was beginning to think it did not much matter what happened to him. Ah yes, one thing mattered, always had, always would. For him to swing would mean that Pascoe had got the better of him. That—he could not stand that.

VI

The primroses were a foam of pale yellow at the foot of Gudda Hill. Mr. Corlyon, fetching wood one evening from the shed in the garden, saw them and realized that spring had come, a late spring that year, a spring held in check by winds that nipped plum and apple-blow, that lay dark over shivering seas.

He looked longingly at the flowers. The smooth bright surfaces of growing things were beautiful: clean petals under a clean sun in the clean air. And the earth out of which they came, into which they sent fine brown roots, that too was clean. Everything, except the foul and gloomy house in which he lived, from which he could not escape.

With a sigh he picked up the wood. He loved clean wholesome things, things that the dew washed and the wind and sun kept sweet. But he must not linger for it was growing late.

He took his load into the kitchen.

A curious thing, due, of course, to the room being in semi-darkness, yet he had fancied—

How could there be a second shadow?

He lit the lamp with hands he had long since controlled to steadiness, stood it on the table which, though clear of tangible objects, was cluttered with the remnants of a meal, then looked about him. Pascoe in the chair by the table—but that was what he had expected to see. A gust of fury made him long to lift the blazing lamp, bring it crashing down on that figure in the chair, but instinct had long since warned him to keep himself in hand. Once he let himself go—and it was growing increasinly difficult not to—he might not be able to get back to the old deliberate self. Hitherto, whatever he had done, had been done after consideration. He must not depart from what had been the habit of his life. He felt it to be peculiarly necessary that he should not.

He stood, therefore, with his hand resting on the table; that it was clenched, the only sign of his anger.

A man long buried, yet sitting at his table!

The apparition had been leaning back. It turned towards the

door as if expectant, and Mr. Corlyon found that he, too, was expectant. He looked, with it, towards the door.

It was closed, but someone on the further side was pushing with a foot, had pushed it back; someone who was carrying—

Mr. Corlyon had known that he would carry a little flagon, a little flagon half-full of wine. He was looking—a sensation of nausea gripped him—he was looking at himself.

VII

In the house on Quayside were two wraiths, the wraith of Pascoe and the wraith of himself; they moved, enacting a fateful drama, re-enacting it for all to see.

All, that is, who were in the house. They acted it where it had happened, reproducing every detail; and the live man amidst these vehement shadows seemed the least real.

This last phase of the haunt had left Mr. Corlyon momentarily unable to plan. He remained looking on in a sort of dull maze.

The shadows were not only in the kitchen. A wraith decanted wine in the parlour, dropped poison into the mulling horn, carried out the brew. Shadows wrestled, the one in a death agony, the other with a face that Mr. Corlyon refused to believe was his. He could not have looked so furious, so—he would not give the thing its name!

Nor were the movements of these shadows all that was happening in the house. Mr. Corlyon was beginning to hear things as well as see. In Pascoe's room were movements, also in his own; steps came and went on the stairs, a weight which he thought of as a heavy body was dragged along the passage.

The house was no longer his. It had become the setting of a scene, the scene of Pascoe's death. He was a stranger in it, a stranger of whom the actors took no notice, a stranger who wandered in and out as might a lost dog. The haunt had pushed him aside, was gradually making of him—yes—of him a shadowy presence.

What could he do? It was he who was being ignored, not they. The rooms were theirs, the house was theirs. Almost it seemed as if they were the living, he the dead.

Over and over again the same drama, but growing in clearness and sharpness. No one with eyes to see could fail to realize that he had killed his brother.

They would not know why, but—what did it matter if they knew, everything . . . ?

VIII

Broken sleep during the early part of the night generally meant for Mr. Corlyon hours of heavy slumber towards dawn. Although this sleep was deep, it was not often refreshing. One morning, however, he woke out of black quiet into a world of sun and breezes. A sail was flapping against the mast—no, it was his blind. He sprang out of bed to find that the boats were dancing on a full tide, and the gulls swooping and crying. A day full as the tide, full of life.

Below him the house lay shuttered in a haunted stillness, but without, in his little garden, the daffodils of the new spring were dancing, the bluebells breathing honey. He balanced the one against the other. The house—the flowers! The air was blowing in at the open window, the keen salt air; but it was not blowing for him.

He knew what he must do.

The haunt had been born of a disordered fancy; but for one tremendous moment the mists had been blown apart, and he was able to see things as they actually were. The haunt was a fungus, a monstrous toadstool of the mind.

He had killed his brother. Pascoe had deserved—not perhaps death, but death had been the only possible outcome of the situation, and, after all, death, what was it? The sacredness of human life? Pah! The Force Behind killed with disease, with cancerous growths, killed by accidents, through carelessness, and with no repect of person. Man was fodder, the appointed food of germs. He was as much their meat as bullocks were his.

Why then all this fuss? Nevertheless, as a matter of justice, Mr. Corlyon was not so sure—not with this wind blowing—that he had been in the right. If he had killed Pascoe in cold blood, and after long consideration—yes; but his blood had been hot. He had been angered to the depths of a nature unable to take things lightly, and while so angered he had struck. He rubbed a bristly chin contemplatively. He had felt too strongly, had put too much of himself into the matter, and the result was that, in killing Pascoe he had damaged himself, his mind; and what he saw and heard were part of the consequent sickness, they were a sort of delirious vision.

They were imagined, they were not real.

The reality was mouldering flesh and white bones, a dead man at the end of the fogou.

IX

He was sick, and he must get well. The conclusion come to, he forgot the trawlers in the foreground, the life on Quayside, the distant curves of Brown Willhay and Rowtor. He looked beyond the hills, wondering. The cure! Was there no cure but the one? He stood for a long time with the wind blowing on his head, on his body; and every moment it seemed to him that his need to escape was growing more urgent. But he could think of only the one way out, and that way . . . He turned back at last into the room. Very well, then, he would do as he must.

He shaved, he brushed his clothes. Then, without further thought he ran down the stairs, out of the front door. He had a feeling that if he did not run he would be caught by what ruled the dark downstairs of the place. He shut his ears, therefore, he almost shut his eyes, he certainly pulled the door to behind him with a suggestive sharpness. It fell into place with a resounding clap, and he, almost feverishly, turned the key.

The faces of the folk were quietly intent on the business of living. Mr. Corlyon marked the urchins playing about the half-doors, the old men on the benches—the children wholesomely grubby, the old men, clean because life had done with them! He drew in deep breaths of air, drew in the goodness of the commonplace.

He had turned up the street. As if acting on a decision to which he had long since come, and about which there was no question, he went—to Morwenna.

CHAPTER XXII

I

THE gate clanged irrevocably on Mrs. Liddicoat. She walked slowly up the road, surprised to find that she was hardly able to put one foot before the other. She was tired, and life had gone out of her. She was so tired that she was dizzy. When she reached her house, she went into the kitchen and sat down on the nearest chair. For a long while she sat there in her outdoor clothes, numb, lost, hardly alive. About her the night fell; in time, the fire went out, and she was alone in the dark. But she was without the energy to move. Why should she? It was finished.

The faint starlight fell through the little window. It had four panes, and the wood of the sashes was a darkness between the squares. The squares moved slowly, very slowly across the floor. Mrs. Liddicoat's eyes saw the dim lights, followed them without knowing what she saw, without knowing anything. Life was over, and she had no feeling, not even grief.

The kitchen grew cold, and the little squares brighter. A shudder shook her, and the numbness began to pass. Light, real light was extinguishing the stars. Life might be over for one, here and there, but over by Rowtor the sun was rising.

II

The house was no longer a shop. No need, then, for her to sit in the public gaze, to sit behind her counter pretending and smiling. She might remain in the kitchen, do what she would, leave undone the foolish unnecessary things that, once upon a time, had filled her days. Yes, when she had been happy, and before, when she had merely been content. Ah, but she had been happy longer then she would have cared to acknowledge. For ten years she had had his friendship—had seen him once, at least, during the week. Now she had lost even that, she had lost everything.

She did not invent tasks for herself. Shutting her door, she sat behind it with her hands in her lap. Her knitting lay on a chair, and she let it lie. He no longer wanted her to make stockings for him.

She had won him, but she had not been able to keep him, and now that the episode was at an end he would want—of course he would, but how it hurt—he would want to forget that it had ever been. His love had flashed for a moment, but because she had had lines in her face and greying hair, it had not strengthened into an enduring flame. A flicker, and it had gone out.

The lines and the white hairs were outside, but she, she who was inside, she was still young. About the woman inside he knew nothing, yet it was she who loved him, she who was sitting hopeless in the dark.

III

Though Mrs. Liddicoat was a robust woman, she lost appetite, lost strength. Jenifer, coming into town, was surprised to find her actually ill, and the consequent fuss caused Mrs. Liddicoat, in self-defence, to make some sort of effort. It would have been easier, more pleasant to drift from one depth to another until the blackness covered you, but she had not finished with life, only with love.

"Men and women are not the same," she told herself, "a man's love blazes up fiercely, but 'tis soon over, a woman goes on lovin.' "

Nor was it as hard lines on the woman as it seemed. Her heart turned to one man, broke into flower for him, and went on blooming. Hers the delight of that unfolding and opening and giving. It was for him; and sometimes he was able to take it, but very often not. Even if he could not, she had had the giving, the joy of it.

But also the aftermath of pain. Ah, well, and that, you had to bear it. It was terrible—that unending ache. . . .

"I love'n," Morwenna told herself, "and he don't want me, and I'm terrible sorry, but I'll love'n till I'm under the turf. My heart do ache with longing, but the longing'll be over one of these days, and I'll still have the love. 'Tis sorrow and sighing now, but I'll be better of it in time."

IV

Though Denny Manhire offered to dig over his mother-in-law's garden and plant it for her, Mrs. Liddicoat was of opinion that a little hard work would be good for her . . . you don't break your heart if you are breaking your back. She would set her own seed potatoes, sow her own onions, and cabbage, and lettuce. It would give her something to do.

She began to feel an interest in the pushing shoots, and every morning, as soon as she had lighted the kitchen fire, would walk up the flagged path with its edging of violets, and scan the beds to see if any yellow-green heads had broken through the clods during the night. Though your personal life was at a standstill, growth went on—a world of plants, busy each with its pushing and leafing.

If only the days were not so empty, and so full of echoes. But you must not look in on that emptiness, you must look out; look at the buds on the pear tree, the fat ones with their promise of fruit, the thin pointed ones that would unroll into leaves, look at Jenifer growing reconciled to life with her kind young husband, at Jenifer who soon would have a new interest. For Mrs. Liddicoat, too, there would be the interest of Jenifer's child. Yes, yes, a little patience.

Ah, easy to say . . .

"I wonder, Mammy, that you don't live at Carnrose now that you've sold the shop. Mrs. Morecambe's take is up at Christmas, and you always said you'd like to try farming."

Carnrose had come to her from her father. Loveday had had the money, and she the land. She—they—had been born in the old roomy house, spent their youth on the farm; but, could she go back?

"Nothing to keep you in Stowe," Jenifer said.

Only the hope that she might get a glimpse of him! His voice on the street as he went by, his shadow thrown on the drexel, the passing of that spare knit figure—nothing to keep her in Stowe? "Perhaps when Michaelmas comes, I may be able to go."

If she went to Carnrose she would take Jenifer with her; Jenifer, and the child, and Denny.

"You'd like to have calves and chickens, Mammy, and come into market Saturdays."

Calves and chickens—yes; but she would not like to come in to the market! She would be hoping all the time for a sight of Gale. Her heart would be burning, and she would be eaten up with the fire of it. As she was now! No, if she went, it would be to bury herself. She would turn her back on Stowe, try to forget its lanes, the rooms in which he had kissed her, the house in which he was still living.

"Well, my dear," she told Jenifer, "I'll think of it."

And as she dug the dark garden earth, and scattered seed, and weeded, she did think.

Living in Stowe was like having an open sore on your face. The wind and the dust chafed it, it had no chance to heal; but if she covered it with space between, if she went away? Yet the hope that at any moment, any divine moment she might see him! How could she give that up?

See him! She thought that if once more he were to cross her threshold she would not be able to speak; she would sink on the floor, and lay her head on his knee, and stay there, just stay there, silent, and feel the pain draining out of her heart. Give up the hope of that? Oh, no. Not when Michaelmas came?

Not as long as he lived.

V

Never had she had such a crop of violets. She would gather a few, make-believe that she was gathering them for his—their—breakfast-table. the flowers had an early-morning smell of dew and earth, but when the sun was stronger they would give out their scent. She would put them in a bowl and place the bowl where the sunlight coming through the window could fall on them. Fresh, sweet, and for his eyes.

She carried a loose handful into the kitchen, began to set the thin stems—one at a time, that all should have their drink—in water.

A hand pushed at the street-door, the door that was never locked. Morwenna looked up from the violets, and as she saw who was coming in, her heart stood still, her body flushed with flame.

Mr. Corlyon walked quickly through the outer room. Without a word he took her in his arms, held her close, held her as if never again would he let her go.

CHAPTER XXIII

I

"Don't look to me as if you'd had any breakfast. Set down here," Morwenna led him to the sofa, "and see me cook something for you." She did not want, after all, to rest against him till the longing had drained out of her, till she was full of new joy. Why, she was full already, in a twink; the sight of him had been enough, and what she wanted was to do something for him, spend herself, give.

She was brimming with glad energy, suddenly full of life; and she would cook him the best breakfast ever man ate.

Mr. Corlyon took the corner of the sofa that was nearest to the stairs. It commanded the linhay and the kitchen, and would enable him to watch Morwenna as she prepared his food. His woman cooking his food! The comfort, the righteousness of it. Her pleasure to give, and his to take. And oh, the relief it was to be with her.

He need not think of the Brown House and its gruesome shadows, and of what was to come. He might, and what was more, he would, live in the moment. Here, he was a man, not a shadow, and it did not matter what Pascoe did.

He, Gale, would save his soul. That was what ultimately mattered. Your fellow men might misunderstand, might condemn, might penalize you, but they could not pass the defences of your spirit, could not get at the real you.

Whatever happened now, he was safe from ultimate disaster.

When Morwenna called him to the table, he ate and drank as he had not since last he sat there.

"You are gone to skin and bone; nothing but a proper skintrell," she told him with a little break in her voice. "My tender soul, what have you been doing to yourself?"

He must not tell her. "Working," he said.

"Then you must give over working for a bit."

His eyes, those eyes that were so tired, looked kindly on her. "It will be for you to say how much I do."

"For me?"

"I have not brought my desk."

She saw the question in his eyes, but did not dare to believe she read it aright. "No?"

"I did not stay for a thing, I just came and"—the question was clear—"and I am not going back."

She answered out of her full and happy, gloriously happy heart. "That is all I want."

II

"Where are you going?"

"To do my marketing, there's nothing in the larder."

"I will come with you."

She felt glad that Jenifer should have insisted on retrimming her bonnet. She was going out with him. All Stowe would see that she was with him, and she must look her best. Ah, it was good to have someone for whom you put on your finest clothes. Yesterday, how little she had cared! "You won't mind waiting about?"

"Not if you are there."

As they left the house, he turned up the street. "You are going the longest way round."

"Any hurry?"

None, of course, and anyway, he might do as he would. It was not until they were in butcher Andrew's shop and she was buying lamb for pasties that she perceived a change in Gale. He was no longer the good and genial listener to whom all the town could talk. Andrew was showing her the little marbles with which he shot his beef:—"and afterwards I take'n out of the brain, and wash'n and put'n by for the next." The Gale with whom she had for so long been familiar would have examined the marbles, asked questions; but this man glanced away. How butcher killed his beef was for Gale a matter of no interest.

Putting the parcels in her basket, she glanced at him. Of what was he thinking? He was looking out of butcher's window at the sea. It was almost as if the dancing glitter of the water fascinated him. When she touched his arm, he moved, but as if in a dream.

Useless to question him. He could talk of outside impersonal things, but otherwise he had always been dumb. His depths were like a well. She thought of them as covered with a slab of blue Delabole slate. Under the slab, deep under, what had been happening?

Nothing in any way connected with her. Of that she was, by now, pretty sure. He did love her, she could not doubt that he did. Oh, yes, in his way, but she must not expect too much. Enough that he was hers to love.

But—there was something the matter with him! He had some trouble; was in difficulty. She could not guess what it was; perhaps time would give her the key. Meanwhile, she must look after him, feed him up, see that he did not work too hard. In the bright light of noon his face showed a scoring of fine lines. He looked older and very thin, and, yes, ill. Something about his eyes—she thought he looked more than ill. . . .

III

That evening, after supper, Morwenna put chairs by the linhay door. "We'll sit out here in the cool," she said, "oh, the many evenings that we have sat here."

He drew a deep breath. "The many evenings!"

"One moment while I get my knitting."

He stood looking after her. It was almost, she thought, as if he could not bear her to be out of his sight. The house was in darkness, but she knew where the knitting would be, and it was easily fixed. A wad of straw, a stout pin.

"If you only knew what 'tis to me to see you standin' there," and she put her arms round his neck.

He drew her close. "Go on loving me—"

They went toward the chairs. "'Tis what I live for. I have been ill since you were here. In bed I was, and for quite a time."

"No? I'm sorry."

"And while I was laid up, I learnt that—"

"What, dear?"

"That 'tis what I live for—to love 'ee."

He put a hand over hers. "Go on, tell me about it."

He had been with her all day, yet he had given her no explanation either of his keeping away, or his return. He had glanced at her, now and again, as if he were not taking things quite for granted, but he had not spoken, and she could feel for him . . . a dumb man . . . If he only knew how little it mattered!

His staying away had had to do with something other than love. She could not feel that anything but love was of real importance, but that was a woman's view, and men thought differently. Each must do as was natural to her or him. Morwenna's weeks a-bed had been a time of quietening-down, of accepting. But she had risen convinced that live as long as she might, she would love Gale, "All I want," she said soberly, "is to spend my days doing things for you."

"You'll take me as I am, Morwenna?"

"Yes, sure I will."

Tempted, he went a step further. "Don't matter what I've done?"

She had put her other hand over his, and between them his fingers, dry and chilly, were growing warm.

"No, don't make a bit of difference to me what you done."

He felt her assurance as helpful, steadying, almost he believed what she said. In this little garden, the air of which was quick with the smell of growing plants, of spring flowers, of violets, of gentle creatures occupied with the business of living, he might rest his spirit. With nothing to remind him of the haunt, with all around ignorant of it existence, he might forget it. Taking it to be a toadstool of the mind, his forgetting would mean he had trodden it under-foot, that it would not trouble him again.

He would turn his thoughts away from it, listen to what Morwenna, his hand warm between hers, was saying.

"I don't believe you know what love is."

He smiled, that half-smile that the moustache hides, and Morwenna's eyes narrowed in understanding. The dear of'n, to think he knew! His thoughts were plain as print—she could have hugged the boy in him, the boy that was so wise and experienced! That he should be pleased with himself and his little courtings, the courtings that had nothing to do with love.

"Men don't love," she said, her soft voice seeming to rise in spirals through the dusk, and again Gale smiled. Not love? That burning sweetness, a craving more imperative than any other, and the satisfying of which gave you supreme happiness! A simple thing, clean, clear, flaming! A thing of the body, but which yet gathered in the personality! Not love, he?

"Men—they go courtin'," pursued the soft voice, "they are head over ears for the time, helpin' you over all the stiles, and so careful over you; but after you are married, it is 'Take and get over yourself.' They do their lovin' with the body—for what they can get, and after that, they'm tired."

Why, yes, of course. Love was passion, and passion was episodic. She had hit the nail on the head. Tired—a man grew tired—

"There's more to lovin' than that." They had the evening, the rest of life in which to talk; no need for any sort of haste. "I know there is. I've a-got to see that, since you turned me off."

"No need to think of that now." His arm went round her shoulders. He could not have come a day sooner . . . even now . . .

She tried to reassure him. "It isn't that, then, for Gale, I see things in a different light these days and I don't care if I am old; no, nor if I ain't 'ansome any more. My feelings for you have gone behind that, deep down into my heart. It wouldn't make a bit of difference whether you stayed away, or whether you came back, I should go on loving you all the time. Whatever you did, whether 'twas black as night, would not trouble me—not the awfullest things in the world! For you have got my heart, and I should not think no more about what you done, shouldn't blame you, nor worry."

Almost, he could have trusted her.

"Your face is butivul to me, but if I never cast eyes on it any moör, I should go on lovin' it through daylight and dark till I was put'n under the turf, ay—and after. Do 'ee see, dear, for

good or for bad, you are all the world to me. If you was to 'buse
me, or 'eave me to doors, or make a mock of me in my own
town, 'twould be all the same to me, and that—well, that is
what I do call love."

Her voice died away, and silence, a lining to the cloak of
night, folded them close. His arm had drawn her near, and the
long kiss he gave her expressed him better than words. She felt
in it the possibility of a devotion less passionate but more
serious than lovers' love.

"I, too, have been ill," he said. "And now I want just what
you have been talking of. If you give it me, I shall get well
again."

"'Tis yours, love, for the takin'."

He had come to her in some way broken, and she was to do
the healing. She was not curious—or not very—but she
did wish she knew the how and when and why. Still—care,
patience, delicacy of handling, and in time he would be whole
again. "And then," she murmured, almost to herself, "then
you will love me."

Under the influence of the night and her warm love, he was
growing cheerful. "If I don't, what has brought me here?"

"Dunno for sure, but 'twadn't love."

"I care more for you than for anybody I've ever seen."

Her voice was tranquil, reconciled. "It'll come. It is bound
to come. 'Tisn't for nothing you've been Good Samaritan to
the people all round. You've a heart—"

"Well, I was fond of Pascoe."

Something in the tone made her feel it would be safe to let
him see what she thought of that one. "you put your affections
on him like they put clothes on a dummy. You'd nothing else,
then."

His mind grasped at the explanation. That was it. He had
needed to love someone, and Pascoe had been there. That
love—not the flaming of the body—but devotion was what
Morwenna offered, what she was seeking to arouse.

His heart, moved to tenderness, grew vocal. "You," he said
softly, "you believed I minded because your hair is grey and
your face a bit wrinkled. I was a liar, a 'bigger liar'n Tom

Pepper,' dear. 'Tis something in you that draws me. All the rest
is wrapped round that something, and does not really count;
but the something—"

She nestled closer. "Yes, sure Gale, and the something?"

"The something is you."

IV

Gale had come to Morwenna much, she thought, as he must
have come long ago to his mother. He had not with him so
much as a nightshirt! Not that it mattered. She had some—old,
clean, and neatly mended, that her sons had left with her; but
there were other necessary garments. "Perhaps you would go
in to-morrow and get them?"

The look which, she had already learnt, was in some way
connected with his troubles, came to the surface. "No! no!" he
said.

"Perhaps you would rather buy new ones?"

He caught at the suggestion. "We are beginning afresh, we
will have everything new."

She perceived that he did not want to go back, not for any of
his things. Very well, she would see what she had put away. He
must not be worried. That was not the way to get him better.
The poor dear, how thin he was! Ah—milk! It was getting late.
She would heat him a cup of milk, and he should drink it last
thing before going to bed. "Dear," she said, with a little thrill
that burned through her, "will you lock the front door?"

He went obediently. "The key won't turn," he called back.

"Lock wants oiling, I expect."

"But you lock up every night, don't you?"

She put down the saucepan she was holding over the embers,
and went to him. In the dark, by the door, she would be able to
tell him why that key had rusted in the lock.

V

You ought to know, by a sort of love-instinct, how many pillows the beloved required for his comfort, but you did not, you had to ask. His little ways, many of them, were new to you, as new as if her had been a stranger.

Morwenna, after giving Gale the cup of hot milk, had gone up to bed. When he had drunk it, he might come.

"I don't sleep well," he had told her.

"Would you rather I made you up a bed here?"

"I should not sleep at all then."

Except for the silks and satins and velvets of the quilt, the bedroom was neat and chilly white; but Morwenna went about her undressing with a prescient smile. She was seeing, not the orderly arrangements, but an untidiness of added objects. Before long, her looking-glass would have braces hanging from one supporter, and a strop from the other. Over the marcella cloth would be spread the contents of a man's pockets; and his clothes would lie in a loose heap on the chair. Gale's traäde! It was to her as if a lime-washed wall were about to be hung with pictures.

She was absolutely happy.

Ah, yes, but shy—rather. Such nonsense to be shy. She had been married before. Not that she remembered, time had washed her clean of memories, had made her new. Ten years between then and now—but it was not the years, it was that she had not known, no, never, what love was.

Downstairs, he was moving about, taking off his boots. She got into bed, and lay, listening. Through her ran little waves of warmth. His step on the stair—that step! She was too happy, she was fainting under her happiness.

He took his coming as a matter of course, as a cheering fact that was almost a joke. "Never slept with a woman in my life," he said looking at her with dancing quizzical eyes, before which her lids fell.

"But you—there was —"

He seated himself on the edge of the bed. "Don't you believe all you hear. Stowe is an awful place for gossip."

She could not look at him, but she clung, encouraged, to her point. "You old rogue, you. Think I been livin' so near and haven't seen? Take your tarradiddles to Bodmin, there is no market for them here."

He gave in to her with a laugh, and she listened to it with a heart that seemed to turn over. His laugh! The laugh with a catch in it, the laugh she had not hoped to hear again! Oh, that laugh.

"Well, well," he said, "at least I never slept with any of them. You can bake that in your cake."

In some ways, the ways that were of most importance, she was to be first with him. Those transient passions had not given him the domestic sharing of board, of bed. Those intimacies, they had not meant sharing a home. He was come new to her, as she to him. "You—" she was too much thrilled to utter clearly her thought. "I wonder if you will like it."

"Like what, my dear?"

He was a tease. "Like sleeping with anyone."

"I shall like it all right." He got up, went over to the dressing table, began to empty his pockets.

Morwenna, high against her three pillows, watched. His coat came off. Not the first time she had seen him in his shirt sleeves. When she had needed help with the bales and packages, he had lent her a man's strength. Standing back, she had watched the play of his shoulders, the ripple of muscle, had admired the beautiful poise of him. She had looked on and longed, but not hoped, no, she had only thought how wonderful it would be if he ever turned to her.

Even now, it was almost impossible to believe that she was not dreaming, that he, her lovely man, was actually there in her room.

Worshipping, she hardly dared to look at him.

The shirt, a white gleam, was yet old and worn. It needed a patch across the shoulders. The dear had never had a woman to make and darn for him, and he was all to larrups. She lost herself in a dream. Ah, the hours, the blessed hours that she would spend, setting stitch after stitch in his belongings—

sewing love into them.

He pulled the shirt forward over his crisp hair, and she saw his shoulders, his deep chest.

She forgot that such things as shirts, as loving service existed. She was swept forward on a tide of humble adoration. She had stood in the outer courts, now the door of the sanctuary was opening, that of the shrine itself.

She lost her breath, looking, worshipping.

VI

He slept before she did, slept uneasily, but still he slept. She was content to lie beside him, take into her spirit the fact of his nearness, listen to the soft, regular breathing. She was more than content.

Her head was against his shoulder, his chest rose and fell under her arm, his feet went down beyond hers, into the depths of the bed. In spite of being so tall, so strong, he was helpless as a babe. It felt good to be awake while he, trusting her, slept; to lie beside him, guarding him from evil.

She knew that she would die sooner than that any hurtful presence should come nigh him. Die! It would be easy now, for he was hers, her man. Her heart had its satisfaction, and that, none, not even God, could take away. Gale was her man, and she his woman.

She was glad the night was not to be wasted in sleep. She wanted to lie and brood over her happiness, re-live what had happened, realize her lover's presence. This was high water— no, there would be many such tides. Every night and all would be spent with him.

The days would be for working in, working for him; the nights for the quiet thinking, the acknowledging that she loved him; they would be for the feel of his arms about her, as she drifted—unwillingly to lose a moment of her happiness— drifted away.

She lay still, conscious only of the rise and fall of his deep chest—lay there, living her moment.

CHAPTER XXIV

I

LOVEDAY POLLARD, of the Ring o' Bells, at St. Columb, knowing Mr. Corlyon well, approved her sister's marriage. Very suitable. She and her husband would come over for the wedding, and Morwenna need not get in any wine, they would see to that.

Gale had accompanied Morwenna when she went to give in the banns. Marriage, as an institution, worked for the good of the tribe. The indissolubility of it gave each new generation a chance to grow in garden earth, behind a protecting fence. He thought it like the priesthood to have laid hands on it, to have made the tribal recognition into a hard and fast law. For him, the ceremonial, the undertaking to do this and that, were unnecessary, but Morwenna did not agree with him.

"Gettin' married is like putting the dough into the oven. It comes out bread. It won't never be just yeast and flour again."

"You're my woman, sure enough, but it isn't the going to church has made you that," and his eye was quizzical.

Though she glowed under his look, behind the physical answer lay another. The fire and sweetness were too intense, however, to get that other spoken.

"'Till I'm putt'n under turf I'm your woman, and—and afterwards. Gettin' married make me look on to that, to when we'm gone."

He mocked a little, tenderly. "You won't like it," said he, kissing her throat, "when you've done with all this."

"I won't, no, indeed. Every kiss I have of 'ee go through me like a knife. I do feel as if I'll die with the joy of it. I want no more than to go on livin' here with 'ee." She drew a deep breath. "Oh, my tender life and sawl, I be too happy."

He smiled at her. "We've many a year yet."

But she said again. "I be too happy."

"Well, well."

"That is why I want to go to church with 'ee, and kneel down—you and me—"

"But old Stokoe—" He thought of the rector's unimpressive figure, and choked gobble of his voice.

"Aw, 'tedn't him, Gale, 'tes behind him. I dunno, I can't tell 'ee. 'Tes only what I do feel."

He was cupping her chin in his long hand, was reflecting idly on the curve of the jaw. Presently, he would bend to the lips, speaking so eagerly, that crumple of soft lips, flowering, folding. He would change eagerness into warmth.

"I can't think as we stop under turf. Them eyes of your'n. Bright as stars, but there's things as they can't see. Why, times out of number, when I been settin' here, mindin' the shop, and there's been nobody in, I've seen you. You in the Brown House, and me here, but I've seen 'ee plain as print."

The explanation came without his looking for it. "You imagined you saw me."

"One day, you had on a coat I had never set eyes on. Grey 'twas, and your fancy being blue, I couldn't believe I saw it. But when you came in that Thursday you had it on."

He turned the matter over. Morwenna was sincere. She spoke according to her belief. His doubts then must be for the reality of her visions. He considered her temperament. Not highly credulous. Her religion was a matter of accepted belief, not of experience. "You thought you saw that tweed suit, but I must have told you I was getting it, or Honey told you that he was making it for me."

"No, nor you didn't, nor he didn't, and when I see you that time, and see your arm in a grey sleeve, I thought I was mistook. But I wasn't."

"But how? I don't quite get you." Queer things at Quayside, and now queer things here. Perhaps, under the surface of life, queer things everywhere, and he awakening to them by degrees. He wanted to understand. He wondered whether, perhaps, these mysterious things were not beyond his grasp . . . whether mankind had not some way to go before, like a mouse nibbling at a cake, it could get through the crust, the outer crust of knowledge. The attitude of stuffy people was "best not to know too much." Having no imagination, they could not see the riches that lay behind the hard crust. But he, very decidedly, he wanted to know.

Morwenna's eyes expressed the difficulty she had in explaining. "Lovin' 'ee, I did want to be with 'ee, and sometimes I was."

"But how?"

"Well, 'twas dark and quiet in here, and the body of me stayed—there," she indicated the windsor chair, "and the other bit of me went to you."

The conclusion she could not put into words was plain. "You think the other bit of you would be alive, even if your body was under turf? That other bit—"

Was there really a part of her, of himself, that could function apart from the body? The grey sleeve that she had seen—how could she have seen it? She could not unless what she said were true, and actually happened.

He must believe that she thought she had seen it, and that the seeing of it had convinced her.

A projection of herself, a discarnate projection. He held the thought in his mind, considering it. "I wonder."

II

"I be too happy," Morwenna had said, and it was true—at times.

When Gale smiled at her, when his hand touched her, when he grew prodigal of kisses, her spirit swooned under its rich weight of joy. After the years of hopeless quiet—this. She looked back at days lived in a sort of half-light. All round her people who thought themselves alive, whose interests lay in pounds and pence, in a streak of damp on the wall, or a new bonnet for chapel. She, too, had lived a poverty-stricken life of shallow hopes, a life that had left her memories, thin as dried leaves; but now, oh, now life was as wonderful and unexpected as a lucky bag.

Not every parcel, though, held a prize.

Gale was worried, kept it to himself he did, but she knew; and 'twas the worry hurried him up. She wanted him to see doctor, but he said there was nothing the matter that sun and dryth and the oncoming summer would not cure.

"And you—"

She? But she was not an Elizabeth Brenton. That one, now, a healer for sure. "I can't put meat on your bones and quiet in your mind."

"You can, for you do."

He was thinking of a ring he had once seen. Brass, it jutted from an old door, jutted, so that a man seeking sanctuary, fleeing from his enemies, might clutch it easily. His hand once on it, he would be safe.

A brass ring, glittering in the sun.

The one in his pocket was of gold and thin, an old ring. He took it out, detached it from the swivel of his chain. "My mother's."

"I warn your mother loved the father of 'ee," Morwenna said. Love must have gone to the framing of him. In the Brown House was a print—she had seen it in years gone by—of the grand place that had been Mrs. Corlyon's home, the place from which she had fled with Handsome Tom. She had loved him more than the things of this world. She had loved him—it seemed impossible that—as Morwenna loved Gale.

"Take off that other ring."

Up till then, she had worn Peter's. It meant to her not Peter, but Tristram, Edgar, and Jenifer. Obediently, she pulled it from her finger. Her children were grown up and had left her, she had only Gale.

"Now," he said, and kissed the plump hand with its pointed fingers, fingers with a sure light clip and grasp.

"Be I to wear your mother's ring?"

"With this ring I thee wed.' "

A lovely thought of his to have given her this ring which had already circled both joy and sorrow. Death had parted the wearer from her lover, had re-united them. Love, death; but she believed in a love after death. To love such as hers, nor man

nor even poor cold God, away there in the empty skies, and
ignorant of love, could put an end.

III

Was there anything in Morwenna's reasoning? A breeding-
ground this earth, a nursery for young shoots of life. The
young shoot transplanted, set in the soil of other planets might
develop beyond imagination; the present stretch of human
endeavour might be to that development as green grass to an
oak—might! Yes, but you could not accept theories of which
there was no proof as facts.

Theories, Gale had been living among theories, theories and
shadows.

If Pascoe, being dead, yet lived, it was in order to do harm,
and surely a better fate than some sort of demoniac existence
awaited the soul? Why, though, should Gale imagine a world
of good beings, of angels? Good and bad here, good and bad
there.

Of that, if he could agree that Pascoe yet lived, he had proof.

Whether or no he lived, the hatred he had felt was still
reaching after Gale. He was always conscious of it; yes, even
here, in Morwenna's kitchen.

It pulled at him, sometimes it more than pulled. He saw, not
the chairs and table, the rug at his feet, but—

Darkness invaded his mind and, in the midst of the night he
would become aware of a gleam, not a gleam of light, but of
phosphorescence. Something would begin to move—figures,
phosphorescent figures.

He was, perhaps, remembering.

Of that he could not be certain. What was of more importance was that he did not know when the darkness would invade
his consciousness. Suddenly, like a loosed curtain, it would
fall, and blot out the day.

When he came out of it, it was to find that the lapse of time
had, sometimes, been considerable.

He had not known what was happening about him, who came and went.

A time between times. A space of minutes during which—yes, it was a sort of unconsciousness—he was at the mercy of events. How if Morwenna, who never intruded on his silences were, one day, to be absent when the curtain fell? How if others—strangers—were to come in?

They would think him mad.

"If I were—er—lost in thought," he warned, "you would not trot off on some business of your own? I mean you would not leave me?"

She hastened to reassure him. Always thinking he was, thinking about the something of which he could not, or would not, speak. "Leave you, Gale, why it makes me happy to be with you."

"You wouldn't think I wanted to be by myself?"

Now you have told me, I never will."

"We'll be married soon." He heaved a sigh of satisfaction. "That'll tie you to me for good and all. Are you willing, Morwenna?"

"Oh, love, of course I'm willin', I'm more than willin'."

IV

The seedlings in Morwenna's garden were as great a joy to Gale as to her. He spent most of his day weeding, destroying slugs, raking; and in the warm showery weather the young things grew with gladdening haste and vigour. Lettuce, onion, and a border of sweetness, a border between the bushes and the flagged path. Every morning, he went with Morwenna to see what had happened during the night; every evening he took into the house the picture of the dim paths with, on either side of them, the plants, the spread of brown mould. The garden exercised on him a spell. Not once when he was digging did the curtain fall between him and it.

It fell when he went into the dark of the house. It fell when he was sitting quiet in the dusk.

He surprised Morwenna by his craving for light. Her thrifty soul gave the extra lamp, the night-light in a saucer, and gave without grudging, but she wondered.

Was it part of his illness, or was it possible that he was afraid of something?

He never, by any chance, spoke of the Brown House, would not let her. Had something down there got on his nerves? Would it help if he were further away?

"I s'pose you would not like to try farmin'. There's Carnrose, and 'twill be empty at Michaelmas."

"Carnrose?"

"The farm my father left me."

The dear woman was offering him his heart's desire. Always his dream to rent a few fields and till them. Carnrose? He knew the farm, inland, but not too far, and a sizeable sort of place. One hind would be enough to run it, and there was Nicolle eating his heart out in Stowe, he'd come. Corlyon saw himself in cords and gaiters, a proper farmer, saw Morwenna making butter, brewing, saltin' in.

But—Pascoe.

Surely having left the house on Quayside, Gale might take this further step. Surely—

Leave the haunt to its own devices?

What was it doing at this moment? He got up, went to the door. No, he would not look. As long as he did not think of the apparitions they were not there. He came back to Morwenna, put an arm round her, held her as if anxious to be assured of her flesh and blood reality. "Farming? No, I don't think I should like it."

Yet, times out of number, he had told her he hoped to spend his old age on the land. Fear, a fear of something beyond her grasp, stabbed. "Then we must poddle along as we are."

V

Not until Gale had been with her ten days did Morwenna admit to herself that he was not gaining ground. During the first week, in spite of his lack of appetite and broken rest, he had seemed comfortable in himself, on the mend. He had talked and laughed with her, had been like a boy out of school. Splendid company he was.

It had not lasted. He was growing daily more absent-minded. When he came out of a brooding silence he seemed to leave behind a part of himself. Also, he looked ill. His skin was losing its pale clarity, his eyes were bloodshot, his expression— she knew that the alteration in his expression was of more importance than the lines and the troubled look. It portended —what?

Sometimes, when she was sitting beside him with her hand between his, he forgot that she was there.

Every morning she woke to an eager hope that he would be better, more his old self. Day-long she watched, still hoping, and at night, while he tossed and muttered, she lifted her heart in prayer.

His safety, his health, his sanity!

VI

"Mrs. Liddicoat!" A voice was hailing them from the street. Supper being over, Morwenna was stacking the cloam on a tray.

"It will be Rebecca French with my share of the week's takings." She opened the kitchen door, let the warmth and light flow through the intervening room, the room was to have been Gale's office. "Come along in, and set down."

"I want to pay you what I do owe you." She came blinking out of the night. A lamp on the table, candles on the mantel-board, and they courting? "Evenin', Mr. Corlyon."

Though Gale, from his seat on the sofa, made courteous reply, her coming was unwelcome. Even when he had Morwenna's full attention, it was difficult to keep his thoughts fixed on her, prevent them from straying down the street.

The kitchen in which he sat grew dim. He was seeing a room in the Brown House. Locked doors and shuttered windows and darkness, yet he saw the room more clearly than that in which he was sitting. How long would a turned key, a hasped window suffer to wall in the shadowy occupants of that room? The time was coming—he felt it creeping towards him . . . a black point in space . . . Whenever he looked, it was appreciably nearer. The time was coming when the shadows, jigging in that confined space, would break through; when the walls would be as mist, and the shadows as strong men.

He must not think of the future, of what would be. Morwenna . . . he must hold on to her, lose himself in her love, in that long, swooning glance.

"How be gettin' on with your shop?"

Rebecca liked to hear it spoken of as "her" shop. Ringlets swinging, she drew up to the cleared table, and opening her purse, took out a piece of gold and some silver. "Not so very dusty." She had sold so many yards of frilling, so much muslin for robes, embroidery for trimming. So much left, and Morwenna's share would be——

Under the business chatter lay her preoccupation with the amazing couple. It did not seem very right for Mr. Corlyon to come and live there before they were married and she was surprised at him. But there, men did not think nor they did not trouble. Made you glad you hadn't got none to trouble you.

People had told her he was looking whisht and, dear life, so he was. Would not, hardly, have known him. Gone all to pieces.

She counted the money into Morwenna's hand; and Mr. Corlyon, rousing from his abstraction, prepared to make out a receipt. But, no. "Then that will be all right," Morwenna said. "We know how each other stand and I shall be seeing you again on Monday."

He wondered if this way of doing business answered. Men put black upon white, but women depended upon words and the character behind the words. To do so must quicken the faculties, for unless you were able to size up the people with whom you were dealing you would lose.

Morwenna went with the other to the street door, and stood there for a moment, hoping. Perhaps Rebecca, who was so cute, would guess what she wanted.

"Well?" The other smiled to herself. "Driven your pigs to a braäve market, 'aven't 'ee?"

"Don't mind for that."

"At your time of life to be scandling the parish."

"Parish might find something better to do than go scandling about me; I am old enough to look after myself."

"Of course you'll do as you've a mind to. Always have and, I supoose, always will."

"Becky . . . " It did not matter what Rebecca said as long as she would talk things over. To go on, with your fears shut up inside—to feel there might be something to be done if you only knew what it was—she could not stand it any longer! "Mr. Corlyon don' seem so well as I could wish."

Rebecca caught the note of anxiety, the anxiety that brought folk to her for help. "You can't expect it."

"Not expect it! Why?"

"You don't knaw?"

Morwenna's mind fled from what the other would have implied. "I'm doin' all I can for him—new-laid eggs and cream and chicken. If I could get him to eat as he belong to, he'd soon get better."

"He can't get better whiles the wish is on him."

Morwenna's voice rang out sharply. "Don't 'ee tell I that."

The witch shrugged bony shoulders. "Have it your own way."

The other hesitated. The fear of witchcraft was in her blood, and she must admit that queer things did happen. After Elizabeth Brenton had charmed the mole it had dropped off her cheek, no denying that.

Gale had nothing definitely the matter with him, and yet was ill. She wanted to believe his getting better only a matter of time, but under what she said, under what she thought lay uncertainty, and under all a black terror. The words and thoughts sailed over that black pit. All day they went to and fro above it, trying to forget that it was there; but at night in the stillness, you had to admit . . .

"Do 'ee think—" she said to Rebecca.

"Think?" the little woman's bright opaque eyes—water-washed pebbles—were scornful. "I knaw 'tis true."

And to Morwenna it seemed so very likely. Almost she believed . . . quite . . .

Ill-wished! Who could have done it? Never had she known Gale do anybody a bad turn. Ah, but they might think he had, and people who had "the power" were easily vexed. So often it was a next to nothing, such as Rebecca's wrath with Mrs. Maddicott on account of her having baked old Spargo a loaf. Yes, they ill-wished you because they fancied things.

"But who'd witch'n, Rebecca? He's loved by everybody."

"Dunno who 'tis, but I could find out."

"I should be pretty and glad it you would." But she could not unless Gale were willing and Morwenna knew he did not hold with such things. "Mr. Corlyon don't altogether believe in witchcraft."

Rebecca stepped off the drexel. "Well, 'tisn't nothing to me. I didn't offer to help you and I don't want to, but—he edn't half the man he used to be."

The black terror drove out little fears and tremors with an irresistible sweep. Gale might deride but she did not care. He must do what was best for him. "Not half the man? No, he isn't," she cried, "he's a proper wreck. Nothing but bones pokin' through his skin. When I look at'n I grieve my life out, I do, but—" she looked anxioulsy at Rebecca, "but it wouldn't be any use tellin' him he'd been witched."

"Aw—leave it to me."

"I can see so well as you do he edn't well and it worry me to death."

"'Tis so plain as a pike-staff."

"What's plain, Becky?"

"That he'm witched. Haven't I seem 'em scores of times? Don't sleep well by night, do 'e? Seem to be hurried up in his dreams?"

"Yes, 'tis awful. Cry out 'e do and make such moans."

"And don't eat enough to keep a sparrow alive?"

"No, that's true. I coax'n and coax'n, but I can't make'n eat scarcely anything."

"And wastin' flesh daily? Aw, I know! Got every sign of it."

"Whoever can it be?" Morwenna's voice was a shivery whisper.

"Would you like for me to tell you?"

"I wish to goodness you would. I'd do anything to get him better."

"Well"—the time seemed to her ripe, "if I was to show him who had witched him—"

"Yes?"

"What 'ud you give me?"

"If I could, I'd give you the two eyes out of me 'ead."

"Pretty lot of use they'd be to me."

"What do you want?"

"Don't want more than the old lace collar and if everybody got their own it belong to me, so I'm doing this, you might say, for nothing."

Morwenna did not hesitate. What was a mere bit of decency when Gale's health, perhaps more than his health, hung in the balance? "You are welcome to that one."

"Very well, then." She turned back. "Bring me down the little old looking-glass that hangs to your wall and I'll tell'n."

Gale, when Morwenna left him, had tried to concentrate his mind on the vexed question of replacing the street cobbles with asphalt—smooth, dry, lasting—or with flags from the Poldinnick quarry. He was in favour, he thought, of the paving-stones. They would be cheaper, yet would last nearly as long. To begin with they might be tried on French Street. He saw them beautifying the crooked thoroughfare, running on—

They would go past the Brown House, not past, no. they would end at the further wall.

He forgot the paving-stones—

"You have been a long time away!" He looked at Morwenna reproachfully. She had declared she would not leave him to himself; but when he needed her, the strong feel of her hand on his, she was not there.

"Been tellin' about you, Mr. Corlyon," interposed Rebecca. "Mrs. Liddicoat say you don't believe in witch-craft."

"To believe I must have proof." He had risen, a tall figure with hair in which the grey was yielding ground, which would soon be white; and Rebecca, glancing at the aquiline features, the brilliant eyes below level brows, hardly wondered that her cousin was foolish over him. After all, if you had to have a man in the house, might as well have something worth looking at.

"No difficulty about that," she said. "I will give you as much proof as you do want."

He smiled, courteous but sceptical. "As you please."

Morwenna had brought the old round mirror from her room, and the other, giving the surface a rub with the black sleeve of her gown, handed it to him. "Look in there—hold it steady, so, like that." She tilted it till the dazzle of the lamp filled it, like a pool, with light. "Now look until you see a face."

"Until I see a face? Whose face?"

"Aw—never mind, wait till you do see'n."

A month ago and Mr. Corlyon would not have humoured the woman, but during that month much that was incomprehensible had happened. His beliefs were no longer fixed. Behind the surface manifestations of life, powers at present undreamed of might be hidden. Sir Isaac Newton had confessed himself a child picking up a pebble or so of knowledge on the shores of its ocean. This woman, what did she know? Her eyes were piercing, uncanny. she might be able to give her thoughts shape, project them on to this shining surface. She might be able to solve some of his problems. No harm in testing her and he could pretend he was doing it for his amusement. He stared at the mirror and staring grew dreamy, forgot Rebecca, forgot the place in which he stood. He seemed to be passing out of time into a world transfused with light, which was all light, nothing but light, when he was caught back by a change in the pool. It had grown cloudy and in the centre was a darker spot. His interest wakened. In the spot, which had spread a little, something was taking shape—the shape had an outline, features—Gale was looking into a furious blood-suffused face, the face of Pascoe when he realized that he was being done to death.

"Pascoe!" he cried and the mirror fell from his hand. The glass in the old gilt frame smashed scattering over the floor. "I—I was thinking of him."

"Ah,' said Rebecca, thrusting forward her eager face, the face that seen beside Morwenna's was as glittering metal to a flower. "Ah, but seein's believin'!"

He realized the need for caution. They must not be allowed to think there was anything peculiar in his having seen his brother's face. "What do you want me to believe?" He was conscious of the hard glitter of Rebecca's eyes. The sort of woman, that, for whom he had no use; of whom, had he been other than Gale Corlyon, he might almost have been afraid.

"You've seen with your own eyes and you must bring your mind to bear on what you seen."

He forced a smile. "At your service!"

"Aw, now—there's no doin' anything with you."

"Well?"

"Can't you see you'm wastin' away and that 'tis 'e that 'av done it? Your own brother, 'tis 'e 'av ill-wished you."

VII

Morwenna had swept up the fragments of broken glass, had seen Rebecca out and come back to Mr. Corlyon. she stood looking anxiously at him, noting without appearing to do so, the dryness of his skin, 'ie troubled eyes, and the fact that his hair was different. It was not unkempt, for she had watched him brush it, but it stared. Long ago, she had watched a mad dog run down the street, and she remembered that its coat have been starey. Gale was ill, but she was used to illness, only— well, there was something strange about this illness, something that frightened her. Why should his brother have witched him? What lay behind it all?

Whatever it was though, she would help in any way she could, yes, any way, every way.

"She say Pascoe have ill-wished 'ee! Can't be anything in it?"

He did not answer, but she was used to his silences. They

told her as much as another man's spreading talk.

"What 'av 'ee done for 'e to ill-wish 'ee?"

He stared at the red and black of the mat, warm beneath his feet. Let her guess, ay, even if she did get a glimpse of the truth.

"Was it money?"

She waited for a denial, but he continued to stare at the mat. So that was it? The brothers had quarrelled. Pascoe had made unconscionable demands and when Gale refused to let himself be robbed, the chap had witched'n. She had always known that Pascoe had it in him to play dirty tricks.

First Jenifer, now Gale.

A black-hearted fellow, Pascoe, a real bad lot . . . and for him to have ill-wished Gale!

"Aw, my dear life—" A little come out about money and for Pascoe to have turned nasty. Sinking down beside Gale she looked at him anxiously. It was no laughing matter.

"I am not afraid."

She was, she was very much afraid; but, in the midst of her alarms, she was able to adore his immunity.

"I am not afraid of anything on earth or—or off it."

She turned the matter over, seeking the way of escape. That he was not afraid might be a help. "Pascoe'll be in Jamaica?"

"He is gone out of our reach."

"Can't we get to him no way?"

"No."

Her clasp of him tightened. Not even Rebecca could take off a wish, unless she were able to confront the ill-wisher. Pascoe could send this devil of mischance across sea and land, work his will on his brother; and they—

"Can't we do nothing?"

"Nothing."

But they would. She sat up, tilting her chin, staring with mother-fierceness. "We'll fight it—you and me—you'm stubborn as a pig and I have a strong will of my own. We'll fight, dear life."

CHAPTER XXV

THE WEDDING GUEST

I

"The day'll be showery," Loveday Pollard said as she stepped into the gig. "But Wennie may be thankful, seein' the time of year, that she 'aven't got Cousin Jack's weather."

"Prince'll get there between the drops," said Pollard.

As the marriage was to take place at eight o'clock, they were starting betimes. The drive across moorland and countryside was all of twelve miles, but Prince would make nothing of it. Pollard would stable him at the Farmer's Arms and, with his wife, go straight to the church. Did not look well to have too much fuss when you were middle-aged. Getting married at any time was sort of foolish and when you were ripening to fifty, the less show the better.

Get the thing over, that was it. Pollard had business to do in Stowe. When he was through with it they would have dinner and a bottle of wine, all hunky-dory, and he and the Missus would drive off home again. His sister-in-law had a bit of money and Corlyon was spoken of as well-to-do. Pretty and sensible of them to put their odds and bits together. Besides, the chap had been going there up in teens of years—best to get married.

II

On stepping with Morwenna out of her house, Gale Corlyon had stepped into a brightness of early morning sun. He had not noticed that the wind was from the south-west and that it drove before it heavy, reluctant clouds; but when they reached the church the clouds had been flung across the sky and the bridal party stepped from grey air into gloom.

The little old church had coloured windows. The people who had built it slept under its flags. It spoke not of life, but death, and Gale found himself unwilling to enter. Darkness— and he did not like the dark; it sent his thoughts to Quayside. Only the fact that Morwenna's hand lay on his arm, that she, dear soul—in her quick, taking-for-granted manner was going forward, prevented him from stopping, from turning back. Before he could decide not to go on, he was through the porch and walking up the aisle. Too late, then. He pressed the hand on his arm, the warm, strong hand, and went on.

But the chilly gloom into which he had been plunged made him uneasy. He had left the grey of the house for morning sun, for the light in which he trusted and which, hot and clear, dismissed his visions as unreal. He had stepped from the healing blaze into a shadow-pool. On the edges of it was a night of dim stone tombs, of vaulted darkness, of black air. Walking up the aisle, he looked eagerly at the eastern window. The outer blackness was pressing towards him, but the jewel of darkly-coloured glass in its surround of stone, would be his salvation. Through the red wounds of its Christ the light would flow.

He had forgotten that the sky was full of the July rains, that a grey opacity masked the sun. The window hung agate-dull on the darker wall and Gale remembered.

He had come thither with Morwenna because—oh, for several reasons.

He had said, "What day of next week, my umuntz?"

"'Twill be give out Sunday for the last time," she had answered, calculating. "And I'd like—I think we better—go to church Monday."

"You are in a hurry."

"Once we'm wedded they can't throw it up to me."

He had been amazed. Throw it up to her? Yet there were people—for instance, if Pascoe had been alive . . .

Pascoe would have snatched at the chance to make Morwenna suffer. Yes, if he knew that she had delivered Gale out of his hands he would be bitterly angry with her. Throw it up? He would do more than that.

Being dead he could not know. That is, if there were no life after death and if the haunting had not a life of its own.

The sepulchral coldness of the church was affecting Gale. He shuddered and it seemed to him that not only he but his convictions were a-shake.

Was Pascoe—dead? The flesh of him was mouldering but the spirit?

"I, Gale Corlyon, take thee, Morwenna Liddicoat . . ." but he did not realize what he was saying. He was listening, not to the parson's voice, but to a sound that came from a distance, a sound as of an opening door.

III

When the bridal party—newly married couple and witnesses— reached the porch, a plump of rain was falling between the black spires of the cypresses that bordered Deadman's Way. The blue of the estuary, the blue of the day, were veiled, a grey world and out of the greyness arrows of rain. As Mrs. Gale Corlyon's bonnet was new and Mrs. Pollard's had a freshly curled feather, they decided to wait for a little. The shower would pass.

The women drew back from the splashing drops. Jim Pollard, wondering if he might smoke, began to stuff his pipe, and Gale, the chill of the stones striking through his soles, stood looking down the straight path between the trees.

And presently he saw that for which he was looking, that which he had known must come.

IV

Up the path, dim as yet because of the grey rain, walked a man. From far away he was recognizable. The rolling gait, the sailor rig, Gale knew him at once. He saw, too, that the fellow had something in his hand. That something, yes, of course, Pascoe would not have forgotten to bring with him the proof. He must be able to show the glass, the dregs of the wine.

This, then, was how he intended to "leave the town know!" Before Jim Pollard and his wife, before the rector now coming out of the church, before Morwenna, he would denounce his brother.

He would stand before them, careless of mortal rain, and tell the story.

With stabbing finger he would point to Gale. "You poisoned my drink. Let 'em search the house—my traäde is in the cave! Let 'em go on, down the old run-way, and they'll find what's there."

And the rector, Mr. Stokoe, would question him.

"But why should your brother"—he would lean on the "brother"—"why should your brother have done this?"

"To prevent me taking what was mine."

The dead—people would say—do not lie. Tergeagle, the dead steward, the man whose wickedness was a household word, had come from his grave to bear witness and his testimony had been accepted without question.

Short-sighted folly! Because he died, a bad man did not become good. But the rector, the Pollards, the townspeople, would believe what Pascoe chose to say, take his version of the story for truth. Not Morwenna, she knew what Pascoe was like.

Ah—he had her on his side. Everyone else, everyone in Stowe might turn against him, but not Morwenna. If he told her he had killed Pascoe she would say, "you had good reason," and "it make no difference to me."

The three weeks with her had opened his eyes. Love o' women . . . such love . . . and he had been blind to it all his days; but it was not too late. He, too, could give. He had not known that he could, but a spring was rising from the depths.

When he got Morwenna alone, he would sing her his song of love, tell her what he had done. Yes, but Pascoe must not be allowed to be beforehand with him, to stand on the church drexel and shout his story. What the others thought and did was of secondary importance. It was Morwenna now. She was his wife—queer word that, sort of solemn. Yes, the solemnization of their union had lifted it on to a different plane, a time-worn ceremony, slavish, impossible promises, but behind these things, the warm sacredness of their love. She had long been his; she was his, now, but in a different sort of way.

So far, no one had caught sight of the graveyard figure rolling up Deadman's Way—coming nearer and nearer—but at any moment they might.

Pascoe had been a shadow, looming through veils of mist; now Gale could see his face. It was the face of a dead man, waxy; but his eyes were open and the spirit that looked out of them had a strange staring life.

Neither lock nor shutter nor the stony bosom of Gudda had been able to keep him where he belonged. He had escaped from the fogou, from whatever spell had kept him jigging from parlour to kitchen, acting and reacting the drama of his death. He was free to range the streets, of Stowe, to dog his brother—

A black hopelessness held Gale for a moment, but only that. for the sake of the hand on his arm—the hand with glinting ring—he must act. "We won't wait any longer," he said, and Morwenna waking out of happy dreams, stepped at once and willingly into the rain.

Loveday saw them move, the tall absorbed man and her eager sister. "I'll stay on a bit," she called after them. They might be glad to be by themselves and, anyway, the rector was talking to her husband and it would not be manners to interrupt.

She walked to the doorless opening and stood looking down the path between the cypresses. The end was closed by a lych-gate. By way of it the dead came to their resting-places. Up that path she had followed Peter Liddicoat—the coffin carried breast high, her sister walking behind it and then, in proper order, the family. When the rain ceased she would go across to his grave, see if it wanted trimming, if the rosebush were still alive.

The shower was nearly over; before long the sun would be out, would be shining on Gale and Morwenna . . . "lucky the bride."

V

As Gale held the swing-gate for Morwenna to pass out of the
churchyard, he looked back; looked carefully along the winding neatly-gravelled path. His heart leapt. Yes, he had
succeeded in turning Pascoe from his purpose. The porch, that
little hood on the face of the church, still held the Pollards and
the rector; the murmur of voices in innocent conversation was
audible; the peace of a soft dropping brooded over the place.

Pascoe had stepped from Deadman's Way on to the daisy-
bordered path by which the living came to offer their weekly
worship. He was following Gale.

Would he follow him through the town?

"Gale," said Morwenna dreamily, "I be Mrs. Corlyon." She
leaned on the sweet syllables. "'Tis a lovely name," and she
repeated it bringing out the music. "Mrs. Gale Corlyon! 'Tis
mine now for ever. They'll put'n on headstone when I'm in
under."

He glanced over his shoulder. Pascoe was on the side-walk.
He seemed to be smiling to himself.

"'Tis a long time"—Morwenna's voice rippled pleasantly
on, "'tis a long time since I was Morwenna Strongman, driving
into Stowe with my father on market-days. Marryin' so quick
I've always seemed more Liddicoat than Strongman. Pittery-
pattery sort of name Liddicoat. But now," she paused, smiling
to herself, "I have got a name that is worth havin'."

He spared her a quick glance. "The years we've missed, my
girl."

It went through her like silver fire that he should call her "my
girl." "We'll make up to one another for they years."

"Blind!" he said, "I've been blind."

"Love," she did not want him to reproach himself, "when
you stepped over the drexel, the night you came again, you put
me in your debt for as long as I live. A woman can't be more
than happy."

He smiled down on her. "'Twill be hard lines if I can't keep
you that."

As long as she had him, no need to trouble. "I only want to be let love 'ee."

They had come by the turning that brought them into French Street opposite the Farmer's Arms. He paused to look back and she supposed he was looking for the Pollards.

       ✻   ✻   ✻

Yes, she thought that, even she, who so loved him!

       ✻   ✻   ✻

"What do you see?" he asked her as she, too, glanced up the road.

"Nobody."

"Nothing?"

"Sun's in my eyes."

"You don't see anyone coming . . . there by corner shop?"

She saw the sharp turn of the road, the rain-washed cobbles, the shine of Mrs. Julian's parlour-window. Nobody in the street, not a soul.

"Don't 'ee trouble. People come when they've a mind to, not before."

Though it was evident she did not see him, nevertheless Pascoe had come. He had chosen the hour of his coming, set it by the clock of their lives. He had waited for the wedding.

VI

Throughout the walk home, Pascoe kept at the same distance. The light passing through him, yet framed a dark outline, showed it thick if not solid, a shape that was yet a shadow. Details were curiously distinct and Gale could see that the skin over the skull, shrinking, had pulled the dry lips into a grin.

When Pascoe grinned it meant that he had been playing a trick on someone. Dead, he was playing a last trick.

It was as if a flash of lightning had illumined the country of his mind. Gale perceived that if Pascoe had denounced him in the sight and hearing of Stowe, it would have been the end—a trial, a hanging and the end. He was not ready for that—not yet.

Living, Gale was an orange that could be squeezed and squeezed again. After the last drop had fallen there was always another. Pascoe would keep him alive . . .

He saw his troubles as scarlet drops on a black malodorous thread. He saw Pascoe, shaping them and laughing, slipping them on the bit of gut. A tooth for a tooth—a life, ah, more than a life.

This haunting, it was not accidental, fortuitous. Pascoe had planned it, had carried out his plans, but Gale had been blind, had not realized the purpose in what was happening. He saw it at last—Pascoe had broken up his good business of an auctioneer, had separated him from friend and acquaintance, plagued him with ghostly bedevilments; Pascoe, finally, had driven him from the Brown House. His home and Pascoe had made it hateful to him.

His life had fallen about him like the shards of a broken pot, of a pot that had been smashed by a malicious hand.

VII

Morwenna gave him the key of the house-door, waited for him to turn it.

"Go in quickly," he said.

"You won't lock it against Loveday?"

"Not against Loveday." Yet as soon as she was over the drexel he had shut it on them, shut it sharply as if to prevent others from squeezing in, had, she fancied, turned the key.

She went through the house into the linhay, went on light feet. It was amazing how young and morning-fresh she felt. Might have been only seventeen.

Her wedding-day. She looked back at Gale, smiling at him, trying to make him feel as blithe. But he was looking anxious. "I shall be glad when to-day is over."

"And we are by ourselves again? Oh, yes, I'll be glad too." She had the dinner to cook, the best damask to get out, the glass to polish. "Won't you set out in the garden, love?"

"I'll stay here."

He was on the sofa in the kitchen. He would have preferred to be in the garden, but he had to remain in the kitchen. He had to wait.

Her work did not altogether absorb her. Whenever she came into the dark kitchen, she stopped and leaned over and kissed him; and, patiently, he kissed her back.

Only when, passing him, she would have fetched china from a wall cupboard in the outer room, did he stir.

He must remain between her and the street-door. He must or—

Danger to her?

Could Pascoe get at her? Not if he, Gale, stood between them.

The sweat was cold on his forehead, a chilly breeze, dank and mouldy, was blowing through the keyhole. What would be Pascoe's next move? But he need not ask himself, for he knew.

VIII

The knocking of a stick on the door, brought Morwenna, running. "They are in nice time, for dinner is just ready."

"It isn't your sister."

"Must be. Nobody else to come in on us."

"I'll go see."

He was quick on his feet, but to-day they dragged. So many paces to the door and each step echoing back to him from the empty room. He did not want to open the door, but he must. Yes, in spite of what he knew would happen.

Voices outside, the voices of people pleased with themselves and the world. He must open.

Jim was carrying a frail out of which stretched the gold-foiled necks of bottles, Loveday bore a ham. Their jollity filled the dark spaces, broke on the wall of Corlyon's spirit.

He let them in, shut the door after them and secured it, followed them to the kitchen.

Loveday, having loosened her bonnet-strings, was helping Morwenna dish-up, Jim had gone into the linhay for a corkscrew. They were all busy as bees, and Gale, standing in the doorway, was unobserved.

He looked where he must look—at the sofa.

On it sat the uninvited guest.

IX

Pascoe was watching Morwenna. When she went to the cupboard, his head turned, his glance followed her.

Gale, from the shadow of the doorway, watched him, appraising the glance. Pascoe owed her a grudge . . . not quite that, or at least . . .

Yes, he did owe it and he was glad to. It provided him with an excuse, helped him to a plan. He would torture Gale through Morwenna.

Her happiness would be another orange for his squeezing.

The violent wrath Gale had not known since he sought sanctuary with her, swept down on him. He wanted to smash, to tear. The crash of glass and china, the cracking of wood and of heads, would have been calming. To fight . . .

But here was something he could not fight. A black wave rose out of the depths, extinguished the flames, engulfed him. He was helpless.

An appeal? His thoughts were an appeal, but the wraith of Pascoe, grinning, continued to look at Morwenna.

Gale's soul was an intense concentrated plea. He was so lost he hardly heard Morwenna's voice. "Draw up your chairs. Loveday, you sit on the bench and carve the ham and I'll cut up the chicken." Apportioning the work, she gave her husband the task of cutting bread. The dear of'n was too absent-minded to be trusted with anything else, but he could manage that.

And Gale, standing, had sliced half the loaf before she stayed his hand.

For round that table were not four people but five. Loveday and Morwenna were at the ends, Jim opposite, and between himself and Morwenna—the wedding guest.

In the grey air of the room, a shadow, a darker shadow than was thrown by the people, the furniture. they had shadows that were obedient to light, that gave place, but not this.

Between himself and Morwenna! Corlyon would have pushed him away if he could—a phantom chair and on it the wraith of a dead sailor—but he knew the uselessness of attempting that. His hand would pass through cold air—

The Pollards were talking of their morning in Stowe. They had not sensed that alien presence; but Morwenna glanced—it seemed to Gale that she glanced uneasily—at the space which was not mere space. She did not see Pascoe, not yet, but . . .

Undoubtedly, she would in time.

"Set down, dear love."

"In a minute I will."

He had brought Pascoe in, he must take him out, yes—out of her life.

He must. Though every fibre of him was in revolt, he must.

He looked down on Pascoe, "Come," he said.

"Where be goin', Gale?"

His glance swept the table, the faces, but he could not look at her. "Go on with dinner. I—I shall be back in a minute."

She turned, put her hand on his arm, lifted her face.

"Don't 'ee be long," her voice pleaded, her eyes—he could not bear it! "My tender sawl, don't 'ee be long."

He took her hand from his arm, looked at Pascoe to make sure that he was following and went out.

CHAPTER XXVI

I

BIT by bit Pascoe would filch from Morwenna her happiness.

Gale Corlyon had lived through long-drawn-out suffering, a torture that was always as great as he could bear, that when he had adapted himself to one set of strains, wrenched at him from a fresh angle. The thumb-screw, the rack, splinters in quick of the nail, those were physical, but the agonizing of a soul . . .

Of Morwenna's soul? No, that was the bit over, the—unendurable.

Standing with the bread-knife in his hand, cutting slices as automatically as the reaper cuts a swathe, he had hardened his heart. Nothing he could not do. Nothing of which he was afraid. This? It was an adventure.

He must cling to that thought of the adventure, must not let his mind slip away, back—must not think of Morwenna.

When he laid down the knife, his eyes were a sword-grey, his chin a stiffness below the line of lip. When he took Morwenna's hand from his arm, a thread of scarlet ran from the lip.

II

Mr. Corlyon walked down the street. He passed along Quayside until he came to the Brown House, but he did not go in. He looked over the latched gate at weedy path and deserted home. A house of the dead.

Pascoe was behind. The fellow had understood and was waiting to follow where his brother led, accepting for the last time his dominance.

A long while since, on an impulse, he had killed Pascoe, so long he had almost forgotten . . . had the provocation been so bitter, so intense? Pascoe had wronged him, taken his money, but what of it?

Money—yellow metal in a bag. They had quarrelled, as boys quarrel over marbles. "Yours—mine. I'll jolly soon show you." He had seen red—a momentary madness—and then the blow. To think that out of that madness should have come this egregious coil. To-day it seemed to him to have been all about nothing.

Yet he had to untie, no, cut it.

III

The tide was making, but the path at the foot of the cliff was still firm and dry. Gale Corlyon, having assured himself that Pascoe was following, turned towards the sea. Round one bluff, round others, till he was stopped by a ripple of water, of flat pale water, on the edge of which grey and white sea-birds were playing a game. They ran forward, let a film of water spread over their quick brown feet, then all together they ran quickly back. Many the time he had stood to watch their antics, and again he watched.

The shadow of the dragon lay on the rippled sand and he remembered that it was waiting. It had been waiting since the river ran into the sea.

From the land towards which it looked, he had come to it and Pascoe was coming.

The birds, rising suddenly, flew out over the shallow sea, and Gale realized that his feet were wet. He could smile at that. The mists that came up from the water, the rain that fell, the damps of autumn, they had no longer any power to harm.

Round the dragon rock, a wave came with a spreading swirl. It poured through the opening of the cave and Gale, rousing himself, called over his shoulder. "Come," he said, "or the tide will be in."

As the water drained away, he sprang for the opening under the trails of weed. The sand gave beneath his foot. He swung himself over the edge into water, water that was sinking, running out; swung himself into warmth and a riot of colour.

Through slits high in the weed the sun was pouring into the

cave. It glowed on the yellows and metallic peacock tints of the wall, on the blue of the escaping wave, on the rock-basin.

Drip, drip, drip-er-drip. Drip, drip, drip-er-drip. Light on that dimple of water, light that turned the rose-red lining of the bowl into flame.

His own place and it offered him this welcome of fierce, hot colour.

Pascoe had followed him into the cave. Corlyon looked for him, but the rock-hollow, blazing with the sun of early afternoon, was shadowless. Pascoe must have gone on.

Ah, yes, Pascoe understood, he too, that it was a life for a life; no more than that, no less. The final settlement of their accounts had brought him here. They had come in by a door the tide was closing and Pascoe knew.

Something in Gale Corlyon stirred, breaking against the grip of his will. Morwenna would be looking out for him, waiting . . .

He had spent his days serving the community, but at long last he had stretched out his hands to take.

The clamour of his desire rose to the brazen skies.

Something for himself, this one thing . . .

IV

The dark weeks through which he had passed—a nightmare rout—ached through his mind. Shadows growing into fiends, obsessing him, torturing; a hell's-broth of boiling memories. Hell—it had been that!

Morwenna would have shared hell with him, ay, done it gladly.

The water was swirling cold about his feet. He went deeper into the cave, stood by the bowl of dimpling flame.

Morwenna would wait for him till the stars fell and the night was black.

It might be true that he would see her again—then; or it might not.

But he must wait to know, here—where the sea was closing the door.